The McKenzie Files

Barry K. Nelson

The McKenzie Files

Copyright © 2017 Barry K. Nelson

Content Editor: Maddy Drake
Copy Editor: Amanda Berthault
Cover Art: Barry Nelson
Cover Design: Macario Hernandez
Editor-in-Chief: Kristi King-Morgan
Formatting: Kristi King-Morgan

ISBN-13: 978-1-947381-04-9
ISBN-10: 1-947381-04-0

Dreaming Big Publications
www.dreamingbigpublications.com

PROLOGUE

Leon Maseklos felt a painful stiffness in his knees as he walked. That was understandable. Considering the fact that he had just woken from a frozen sleep of nearly three hundred years. His body shivered against the cold air of the massive ship's dark corridor. He regretted not choosing an additional garment to bolster the gray coveralls he wore, but expected to soon disregard the cold as his excitement mounted.

There was only one reason why he was woken from his long slumber: robotic probes launched from the ship have finally discovered a suitable planet for colonization. As the head of this expedition, it was his duty and privilege to wake first. After he confirmed the probe's findings, he would rouse several key crewmembers from their cryo-suspension tubes. Then the work of colonization could begin.

There were six other vessels identical to this huge, rectangular ship, each carrying a large cargo of sleeping passengers. They were part of an expedition fleet whose mission was to relocate the select human populace of Earth to a new home.

In 2059, a gargantuan mass of jagged metal and ice had entered Earth's star system without any advance warning. Measuring more than forty miles in diameter, the intruder purposefully sped past Jupiter and Mars on a direct course to its intended target.

Earth.

Reports stated that the object impacted with a force that surpassed a nuclear explosion. Harrisburgh, Pennsylvania and a huge portion of its metropolitan area were obliterated. The horrendous death toll was too high for anyone to accurately count. Earth's environment was soon plunged into a global winter-effect as tons of soot and debris from the blast formed thick clouds that blocked out the life-giving sunlight.

The worst came a month later when a mysterious viral outbreak quickly spread. Victims suffered fatigue and loss of muscle coordination; paranoia and psychotic behavior soon followed. Its most horrible effect was infesting its victim's faces with bleeding cold blisters. The majority of victims died within days. It was largely believed that the viral organism was somehow released into the atmosphere by the object. But that theory was never scientifically proven. Because of its ghastly symptoms, the illness was named the Pandora Simplex.

Earth's scientists committed a global effort to find an effective serum against the virus, but they were hopelessly stymied. Within a year, forty-five percent of Earth's population was dead. Unsuspecting travelers even carried the virus to the numerous colonies established on the planet Mars. The virus and the frigid conditions on Earth were threatening to exterminate the human species. Their only hope for survival was to turn to the deep space exploration program that was currently under development. Thousands of healthy volunteers were gathered and placed under strict quarantine aboard space stations orbiting the sister planets. Fleets of huge rectangular ships were constructed and loaded with the necessary supplies and equipment to build new worlds.

Then in 2069, the surviving Humans began their mission to find a new home. Six separate fleets of ships disembarked for different destinations in the vast darkness of space.

The door to the ship's main bridge slid open. Leon strode past several rows of blinking instrument consoles to reach the data analysis station. With the touch of several buttons, he summoned the desired information onto a monitor. The long-ranged probes had indeed discovered a suitable planet. Its mass appeared to be slightly larger than that of Earth. A global body of water separated several mountainous land formations. The atmospheric composition was within the desired parameters: large amounts of oxygen mixed with nitrogen and a small amount of argon. Present temperature, seventy-two degrees. Soil and water analysis yielded no toxic materials or potentially harmful microorganisms.

At least nothing as deadly as the Pandora Simplex.

Leon nodded in satisfaction. This would be the world where Human civilization would get a fresh start. Now, after all these years in a deep cold sleep, the members of this expedition team would wake to the challenge of establishing a colony, then build the first of many cities across this planet. During the construction, the exploration of deep space would continue. If there were other hospitable planets out there then they would be claimed as well. And perhaps this team could establish contact with the other five teams that embarked on their own journey.

CHAPTER ONE

"Does it always rain on this damn planet?" Sergeant Colin McKenzie asked himself.

The young black male sprinted through the soggy forest behind the other members of his platoon. His hands maintained a firm grip on his AR-20 laser rifle as his boot squelched against the soft ground. He silently cursed the heavy, plastic protective vest that made his six-foot tall frame feel as though he were carrying a heavy brick over each shoulder. The vest's dark green color scheme matched his rain soaked fatigues and knee high boots his trousers tucked into. The thickness of the vest provided him with a limited degree of protection, but its weight restricted his movements.

The heavy downpour was also working against Colin. It was irritating, the way the cold raindrops continuously pelted his helmet and face, making it difficult for him to see his destination. Of all the planets in the United Protectorate, Colin was unlucky enough to be stationed on Meridan, a sparsely populated planet with an environment comprised of weed-ridden fields and swamps infested by hordes of insects and parasites. The climate was always chilly, with the average temperature in the low fifties, though Colin felt the frequent rains made the climate feel much colder.

Colin's squad approached their destination. He joined the other troopers as they took cover behind a line of trees and shrubbery, diving to the ground to take his place behind the broad leaves of a tall fern. Lying on the muddy ground, Colin peered around the foliage to detect any movement up ahead, only to see ivy covered trees and more tall ferns. Nothing moved. If there was any enemy activity out there, then he was certain that the noisy rain was concealing the sound of their movements.

Colin glanced over at his comrades. They were all quiet and still, expecting to engage in a raging firefight at a second's notice. To Colin's far right his superior officer, Lieutenant Paul Yates, crouched down behind a tree, his laser rifle aimed toward the forest beyond.

Colin's personal communicator, a small, oblong device with a keypad and a thin display screen strapped to his wrist, transmitted the lieutenant's voice.

"McKenzie, see anything?"

"All clear on my end," Colin spoke into his communicator. But Colin knew that not seeing their enemy did not mean that there was no threat. The Brelac were as stealthy as they were brutal.

Like most troopers, Colin knew very little about the Brelac, as they remained silent about themselves and their objectives. When the Brelac had encroached upon the United Protectorate over a year ago, they attacked with the force of a tidal wave. The Protectorate was overwhelmed by the alien military force, though troopers fought back bravely on both land and in space. However, they had been pitifully unprepared to deal with the Brelac's ferocity and advanced technology. The Protectorate suffered a year of crushing defeats. Seven star systems and twelve planets had been completely conquered by the Brelac. Many large cities, with their gleaming towers and bustling populations, were reduced to rubble. Now, it would seem that Meridan was next on the Brelac's list.

Colin was startled when he felt someone touch his right shoulder. He twisted quickly, swinging his gun around.

"Take it easy, pal," the trooper assured him, his hands held up defensively. "It's just me."

Ed Driscoll. Out of all the men in his platoon, he was Colin's closest friend. He seemed to be near Colin whenever possible, almost to the point of being a nuisance. Back at their main base, Helios, Driscoll would eat with Colin, help him with weapons maintenance duties, and stick close by in the off-duty taverns and recreation halls. All the while denigrating the other members of the platoon. There were occasions when Colin almost felt like Driscoll was keeping him under surveillance. It was no surprise to Colin that the man would be shadowing him even here during an impending battle.

"Let's move out," Yates whispered through their communicators.

Colin nodded to his friend, and motioned to the men on his left. The troopers began to advance cautiously among the wet trees and foliage.

The squad approached their destination at the top of a small, rocky hill. A black, rectangular aircraft rested at the bottom of a rock pile, its nose buried beneath a mound of soil. The broad wings were sheared off. Bits of metal wreckage littered the area, and thick billows of black smoke rose out from the ship's two damaged engine ports. It was a Brelac shuttle, shot down by a Protectorate fighter patrol. The squad's mission was to investigate the crash site and see if any Brelac had survived, and to capture any cargo that was found to be reasonably intact.

Yates ordered the soldiers to spread out and descend the hill. Colin kept his dark brown eyes on the shuttle as he carefully made his way down, alert for any movement. Yates raised his hand, and the squad stopped twenty feet away from the shuttle.

"A type three enemy shuttle," he announced after making a brief inspection.

The small craft had only one way to get inside: the main hatch located underneath the cabin. Since the platoon had no means of lifting a ship of this size, they would have to create their own door.

"Bossar, Craven. Take demo charges and blow the hull," Yates ordered.

The two men rushed up to the ship. They took small packets from their weapons belts. The devices were magnetic, allowing them to attach them to the ship's hull. They pressed small buttons on the side of the devices, and then ran to rejoin the rest of the platoon.

"Hit the ground!"

The squad ducked and covered their heads. The devices exploded, their twin blasts potent enough to rip a gaping hole into the side of the ship. Colin raised his head. He watched the smoke clear from the hole. Still no sign of any Brelac.

"Usher, Sealman, Driscoll, Craven," Yates ordered, "you're with me. The rest of you stay alert."

Driscoll placed his hand on Colin's shoulder. His grip was firm. "Time to go to work, pal. Looks like it's just you and me."

Driscoll rose up and joined the other three troopers as they escorted Yates over to the hole in the side of the ship. Colin felt relieved to be momentarily free of Driscoll's imposing presence. He stood and watched Driscoll and the other men. Yates entered the ship first, the others following close behind. Colin waited, keeping his rifle aimed at the ship.

After several tense seconds the lieutenant relayed their status into Colin's communicator. "So far we're all clear. Still no Brelac. Everybody move in, but stay alert."

Colin slowly advanced toward the ship. When he was close enough, he peered inside the hole in the ship's side and caught a glimpse of the shuttle's cargo. There were eight tall, white cylinders standing on what appeared to be a magnetic platform. The platform's strong magnetic field may have prevented the cylinders from falling over during the crash but it did not protect them from the damaging impact. Three of the cylinders were cracked and oozed a bright yellow liquid that soaked the shuttle's floor.

"Wonder what's inside these containers?" Sealman asked.

"Beats the hell outta me," the lieutenant replied. "They're leaking shit all over the place. If there are any Brelac here, they might be in the cockpit."

"Let's hope they're dead," Usher muttered. "What about these cylinders? Can you see what's inside?"

"No. Maybe we can break one of them open," Yates suggested. "Driscoll, Craven. Give us a hand. Sealman, Usher. Go check out the cockpit."

Driscoll placed his hand on Craven's shoulder. Craven suddenly screamed and fell backward. The instant Craven hit the floor his torso shattered. His plastic combat armor easily splintered into minute fragments, followed by his head and arms.

The other men stood in horrified silence. Yates spun around and aimed his rifle at Driscoll. Driscoll delivered a forceful kick to the lieutenant's chest and knocked him through the blown-out hole and out of the ship. Yates fell onto his back against the soggy ground, splashing into a large puddle of mud. He quickly rolled and aimed his rifle at Driscoll a second time. Colin spun and aimed his rifle at Yates and opened fire. Four crimson bolts of laser fire easily ripped through the lieutenant's body. The man emitted a painful grunt and lay motionless.

Colin was unsure if Yates was dead or simply wounded. But he didn't have enough interest in the man's condition to check. All that mattered was the mission he shared with Driscoll. It was their job to do everything in their power to prevent the United Protectorate from capturing the cylinders aboard this Brelac ship. And in order to accomplish that aim Colin was well prepared to use every power at his disposal.

A trooper standing near Yates raised his weapon. Colin moved faster, firing two laser bolts into the man's chest, and the trooper dropped to the ground. Someone pounced on Colin from behind, wrapping a strong arm around his neck in a strangling hold.

Colin's entire body rapidly warmed. A powerful surge of energy erupted from him, and he and his assailant were bathed in a flash of light and an explosion of sparks. Blue fire licked at the screaming man on Colin's back, and Colin shrugged himself free of the burden he carried. He turned briefly to glimpse his handiwork. An acrid smoke stung his nostrils, the flames on the body already being extinguished by the heavy rain. All that remained were fragments of charred flesh and globs of melted plastic clinging to a blackened skeleton. *Idiot!* was Colin's thought. His contempt of the man that foolishly sought to challenge him was brief. Colin forgot about him the moment that he turned his back on the remains to deal with the man's comrades.

Sealman fired his laser rifle at Driscoll. Driscoll staggered back as three bolts burned into his chest, and raised his rifle at Sealman. His wounds slowed his movement, giving Sealman ample time to dive behind the collection of cylinders. Driscoll fired off a volley of laser bolts that burned easily through several cylinders but failed to hit Sealman. Two troopers outside the shuttle opened fire at Driscoll. Driscoll thrashed about as several bolts hit him squarely. He let out a defiant shout and feebly raised his weapon, and then stumbled and fell forward. His riddled body lay halfway out of the ship, his blood-soaked armor pelted by the gray downpour.

Colin glanced down at Driscoll and doubted the man could have survived such an assault, but knew there was no time to mourn. Colin looked around at the multiple hostile targets surrounding him. He moved to act but was suddenly attacked from behind. Colin felt a sharp and powerful impact jar the back of his head. He collapsed face down onto a mound of mud.

Colin turned his head to face his new assailant. A baby-faced trooper stared wide-eyed down at him. His rifle shook rapidly in his nervous hands, the barrel never leaving Colin's face. Colin grinned, knowing the frightened young man posed only a small threat to him.

He knew he could kill this trooper as easily as he did the first.

Colin pushed himself to his knees and lifted his hands to attack when four blue laser streaks hit the trooper in the neck and head. The last shot easily split the top of the trooper's helmet and the head underneath. The man fell to the ground, blood and brain matter mingling with the rainwater and wet soil.

Colin twisted his head to look toward the shuttle. The shuttle's two Brelac pilots were barreling through the open hole in the side of the ship, baring their teeth as they surveyed the troopers outside.

The dark, scaly reptilian creatures stood nearly six feet tall. Their large, lizard-like heads grinned with mouths full of long, sharp teeth, and thick plates of scales covered the sides of their heads where eyes should have been. They had thick, broad-chested bodies covered in boney plates. Rows of long, sharp spikes ran along the sides of their torsos. They stood on muscular, reverse-jointed legs similar to those of a canine, with feet ending in three short toes and long, curved talons that clicked sharply against the ship's metallic floor. Their clawed hands clutched the typical Brelac field weapon: long-barreled plasma rifles—weapons far more powerful than Protectorate lasers. The plasma rifles were notorious for their ability to kill targets from a longer range and could burn through heavy armor easier than lasers. Weapons belts strapped around their waists carried holstered pistols, cylindrical grenades, and bayonets with long, gleaming blades.

The two Brelac thrashed their long tails and immediately opened fire at any trooper that moved, and screaming troopers scattered as they returned fire. The Brelac managed to gun down three troopers before a trooper skillfully sent a laser bolt into one Brelac's head. The wounded Brelac stumbled backward as his body absorbed the firepower from other trooper's rifles.

The Brelac's partner shot and killed a trooper standing just behind Colin. As the man's body fell to the ground Colin saw that the Brelac was now training that plasma rifle in his direction. Colin knew that in the midst of a group of hostile, armed humans the Brelac was not taking the time to distinguish between enemy and ally. Colin pointed his hand toward the Brelac. A blue flash and a stream of energy flew from Colin's hand. It created a spray of sparks the moment it struck the Brelac. Colin's firepower was joined by dozens of laser bolts as the troopers concentrated their fire to bring the Brelac down.

Colin tried to stand up but was knocked down by the butt of a rifle crushing down across his neck. Colin looked up and was surprised to see that Yates had survived his wounds. The lieutenant stood over Colin, slamming the butt of his rifle into Colin's face.

"I'm gonna bash your damn face in, freak!"

Yates continued to rain down a series of quick blows to Colin's face. He held the rifle over his head and pulled his leg back to send his boot slamming into Colin's stomach.

"Son of a bitch!" Yates screamed. "I'll kill you!"

Colin's face burned with pain as the lieutenant continued to beat him. Each painful blow felt as if fragments of his face were being torn away from the inside. Blood and rainwater soaked his eyes. His vision began to blur and he lost sight of his enraged attacker.

Then everything went black.

CHAPTER TWO

Doctor Howard Fenlow walked hastily through the busy corridors of the highly restricted military base of Cerulean, concerned whether his black pants and slightly wrinkled gray shirt beneath his white lab coat would be suitable enough for the briefing he was about to give. He ran a hand through his shoulder-length blond hair, frowning. He'd slept in and was running twenty minutes late. He had no time to make a better selection from his wardrobe.

Fenlow's apartment was located in Navarone, the capital city on the planet Maseklos Prime, less than two miles from Cerulean. The planet was the center of the United Protectorate, named after the famed scientist and explorer, Leon Maseklos. A convenient location, in Fenlow's opinion. One of the reasons why Fenlow chose to reside in Navarone.

It also makes last minute commutes on mornings such as this possible.

Fenlow approached the entrance to his laboratory, the door flanked by two armed troopers in grey fatigues, their trousers tucked neatly into black, knee-high boots. They stood silent, holding their laser rifles to their shoulders.

"I suppose everyone is inside waiting for me," Fenlow said, running another hand through his hair.

"President Drennen was about to send us to find you," a guard replied, his voice monotone.

The door to the lab slid open with a hiss to a large room with a row of four long, dark counters. Fenlow grinned slightly, admiring his workspace, and briefly glanced at the dozens of glass beakers and small, metal racks holding test tubes, each containing liquid and crystallized substances in reds, blues, and yellows. The fourth counter held seven jars lined up in a neat row, with lumps of pale-colored flesh, dissected brains, and small tube-shaped organs clearly visible through the polished glass. At the end of the counter was a large, shiny, metal sink and faucet. Along the left wall were three gray metal cabinets with more shelves holding jars of chemicals, glassware, and surgical instruments—shiny metal forceps, scalpels, and surgical saws, all sterilized and neatly arranged on black plastic trays. Fenlow looked toward the end of the room to two tall, gleaming white cylinders.

There were several persons waiting for him. A middle-aged woman instantly caught Fenlow's eye. She wore black shoes, pants, and a pink shirt under her black blazer. With short brown hair and green eyes, President Sandra Drennen of the Central Commission and Commander of the United Protectorate military forces did not appear pleased with having to wait.

Fenlow silently admired Drennen for her accomplishments. She'd been elected president at the age of thirty-nine, and now while serving a second four-year term she was cursed with the monumental task of holding the Protectorate together during this war. Fenlow knew Drennen to be a highly intelligent and articulate person. Her personality was quiet and sensitive, yet strong enough to bear the torment of her people on her shoulders without losing her sanity. She was holding her own for the present time, but Fenlow knew that the Brelac were too powerful, and that the Protectorate would eventually lose.

At her right stood Secretary of Defense John Crane, a thin black man in a dark gray suit. He impatiently ran his fingers through his thinning hair. There were also three members of the Central Commission present, part of the legislative body that helped Drennen govern the Protectorate. Joining them were four generals, among them Major General Verne Larkin dressed in his dark blue uniform with the band of medals on his left lapel, a dark blue cap with the gold eagle emblem worn proudly on his head.

Fenlow maintained a relationship with Larkin that could best be described as tolerance. Months ago, a commissioner had informed Fenlow that Larkin considered him to be too arrogant and demanding for a person sitting out the war in the safety of a lab. Though Fenlow personally felt that a lot of Larkin's disdain stemmed from the general's distrust because of Fenlow's long employment with Carp Technologies.

Carp was a large corporation that owned laboratories and factories on seven planets throughout the Protectorate, and was the leading producer of advanced electronics, biotechnology, and hardware for military use. Their motto was that they are committed to holding the lead in the race for human advancement.

Seven years ago, a movement had evolved on several colony worlds to break away from the central government on Maseklos Prime. Many citizens did not agree with this quest for independence. But under the support of a new political group called Vendetta, the movement had been able to gain thousands of supporters. After growing weary of spouting demands to Maseklos Prime that would go unheeded, Vendetta took a drastic step and directed the rebel planets to declare their independence. A civil war then erupted within the Protectorate. For two years, vicious battles were fought in space and across each rebel planet. The cost was the loss of thousands of lives and massive property damage. The growing market for weapons lead to Carp being charged with reputedly selling arms to both sides. But the end result was the eventual defeat of Vendetta's forces, and order was quickly restored throughout the Protectorate.

After the war, Vendetta's activities became more covert. The more fanatical members of the group waged a war of terror against the Protectorate. Their tactics included bombing vital government installations and assassinating key political and military figures. Their activities were gradually curtailed by the Protectorate's military intelligence internal security operations. Most of Vendetta's major resistance cells were eliminated. Their higher-ranking leaders retreated into seclusion, taking with them any hard evidence that may have linked Carp Technologies to Vendetta's activities during and after the war.

Now, seven years later, General Larkin still remained suspicious and hostile toward Carp Technologies. And that meant Fenlow as well. Though the doctor paid little attention to Larkin's resentful attitude, he considered the man to be a small component within a larger machine. And Fenlow's rightful place was at the controls of this machine. Larkin would have to choke on the fact that he and his superiors needed the technologies and services that Fenlow and Carp provided.

There were two men in white lab coats standing at the rear of the group. Fenlow frowned slightly at his assistant, Doctor Blair Van Doren, a young man with cropped blond hair and a muscular five-foot-nine-inch-tall frame. Dressed in white sneakers, blue pants, and a grey sweatshirt beneath the starched lab coat, Blair was dressed more casual than Fenlow would have preferred for this occasion. Fenlow's second assistant, Doctor Arnold Trevor, was an accomplished computer scientist whose work was regarded simply as ingenious. At the age of seventy his face was mapped by thick wrinkles, and thinning white hair hung past his shoulders. Dressed in black shoes and a gray suit and tie his white lab coat made him appear as an undead specter in search of a decent grave.

"I hope that we didn't tear you away from anything more important than this little meeting," Drennen said, breaking the silence, the sarcasm in her voice obvious.

"I apologize for my tardiness," Fenlow said quietly. "I slept a bit too late this morning." He expected to receive no more than a harsh scolding. Being the Protectorate's top scientist in the fields of electronics, bio-chemical engineering and genetics did earn Fenlow a certain level of leniency.

"As long as you're not too relaxed to sleep through the war," Larkin said, his eyes narrowed.

"We didn't come here to listen to any banter between you two." Drennen held up a hand. "I assembled this group here to learn if Doctor Fenlow has made any progress with this new project I've heard so much about."

"I've made great progress," Fenlow proudly addressed the officials. "I'll make this as brief and clear as possible. As you know, we've learned very little about the Brelac since the start of the war. But, as time moved on my research has revealed some startling facts about our mysterious enemies. Extensive examinations performed on several dead Brelac specimens have revealed that on a basic genetic level they are quite similar to humans. I've run genetic scans on twenty specimens and picked apart every segment of the Brelac genetic sequence. My scans revealed that each one was genetically identical to the other. This suggests that the Brelac could employ an advanced in-vitro organism replication technology to bolster their forces. In fact, their entire race could be comprised of what I call Reploids."

"That makes sense." Larkin nodded. "They do have us vastly outnumbered. They could artificially produce an army quicker than we can recruit and train our troops."

"It gets worse," Fenlow continued. "Since the Brelac have such advanced technology we can assume that they can use it to reproduce other forms of life to suit their purpose. I bring to your attention the recent wave of terrorist activities that have plagued us of late."

"And it could not have happened at such a worse time," Drennen said bitterly. "Military facilities being bombed, officers kidnapped or killed outright. Just last week there was a shooting on the street near the capital. Twelve dead, nine others wounded. And all these acts perpetrated by seemingly harmless citizens or military personnel. We think that Vendetta has picked this time to make a resurgence."

Fenlow nodded. "That's what I would have thought too, until I received a report on an incident in the Hollander System. It seems a police officer took several hostages inside of his precinct, and then set off a bomb that destroyed the entire building. None of the hostages or the officer survived. Then I read two other reports of terrorist activities where police managed to kill the perpetrators. The terrorists involved in these incidents perfectly matched the physical description of the police officer on Hollander Three. I took the liberty of examining two of their bodies. They were both identical, even down to the genetic level."

"That's unthinkable!" Drennen's eyes widened. She turned to stare at the others in the room before looking back at Fenlow. "You mean to say that the Brelac are somehow able to replicate humans and use them against us? If that's true then they could strike us anywhere."

"There's one more detail that could make the situation a whole lot worse," Fenlow said slowly.

"I came here in hopes of hearing some good news," Larkin said. "Instead you're giving us all bad."

"It's not entirely bad," Fenlow assured him. "Follow me and I'll explain."

He led the group over to the two white cylinders at the back of the room. "A week ago on the planet Meridan, a Brelac shuttle was shot down near Helios base. A squad of troopers investigated the shuttle and found a large group of cylinders just like these. They are incubation units containing human Reploids. During their investigation of the crash site, the troopers were attacked by two Reploids posing as members of the squad. It was reported that one Reploid killed a trooper by freezing him to death."

"*Froze* the trooper to death?" Drennen asked.

"With a touch of his hand," Fenlow said, wiggling his fingers. "His combat armor and flesh were rendered so brittle that they shattered like glass. The second Reploid somehow generated enough energy to nearly incinerate another trooper. That Reploid was captured, the first one killed. During the melee several of the other cylinders in the shuttle were severely damaged. The Reploids that they contained did not survive. Only these two remained intact."

Fenlow turned and hurried over to a table on their left and returned with a small plastic dish. Inside the dish sat several tiny transparent envelopes. Fenlow picked up one of the envelopes with great care and held it up for the group to see. The envelope contained a small, silvery disk-shaped electronic component no bigger than a dime.

"This was one of the weapons that the Reploids used to kill the troopers. My assistant, Doctor Blair Van Doren, aided me in performing the autopsy on the dead Reploid. I'll allow Blair to explain our findings."

Blair stepped forward and nervously cleared his throat. He opened his mouth but no words came out. He steadied himself and tried again. "During…during our examination of every Brelac specimen, we found components similar to these embedded deep within their brain's frontal lobes and occipital bones." He licked his lips. "Each Brelac had ten of these components embedded within its brain. As you know, the Brelac have no physical eyes. These components are a form of psionic implants. Apparently, they're designed to increase and focus the brain's level of psychic activity. This is how the Brelac are able to see. Psychic vision."

"So they don't need bifocals," Larkin said, shaking his head. "What does this have to do with those Reploids? And how can we use this to our advantage?"

"These components were taken from the slain Reploid," Blair explained. "They're more advanced than the standard Brelac implants that we've examined. They're designed to boost the brain's level of psionic power to a much higher degree. It's our theory that the Reploid's freezing ability was psychic in nature. A mental ability that was somehow created by these implants."

"Imagine if every Reploid infiltrator had such a deadly psychic ability," Fenlow added, "or every Brelac soldier. The power to read minds from a distance for vital information. As well as the power to kill in an unlimited number of paranormal ways."

The distressed look on Drennen's face made it clear she was not pleased with Fenlow's report. "It would be impossible to fight against such a covert threat backed by this technology," she said. "Is there any way that we can use these implants for our own troopers?"

"I'm afraid that these implants are useless to us," Fenlow said, almost regretfully. "We've already tested them on chimpanzees. The sudden massive increase of psionic energy quickly burned out their entire nervous systems. But the Reploids apparently have a special cellular adaptation that allows them to completely regenerate damaged nervous tissue at a rapid pace. This would effectively counteract any injury inflicted by the psionic energy surge. We're studying tissue samples taken from the live Reploid that's in our custody, trying to isolate the gene that enables his neural regeneration. But," Fenlow paused dramatically, eyes flicking to the faces of each listener, "in the meantime we can put him and these other two to work for us."

"Put these creatures to work for us?" Larkin's face, already a bright red, turned a shade darker. "Weren't they created to fight against us? What do you plan to do, bribe them?"

"No, reprogram them." Fenlow crossed his arms proudly. "We have discovered that the Reploid's brains also contain six implants that we call access memory chips. Apparently the Reploid's programmed memories are stored in these chips and downloaded into their brains as they first awaken. Since these two arrived to us in an unconscious state, I believe that their programs have not been downloaded. This gives us the opportunity to program them to serve us instead of the Brelac."

"And what about the captured Reploid that was already functioning?" Drennen asked.

"That Reploid is under heavy sedation," Blair explained. "I can surgically remove the memory chips from its brain. Doctor Trevor can then delete the chip's current data and enter his own programs."

With a stiff stride Trevor stepped forward. "It won't be an easy job. In order for the Reploids to blend in as one of us the Brelac had to program them with every aspect of an intelligent human mind. They simulate emotions. They have different attitudes and memories of past experiences. Each Reploid is a unique individual. I believe that I can reproduce these highly intricate programs, imitating every aspect of a normal, mature, human mind."

"We believe that the Brelac abduct human victims and replicate them," Fenlow explained. "Somehow, they copy as much data as they can from the minds of the originals and program the data along with programmed instructions into the Reploids to act against us. The originals, having served their purpose, are probably destroyed."

Silent up to this point, Secretary Crane cleared his throat. "Sounds dangerous. This whole idea of trying to use these walking weapons could blow up in our faces."

"It can't hurt to try," Larkin said, slowly nodding. "We could certainly use anything to help turn the tide of this war. God knows that we're sending everything we've got against the Brelac and we're still on a crumbling defensive. But if these Reploids are going to be any good to us then we'll definitely need more than just three. Is it possible that we can produce our own Reploids? As well as these psionic implants?"

"At the present, Carp's research into advanced cloning in limited," Fenlow replied. "We can only produce cloned children through surrogate host mothers. These Reploid creatures are created through an advanced in-vitro process we have yet to understand. Inside these cylinders, the Reploids are immersed in a highly concentrated nutrient liquid and fed through an intravenous mechanism. It's possible that the Brelac can produce these creatures full grown and fully developed in a matter of weeks. As for the psionic implants, we're just beginning to understand how they work. It will be some time before we can reproduce this technology. The research section back at Carp's main starbase has put our top people to work on both problems. I'm confident that a breakthrough will come in a few months."

"And at what cost?" Larkin demanded. "I doubt that Carp is willing to sacrifice their corporate bottom line for the sake of the war."

"The cost for this project will be determined when Secretary Crane negotiates with our board of directors." Fenlow frowned. "Our costs for manpower and materials for our research and development demand that we be fairly compensated. Even so, Carp is fully committed to the United Protectorate's war effort."

Crane stepped in quickly, seemingly to defuse the tension. "We don't doubt your company's commitment to our cause, Doctor Fenlow. And General Larkin would have to admit that Carp has made several significant discoveries that have placed us on better ground with the Brelac."

"Perhaps Carp *has* been useful in reproducing captured Brelac technology for our own use," Larkin admitted, looking away. "Some of which I'm still getting used to. Like the hyperspace technology you introduced a few months ago. But I'd still like to see Carp try to be a little charitable during these tough times."

"We'll have time to bicker when things improve," Drennen said. "Right now I have to decide on whether to approve this project. And I honestly like what I've been hearing. Are there any objections?"

"I'm still leery of the idea of experimenting with enemy Reploids armed with dangerous abilities," Crane replied. "Especially here on our home world. Something could go wrong. Perhaps it would be safer to transport them to Starbase Lodestar until all tests are complete. Located out in deep space it's the ideal facility to develop this project."

Drennen nodded. "Any objections to the idea, Doctor?"

"I can live with it," Fenlow said.

"Then it's settled," Drennen declared. "I just hope that this will be worth all the time and effort involved."

Larkin took a final glance at the two cylinders. "If there's nothing else then I'd like to get back to the war."

"Have the Reploids transported to Lodestar as soon as possible, Doctor," Drennen ordered. "Keep me posted about their development."

She turned to the door. Larkin was already rushing out of the room, the other generals and commissioners behind him.

*****

Fenlow returned to his apartment building late that evening. He approached the door and entered his personal identification number on a small glowing keypad at the right of the jam. The door slid open with a faint hiss. He slipped in and the door closed and quietly sealed behind him. He reached for a small, two-button panel mounted on the right wall. He pressed the top button and four long, white bars mounted six feet apart on the ceiling emitted a glow that illuminated the entire room. The living room was small with modest furnishings, the lights reflecting off the back of his dark brown, leather sofa and reclining chair, both items perfectly matching the brown carpeting. The chair faced a large flat screen television mounted on the wall. At the right of the chair sat a small, round glass top coffee table standing on four wide metal legs.

The far left corner of the room merged into Fenlow's small kitchen, the floor covered by white tile. The black countertop with a sink in the middle partially obscured the view of the gleaming, stainless steel stove and the refrigerator at its right. Past the refrigerator sat the open door to his bedroom.

On the right side of the living room was a sturdy worktable. The wooden desktop held several beakers and test tubes filled with various chemical solutions, and a computer next to a small stack of jumbled papers. A chorus of loud beeps constantly emitted from the computer. It had recorded a subspace message received through its uplink modem. Fenlow looked longingly in the direction of the bathroom, the open door at the left of his worktable. But he decided to take a moment to watch the message, hoping that it would be short. He sat in the high-backed leather chair in front of the computer's black monitor and pressed a key.

The image of a blond middle-aged man in a dark suit appeared on the monitor, sitting behind a desk with his hands folded in front of him. Fenlow frowned. It was Walter Carnaby, the Chief Executive Officer of Carp Technologies—and Fenlow's immediate boss.

Under Carnaby's leadership, Carp Technologies had become the largest corporation in the United Protectorate. He had initiated several successful takeovers of smaller rival companies, absorbing their key personnel to strengthen Carp's position as a corporate leader. Still, Fenlow often wondered if the man was indeed worth the eighty million dollars in salary and stock options the company paid him.

But Fenlow was a scientist, devoting little time in boardroom moving and shaking, and focused on research and development. As long as Carnaby continued to foot the bill.

"Howard," Carnaby greeted buoyantly. "I was trying to contact you earlier, but I guess you were out. I just met with the board of directors. We're concerned about the Brelac stepping up their aggression. Protectorate forces are falling back on several fronts. This means that we're forced to advance with our own plans. I'm making the preparations for Operation Broad Axe. I need you to step up your efforts in the field so that the plan can go through. I'll be expecting a report from you soon. Perhaps we can trade good news."

The monitor went black at the end of the message. Fenlow gave a tired sigh.

Advance operation Broad Axe so soon? Is Carnaby insane? Perhaps the Brelac are starting to worry Carnaby and the other stiff suits back at Carp's starbase headquarters.

Whatever the reason, it was Fenlow's job to help insure that Operation Broad Axe was a huge success. But advancing the plan now would force him to take some extremely drastic measures.

But not now. At the moment Fenlow was concerned about going to the bathroom, then eating the slice of lemon pound cake in the refrigerator. Fenlow headed for the bathroom door.

CHAPTER THREE

Fenlow was not enjoying his stay in the desert region of the planet Talos. He'd expected it to be hot, but actually having to endure the smoldering heat exceeded his expectations. His hot weather attire of a thin, blue, short-sleeve shirt, denim shorts, and sandals provided him with little comfort. The heat seemed to penetrate every pore of his skin, and he used one hand to wipe the beads of sweat from his brow, knowing that he would repeat the process within minutes.

He peered through the heavy, long-ranged binoculars hanging around his neck. He made a quick visual scan of the north and saw nothing of importance. Just a bleak scene bathed in the red glare of the sun. Nothing but miles of sand, rocks, and hills. The east revealed the same image. Looking to the south, he saw moving figures in the distance, nearly a mile away from his position: a small group composed of humans and Brelac.

Fenlow turned and walked toward his all-terrain motorcycle. He sat down on the black leather seat, uncomfortably hard and hot, as he turned over the small fusion engine. He held a tight grip onto the handlebars as the engine revved. This was the first time that he had ever driven such a vehicle, and losing his balance and falling over was his greatest fear. The motorcycle performed quietly, but its enlarged wheels with thick, cube-shaped treads provided a bumpy ride. He gunned his motorcycle forward at top speed, churning up huge clouds of dust in his wake.

Drawing rapidly closer to the target area, Fenlow saw the group more clearly without the aid of his binoculars. Two troopers stood near what appeared to be a small transport shuttle. The troopers had rifles trained on five Brelac soldiers kneeling on the ground with their clawed hands folded behind their heads. A third trooper lay against the shuttle with a bleeding abdominal wound. His vest had been removed to expose a blood-soaked shirt tied crudely around his torso, and his face was soaked by water dripping from a rolled up wet rag placed across his brow. Fenlow could only imagine how they were sweltering under those gray, bulky armored vests and gray camouflage fatigues tucked into those knee-high boots. Their sweat soaked faces turned to him as he approached.

Fenlow stopped his cycle a few feet from the group. He waved his hands in the air to try to fan away the dust cloud that his motorcycle had produced. As expected, one trooper aimed his rifle defensively toward him. Fenlow smiled cheerfully.

"Good afternoon. My name is Howard Fenlow. I'm a doctor from the Ninth Medical Corps out from Starbase Horizon, stationed over Planet Keldorn. What happened here?"

The young trooper aiming his rifle squinted as beads of sweat rolled down his face. He seemed to be in a jumpy state. "Our squad set up an ambush in the hills for a gang of these bastards. We killed three of them before the group scattered and ran off. Fortunately we were able to capture these five. The other members of our squad are out trying to take down the rest of them."

"You say you're a doctor?" another trooper asked. "Baker there could use your help."

Fenlow quickly dismounted and walked over to the injured man. Baker was unconscious. Fenlow examined his wound.

"This is serious," he said. "Your friend needs surgery as soon as possible if he's to survive. In the meantime I've got some medical supplies in my cycle's storage compartment. I can try to stop his bleeding and keep him stable until we get him to a proper medical facility."

"Do what you can for him, Doc."

Fenlow strolled to the back of his motorcycle and opened the storage compartment. The trooper pointing the rifle kept his gaze locked on Fenlow. His lips were pulled tight, almost in a sneer.

"Just what are you doing out here, Doc?"

"I was part of a medical team just arriving to this planet," Fenlow replied without looking up. "We were being transferred to Norcross Base in Sector Eight when our ship was forced down by Brelac fighters. We survived the crash and had to scatter when Brelac troops chased us. They're relentless monsters, you know. I was damn lucky to shake them off. I hope your squad returns soon. If the Brelac should pick up my trail then we'll definitely need some extra firepower. Which way did they go?"

The trooper turned his head to a group of hills on the horizon. He motioned toward them with his chin.

"Over that way, about two hours. It shouldn't take them long to track down the rest of the Brelac."

It only took a second for Fenlow to take the laser pistol hidden in the cycle's storage compartment and squeeze off a shot at the back of the trooper's head. The laser bolt burned a large hole through the top portion of the man's skull, killing him instantly. The second trooper looked on in shocked disbelief as the body dropped limply to the ground, the dead trooper's head smoking. Fenlow quickly fired four laser bolts into the second trooper's chest. The man stumbled back and fell. Fenlow glanced at the wounded man lying against the shuttle, half-turned away, and then sent a bolt through the pale forehead.

Fenlow turned and approached the five Brelac prisoners, listening to their heavy, hoarse breathing. He held his pistol out in front of him. He casually let the weapon slide out of his fingers and drop to the ground in a small plume of dust. He brushed his hands together and put on a sly grin

"Let me introduce myself again. I'm Doctor Howard Fenlow. I was wondering if you could help me make a house call."

CHAPTER FOUR

"I'll kill you!"

Lieutenant Yates' voice echoed, repeating those harsh words over and over. Torrents of rain drenched both their bodies as the lieutenant sadistically pounded him with the butt of that laser rifle. Colin saw his own crimson blood streaming from his nose and quickly mixing with the rainwater soaking his face. But under the impact of the lieutenant's every blow Colin felt no pain. He did not feel the rainwater that drenched his body. He could not hear the blasts of firepower around him. He heard nothing but the words.

"I'll kill you! I'll kill you!"

Yates' rifle butt delivered a crushing blow to Colin's nose. Colin saw his own body convulse under the impact.

"I'll kill you! I'll kill you! I'll kill you!"

The deafening sound of an explosion filled Colin's ears, and a powerful force shoved his body forward. A second later a sharp pain spread along his back and through his ribcage. Then everything went still.

He opened his eyes. He was not on the rainy planet of Meridan, being mercilessly beaten by Lieutenant Yates. Instead, he was shocked to find himself in a dark place, lying on his back. A steady stream of air rushed into his face and through his black, short-cropped bushy hair. He raised his hands and tried to reach out. His hands pressed against what felt like a hard plastic surface. Colin twisted and turned his body around, trying to feel his surroundings. His probing hands revealed that he was confined in a small, round container, his body on a cushion with a soft vinyl surface.

Colin panicked. Thoughts flashed through his mind. The lieutenant could have stopped the beating, took aim with his rifle, and fired. Colin feared that this confinement was the aftermath of his death. Or worse, being mistaken for dead. For all he knew he could be in a coffin, either already buried or awaiting burial, or even possibly awaiting cremation. Either scenario brought Colin to the same conclusion. He had to find his way out.

"Hey!" he shouted. "Somebody! Help!"

Colin was surprised his voice seemed to carry beyond the interior of this small, dark coffin. He took a deep breath and focused on the flow of air he felt on his face. His fingers felt along the inside edges of his coffin, jerking his hands back from the touch of a broken plastic edge sharp enough to cut his skin. He continued feeling around the opening and pushed forward. A large section of the plastic in front of him moved. He looked about and noticed a dim red light far above his face. It barely provided him with enough glow to make out the inside of a small, dark room.

He attempted to climb out of the coffin, though his numb legs made it difficult. Halfway out of the coffin he felt a sharp pain in his left arm. He looked down to find a plastic, transparent tube inserted into his left arm. The other end of the tube led back to a small grey box mounted on the inside wall of the coffin. The box had a small digital display and a keypad with six buttons. Colin examined the screen closer but the blank face gave him no answers. He yanked the tube out of his arm and was rewarded with a brief sting. A small pool of blood bubbled up from the hole on his arm, and he was amazed that he did not feel any greater pain when he examined the long, thick needle on the end of the tubing.

He stepped out, stood up and stretched, and then paused to glance down at himself. He found himself dressed in his green camouflage field uniform. His short-sleeved shirt exposed his arms to a chilly draft. The legs of his trousers were jammed tightly into his green boots. He was grateful for not wearing that cumbersome armored vest that he hated. Lying on the floor close to the wall in front of him were two other dark-colored cylinders—not coffins, he realized—next to the one he'd emerged from.

Each cylinder rested on a thin metal platform, a thick, black strap wrapped across the top and bottom of each. A sturdy metal hook at the end of each strap was connected to a clasp at the side of the platform. On the left side of the cylinder the straps protruded from small, motorized wenches, holding the cylinders securely in place.

Colin looked around and examined the room. The metal-paneled wall close to the three cylinders was buckled and torn, and two large, twisted metal beams protruded through from the other side. Along the wall from floor to ceiling were large splinters of twisted metal jutting outward, one emerging from the floor at the right side of Colin's cylinder, the surrounding floor littered by metal shards. Colin figured that it explained the damage, as well as the impact he'd felt. He rubbed his side, thankful that the fragment had not penetrated a few more inches to the left.

Colin suspected what the other two cylinders might contain. He knelt down near the one in the middle and ran his hands across the smooth, cold surface. His fingers met a small metal bar on the right side. He spied a piece of metal, two feet long and roughly triangular in shape, lying on the floor. He picked up the hunk of scrap, being careful of grabbing its sharp edges with his hands. The metal was fairly heavy but Colin was able to lug it over to the cylinder and bring one of its pointed edges smashing down against the small bar. The bar held firm. Colin raised the crude tool again and brought it down onto the bar again twice until the bar snapped off, bouncing against the floor with two faint clinks. Colin put his tool aside and slowly opened the cylinder's lid.

A tall, unconscious woman lay inside. Black hair obscured her face and hung down past her shoulders. She wore a green camouflage uniform and boots similar to Colin's, and also had a plastic tube inserted into her arm. Whatever the tube's purpose, Colin imagined that she would be grateful if he removed it. He gently pulled the tube out of her arm, and then shook her, but she remained unconscious. Frowning, he shook his head and turned to the next cylinder.

Colin used the scrap metal to break the lock off. Inside was a young man with short-cropped blond hair. He had a youthful face, appearing to be in his late teens or early twenties and looked short. Colin estimated him to be no more than a few inches over five feet. Colin removed the tube in his arm and tried to rouse the youth. Like the woman, the young man remained in a deep, oblivious slumber.

Well, I tried. But I want to know what the hell's going on, and I'm not about to wait around for answers. I need to get out of here.

Colin crossed the room and approached the half-open door. Apparently, whatever force had damaged this room also affected the door. Outside the room rang a loud wailing noise.

An alarm of some sort.

Colin heard the sounds of panicked shouting and running footsteps. He stepped through the doorway and entered a small corridor filled with an acrid smoke and the strong odor of burning rubber. The column of dim lights running along both walls provided little aid for his vision through the thick smoke. A single inhale of the smoky air caused him to cough instantly, and his eyes started to water. He stopped and wiped his tearing eyes with the back of his hands. He swiveled his head left then right, then decided to head to the right toward the sounds of shouting, hoping he would have a better chance of finding someone by heading into the heart of whatever chaos he was in.

A man suddenly rushed up to him through the smoke dressed in a pilot's uniform of a dark blue shirt under a matching jacket. There were small gold insignias of a pair of wings over captain's bars on his shoulders and a gun belt strapped to his waist.

The man halted. "Who the hell are you?"

Colin hesitated. Then he started back the way he came.

"This ship is restricted to authorized personnel only!" the man snapped. He reached for the weapon holstered at his right side.

Without thinking, Colin swiftly hurled his fist into the man's face. The man staggered back into the wall. Colin chose not to follow up on his attack. Instead, he darted past the man and down the corridor.

"Intruder alert!" Colin heard the man's voice cry out. "Intruder on board!"

At least I know I'm on a ship. But what am I doing here? And why were the three of us shut away inside of those cylinders?

Colin came to a large open ramp and realized the ship was still on the ground. That came as a relief because now his escape could be easier, depending on what was waiting for him at the bottom of the ramp. Taking a quick glimpse of his new surroundings, Colin saw that he was in a large air bay, appearing to be located underground. Rows of blinding white lights were mounted high along the rock walls. Dozens of triangular fighter craft were parked on both sides of the painted white runway. Dozens of men and women wearing blue coveralls with tools in hands ran back and forth between the fighters. Colin glanced behind him at the wedge-shaped vessel he had emerged from and saw a huge mass of flaming wreckage imbedded in the side of the ship's hull. Two men carrying red fire extinguishers each shot streams of white chemical foam trying to put out the fires.

Someone suddenly grabbed Colin from behind, and a heavy weight forced him down. The attacker wrapped his arm tightly around Colin's neck, cutting off his air. Colin desperately tried to wrestle free but he was helpless against the man's strength. He managed to throw himself to the side, rolling down the ramp with his attacker clinging to his back. The man's added weight smashed Colin's face painfully against the hard metal surface of the ramp.

Several troopers scrambled left and right, getting out of the way. A few stopped to watch the struggle. Three troopers broke away from the crowd and rushed over to the ramp. They grabbed Colin's arms and jerked him upright and then dragged him toward the stone wall of the air bay, slamming his face against it.

"Who are you?" a loud voice shouted into Colin's ear.

Colin did not respond. The men pulled him back and slammed him into the wall a second time, pressing his face against the hard rock. Colin felt something wet slide down his lip. His tongue absorbed the bitter taste of his own blood. His nose, already aching, was now bleeding.

"Who are you?" the bellowing voice demanded. "How did you get into this base?"

"I'm Sergeant Colin McKenzie. Assigned to platoon three six seven. Fourteenth Combat Division."

"I'm not impressed, Sergeant!" the voice snarled back. "I'd be more impressed if you tell me how you got aboard a ship that's restricted to authorized personnel only!"

"That's what I'd like to know," Colin replied desperately. "I just woke up there."

The men pulled Colin back and slammed him into the wall a third time. The pain in Colin's face instantly overshadowed all other sensations throughout his body. His legs buckled and for a moment he was glad the troopers held him up.

"Stop!" yelled a young but commanding voice.

Colin managed to turn toward a young, blond-haired man dressed in casual blue denim jeans, a red sweater, and white sneakers, accompanied by an older, white-haired man dressed in a pressed gray suit. His face was mapped by thick wrinkles.

"Let him go," the man commanded.

"Let him go?" one of the troopers protested. "This man's under arrest for trespassing aboard a high-security vessel."

"That won't be necessary," the old man said. "He's with us. He's part of our cargo. I can personally vouch for him."

The troopers hesitated for a moment, then released Colin and stepped back.

Colin rubbed his nose, and his fingers came away red.

The young man approached Colin. "Who are you again?"

Colin wiped more blood away from his nose. "I already told you. I'm Sergeant Colin McKenzie. Platoon three six seven. Fourteenth Combat Division. Who the hell are you?"

"I'm Doctor Blair Van Doren," the young man answered. "My associate here is Doctor Arnold Trevor. He's a computer specialist. Are you alright?"

Colin's patience was wearing thinner with each second. "I'm not okay," he groused. "I just had my face imprinted against a damn wall."

"I apologize for that," Trevor replied humbly. "This ship is under a high security restriction. I'm afraid that Captain Gains here overreacted to your unexpected presence. It would help if you could tell us how you arrived here."

"I just woke up inside this cylinder. I was having this dream, and then I felt something hit me. That's when I woke up. The cylinder was pretty badly damaged."

Trevor nodded. "Sounds logical. Earlier there was an accident here. A heavily damaged ship crashed into ours. The impact must have damaged your containment cylinder and awakened you."

Colin was satisfied with that explanation; it was one question among many that he needed answered.

"What about the others?" Blair asked. "Did you notice the other two?"

"They were both unconscious. I tried to wake them but they were too far out of it."

Blair and Trevor both rushed past Colin and up the ramp into the ship. Colin hesitated. He looked back and forth between the retreating doctors and the milling troopers, and then quickly headed up the ramp.

Inside the storage room Blair was examining the cylinder that contained the sleeping female. "The cylinder's lock is broken off," he said. "Her intravenous tube has been removed." He held out the dangling tubing.

"I know," Colin said casually. "I took it out."

Blair examined the cylinder containing the young man. "Did you remove this one as well?" he asked, his face red.

"Yeah, just like I took out mine," Colin admitted. "I wasn't sure what they were for."

"These tubes are part of a timed intravenous unit installed within these cylinders," Blair explained with a tone of annoyance. "The units are supposed to pump a dosage of sedatives into their recipients every two hours."

The woman emitted a faint moan. Her head swiveled left to right. The young man slowly lifted his arms.

"It's a moot point now," Trevor sighed. "They're both waking up."

"What was the purpose of keeping us sedated?" Colin asked.

"To ensure your safety during our trip to Lodestar," Trevor answered. "Unfortunately, an increased Brelac presence in this sector forced us to seek refuge here in Scorpis, a small base on the Planet Voran. We're only six hours from Lodestar, but it appears that even here we're shadowed by the threat of the Brelac."

The woman opened her eyes and looked about. Her eyes widened as she took in her surroundings. "What happened? Where am I?"

"You're aboard a cargo cruiser presently resting within a small base on the planet Voran," Trevor repeated.

Blair helped the youth out of his cylinder while Doctor Trevor assisted the stiffly moving female. "How do you both feel?"

The woman answered first. "I'm okay. I just feel a little dizzy."

"Me too," the young man answered, rubbing his head. "How long have I been out?"

"Only a few days," Blair said. "But we didn't expect you three to be up so soon. Do any of you remember anything before you came here?"

"I remember being on duty at Helios," the young man calmly explained, looking down at his hands, "at a communications outpost on Meridan when the Brelac attacked."

"What was your job?"

"Trooper Kelly Lytton, Technical Master First Class." He held out his hand, and Blair took it. "I was repairing a computer terminal in the central command center. I must have been shot because I don't remember anything beyond that."

"Same here," the woman said with surprise. "All I remember was that I was coming back from a mission. And that's it."

"What was the mission?"

She looked confused. "I…I don't remember. All I know was that I was in a fight. I'm a pilot. Captain Diane Christy. Credited with 230 confirmed enemy kills."

"Quite an impressive score," Trevor nodded. "I'm sorry that we haven't been properly introduced. My name is Doctor Arnold Trevor. I'm a computer-programming specialist. My young friend here is Doctor Blair Van Doren. The reason that you are all here is that you were seriously injured while on duty, each of you hanging close to death. Our only chance to save you was to conduct a series of experimental operations. These operations not only saved your lives, but also endowed you with certain paranormal abilities, each possessing a different power that we hope to use against the Brelac. How effective you are against the Brelac will determine if more of your kind will be created."

"What kind of paranormal abilities are you talking about?" Kelly asked. "And how do we use them? I don't feel anything out of the ordinary."

"You will when the proper time comes," Trevor said.

Colin narrowed his eyes at Trevor. "Some of what you're saying makes sense so far. But why take us all the way to Lodestar?"

"As a security measure," Trevor said. "You three are part of a highly sensitive military project called Silencers Squad. Its success is all too important."

Diane shook her head and rubbed her hands over her arms as if she was cold. "Only three of us? You're not going to send us out on any suicide missions, are you?"

Captain Gains entered the room and quickly approached Blair and Trevor. He made a sideways glance at Colin, and then cleared his throat.

42

"I've inspected the hull and used the ship's sensors to run a full diagnostic. We were lucky. The crash only breached a small section of our hull, and we can easily seal this entire section off during our flight. Also, the flight controllers just told me that their scanners show the enemy traffic around the planet has abated. But that might not last very long."

"Then we'd better leave now," Trevor said.

Blair pointed to Colin, Diane, and Kelly. "What about them?"

"Our friends here are already awake so we have no choice but to have them sit up front with us," Trevor sighed.

The group followed Gains out of the room through a corridor on the left and up a short flight of steps. On the next deck they assembled in the small passengers compartment. On both sides of the compartment were rows of four black seats with safety straps that dangled to the floor.

The ceiling was too low for Colin's comfort. When he entered he had to bend down to keep from bumping his head. Looking ahead he saw that Diane was forced to do the same thing. Colin wrinkled his nose at the odor of burning rubber from the smoke that had penetrated this section as well.

Gains headed for the pilot's section. He strapped himself into the single seat in front of a small instrument panel with a large, dark, square display screen below a large, panoramic forward window. The screen was flanked by rows of glowing buttons and switches. Protruding from the panel, in front of the display were two black control sticks with thick rubber handgrips.

Colin took the seat at the left behind Gains. The seat was soft and warm as it absorbed his weight. Diane sat at his right. Blair assisted Colin with the wide safety strap. The strap ran from the top left of the seat and pressed tightly across Colin's chest. There was a loud, sharp click as Blair inserted the strap's latch into the buckle at Colin's right hip. Blair then moved on to assist Diane and Kelly, who sat behind Colin. Blair took a seat behind Trevor and Diane and strapped himself in.

Gains reached over and pressed three buttons at the left of the display, and a faint yellow glow emanated from the screen. The loud whine of the ramp raising filled the ship's interior. A loud hiss came from the back, and a light draft of air blew through the compartment as the hatch slid shut. Once the ship was sealed tightly, the whine was replaced by the powerful thrum and vibrations generated by the ship's engines.

Gains pressed a button at the right of the display. "The wreckage is cleared away," his voice announced over two round speakers in the ceiling. "Now sealing off the lower deck."

Colin could clearly see into the cockpit and through the panoramic window as the ship slowly rose into the air. He quickly lost sight of the people working below amongst the triangular fighters at the left and right. The ship slowly headed for the white runway, then turned and faced the gaping exit to the subterranean base. There was a booming pop from behind them, and Colin was thrust back against his seat as the ship sped out of the air bay.

By Colin's view the ship was flying less than a quarter mile from the rocky ground while Protectorate and Brelac fighters continued to battle overhead. Gains explained his plan to try to keep low and hopefully fly under the skirmish until the ship cleared the area. Then he would pilot the ship safely up into space.

Colin glanced out the window and hoped that Gains tactic to escape the Brelac's attention would work. After several minutes of uninterrupted flight, he stopped gripping the armrests and settled back into his seat. The ship traveled silently above the rocky hilltops and groves of tall green trees for five minutes without incident. Colin closed his eyes, finally feeling relieved and confident they would soon arrive safely at Lodestar.

A violent tremor suddenly rocked the ship, making it veer to the right.

"We've got trouble," Gains reported. "We were hit by enemy fire. Shields are holding, and no internal damage reported. Scanners have picked up four Brelac fighters on our tail. I'll try to outrun them."

Diane released her safety belt and rushed into the cockpit. Gains didn't acknowledge her.

"Maybe I'd better take over," Diane said. "I can handle our friends outside."

Switching pilots at such a crucial time did nothing to help Colin hold on to his feeling of security. "Sit down, lady!" he cried out angrily. "Let the man do his job."

The ship made a sharp turn and headed into the sky. Gains thrust the ship into wild zigzagging maneuvers to avoid the enemy's fire. Another tremor rocked the ship, more violent than the first.

"Engine trouble!" Gains cried out. "Hang on back there. This might be a little rough!"

Diane stumbled back to her seat as the ship descended rapidly. Colin watched, detached, as Gains jerked the twin control sticks back sharply but gained little response. The ship plowed into the ground and skidded for a short distance, and huge chunks of dirt and rocks hurled into the air as the ship's bow split the earth. The ship's momentum came to an abrupt halt when it crashed into the base of a large hill, and the loud wail of an alarm filled the compartment.

*****

Colin's body throbbed with pain. He groaned and opened his eyes, running a hand across his face to brush off the layer of dirt that had settled over his skin. He was fortunate that he'd been strapped in his seat instead of being bounced against the bulkhead. He was amazed that the ship had not exploded after enduring the massive impact of the crash. He coughed against the thick cloud of dust filling the compartment, and slowly turned to look over at Diane. She was slumped over against the thick safety strap.

He glanced into the cockpit. The forward window had shattered, and large splinters of plastiglass littered the cockpit. Small piles of dirt and smaller rocks covered the instrument panel. Gains leaned limply to the left, his left arm hanging down to the floor. A stream of blood ran out of his ear and down the side of his face. There was a large rock resting against his chest.

Colin didn't like that Gains wasn't moving, and from where he sat he couldn't tell if the captain was even breathing.

Colin started to unbuckle his safety strap, then paused and glanced up at the sound of scuttling through the broken forward window and saw a mob of ragged figures rushing through. Men and women dressed in dirty robes and capes, a few clad only in short loincloths.

What the hell?

One man detached himself from the ground and headed toward Colin. Tall and muscular, his uncombed black hair grew far past his shoulders. He wore a pair of dirty ragged shorts and a hooded robe made from the scaly hide of some reptilian creature. His massive fist flew straight at Colin's face.

Colin closed his eyes as intense pain flooded his head and blurred his vision. He did not register the sensation of falling back against his seat as everything went black.

CHAPTER FIVE

Two Brelac guards dragged Fenlow by his arms through the dark corridors of their base. After freeing the five Brelac prisoners back on Talos, they'd taken him prisoner and transported him here. Fenlow had not been informed as to which planet or base he was on, but names and locations were unimportant to him.

Fenlow had a special purpose in mind.

Fenlow had expected to be subjected to some form of physical abuse the moment he arrived. He'd firmly stated his motives and suspected that the Brelac had gone as easy on him as they could during his interrogation. If repeated blows with electrically charged metal rods and being slammed against a stone wall could be considered soft treatment. He endured his punishment with dignity, reminding himself that if he survived and got what he wanted from the Brelac, then his suffering would be well worth it.

The guards taxied him through a set of twin swinging metal doors and into a cold and dark banquet hall. Fenlow's nose immediately caught a strong, sweet odor in the air. As the guards dragged him forth that odor was replaced by an oily smell. There were other tables situated throughout the room with more Brelac eating and drinking heavily. Others stood around the dimly lit room holding conversations.

Several Brelac were seated behind a long table, a large meal set out before them. Fenlow warily eyed the feasting creatures as he was dragged into the room. On large silver platters were sides of partially cooked reddish meat with rows of rib bones protruding. There were platters with stacks of long, pale serpentine flesh. Large, shiny metal pots contained steaming, pink-bodied insects the size of lobsters, with rows of long red legs on the sides of their bodies. The diners were heartily eating and drinking their fill, gulping out of metal goblets filled with liquid topped with blue foam. All activity ceased upon their entrance. One of the Brelac seated behind the banquet table belched.

"What do we have here?" the Brelac growled in a deep guttural voice. "Looks like an unexpected dinner guest."

"My invitation was probably lost in the mail," Fenlow replied. "Things are pretty hectic these days with the war going on."

The guard on Fenlow's left quickly slapped his face with a crack that was as painful as it was loud. The guard growled and jerked up on Fenlow's arm, gaining a high-pitched whine from the doctor.

"The prisoner was aboard a Protectorate shuttle with five of our soldiers," he reported in a slow, deep voice. "They have all stated that they were being held prisoner on the planet Talos by Protectorate troopers. Then this man came onto the scene. He killed three of his own comrades and turned his weapon over to our soldiers. He insisted on being brought to see our superiors. Says his name is Doctor Howard Fenlow. Insists that you know him."

49

The Brelac left his seat and sauntered over to give Fenlow a closer inspection, his long claws clicking against the stone flooring with each step. He stopped inches away from Fenlow and sniffed at him, his tail twitching sporadically. The long, wide nose worked its way up from Fenlow's legs to his face. Fenlow turned his head away when the Brelac exhaled; the creature's breath had a pungent odor resembling hot, dead fish.

"Are you sure he's not wired to blow?" the Brelac growled deeply. "Or that he's not rigged up with some kind of transmitting device?"

"We've ruled out those possibilities, sir," the guard said. "Once he arrived the prisoner was strip searched and examined with several different probes inside and out. We found no hidden devices of any kind."

"I can vouch for that," Fenlow added with a frown. "My back is still sore from bending over for so long."

"You came here willingly?" the Brelac asked. "Even killed three of your own in the process?"

"It was vital that I meet with someone of a rank higher than that of my two chaperones here," Fenlow explained.

For a moment the Brelac standing before Fenlow remained silent. Fenlow's skin twitched, apprehensive as to what would happen next. He had limited personal involvement with these creatures, but knew that they were as unpredictable as they were vicious. He eyed the rows of long teeth under the curled lips and suppressed a shudder.

The Brelac uttered a deep growl to slowly form a single name. "Fenlow. So, you're the Great Doctor Fenlow. One of the first traitors in the brief history of this war. We finally meet."

"I find the word traitor to be a little too malignant to suit my purpose," Fenlow said quickly. "I'd like to think of myself as an entrepreneur."

The Brelac growled again. Showing more of his sharp teeth. "Traitor, entrepreneur. It's all the same to me. The point is that you're here. The question is, why?"

"I'm here to speak to Bane Mariner. I have a proposition for him."

"You *are* addressing Governor General Bane Mariner. Supreme Commander of the Brelac Empire. And I hope that your proposition is worth my time."

"It is," Fenlow assured him. "What I'm about to propose will greatly benefit both you and my company."

"Carp Technologies," Mariner leaned back on his heels, his tail stretching out to counterbalance his shifting weight. "I admire your company. Playing both sides of the war for their own benefit. All the while maintaining the facade of a benevolent corporation serving your little corner of the universe. I wonder, what your people would say if they knew that you and your company were working with us to create the Reploid menace?"

"I'm…I'm afraid that the Reploid program has been discontinued for the present time. More especially the advanced Reploids. En-route to Helios on the planet Meridan one of your shuttles carrying several Reploid units was shot down by Protectorate forces. Three Reploids were captured by the military. Carp considered this to be a threat to company security and decided to halt the project."

Fenlow withheld the fact that he himself had recommended halting the project. Aided by Carp's resources, Fenlow produced the Reploids in a laboratory within a company research vessel stationed at a secret location in space. Fenlow notified his Brelac contact on a secured channel when each shipment of Reploids would be due for delivery, and would then meet a Brelac transport shuttle at a designated rendezvous point.

Curious about the Brelac's vision without the use of physical eyes, Fenlow had asked to examine their psionic implants. After months of extensive research he'd been able to create a more advanced version of the implants, and promised to deliver dozens of Reploids armed with the implants to help the Brelac achieve a swifter victory. Highly treasonous acts that would certainly earn Fenlow and others within Carp Technologies a swift death sentence.

"Those Reploids in the hands of your military could pose a problem," Mariner stated, cracking his knuckles.

"They're no threat. There are only three of them. The military will make limited use of their abilities, and I've already taken steps to diminish their effectiveness." Fenlow paused. "Carp's board of directors has decided to move forward with Operation Broad Axe. I have to do what I can to insure that the plan is successful. This means that I have to begin some of the more advanced projects that I've been working on."

"And you need my help to pull all this off," Mariner added. He went silent, his eyeless face studying Fenlow. "Let him go," he growled.

Both guards raised their left hands to their heads in a familiar military salute and exited the hall with haste.

Fenlow thought that it was curious how the two Brelac saluted in such a fashion. As if they were mimicking human troopers. He suspected that he would learn a great deal about these creatures by working closely among them in the days ahead.

"Fix this man a seat next to mine," Mariner blared out. "He's my guest of honor."

The attendants serving food and drink quickly provided a place at the table on Mariner's right side, and Fenlow sat as instructed, his hands slightly shaking in his lap. Using a long, two-pronged fork an attendant quickly loaded his plate with three long sections of the pale snake-like meats and two of the centipedes, steam rising from their cooked flesh.

Fenlow stared at his plate. The appearance of the food before him was nauseating enough, but its oily smell combined with a sour milk odor left him near paralyzed. Mariner silently faced him, and a thin stream of saliva dripped out of the right side of his mouth. Fenlow shuddered, slightly spooked in the close sight of Mariner's scaled face and the long pointed teeth in the constant grin.

Fenlow nervously cleared his throat. "I suppose you're not serving any salads."

A faint, hoarse growl came from Mariner's throat. "Nothing so elaborate here."

"I see."

Fenlow looked to the left and right side of his plate and saw no silverware. He quietly groaned in frustration. It was evident that the Brelac were eating with their hands, and Fenlow desired to blend in with his hosts. He gingerly picked up a centipede. It was warm and soft to the touch. He held it up to his face and managed not to flinch away. At least he was able to distinguish which item smelled like sour milk.

A deep grunt came from Mariner. "You look like you were just kissed by Pandora. Don't worry, Doctor. It won't bite you back."

Kissed by Pandora. A strange terminology to use. Perhaps an example of their alien culture?

But the name, Pandora, stuck in Fenlow's mind. There was something familiar about it. He thought that this would be the perfect time to get a little more background on his allies. He laid his centipede back down on his plate but kept his fingers on it.

"So, I've done a little research and found that you Brelac are Reploids yourselves," he said.

"To a degree we are all the same," Mariner sluggishly droned out, grabbing his own centipede and downing it in one loud gulp. "Our race needed a technological means to insure its continuation."

"A technological means," Fenlow repeated. "And what of your females? I noticed that through all the grunting and growling you all sound male."

"As I have already explained, we are all the same," Mariner said. "We have created the means of producing the perfect military force. Our soldiers originate from templates that are devoid of fear, unhindered by compassionate doubts, and minds that are not mired by the frivolous aberrations that obstruct you humans."

"What about these original templates that you mentioned? I'm assuming that it's some sort of original genetic stock."

"Our original source is centuries old and continues to endure. But its history is not important." He waved a clawed hand. "All that matters is that it serves us as we produce our numbers en-masse in order to achieve our objective."

"And that objective would be?" Fenlow asked, suspecting he already knew the answer.

"Our objective is to spread ourselves across this universe and administer retribution to any and all opposition. Then we will become the only supreme power. That is our mission passed down to us through generations. This is what we will achieve. And *you*, Doctor Fenlow, will help us."

Fenlow pondered Mariner's words, fingertips stroking the soft white flesh of the centipede on his plate. He was still dreading the notion of being forced to eat this thing.

The Brelac mission of conquest and retribution. A chilling thought.

But Fenlow's job was to find a way to work Carp Technologies' interests into the mission so that their own plans could materialize unscathed. And with the Brelac's help his job would be much easier.

"I'll help you," Fenlow told him, nodding.

He took a long look at the centipede he was holding. He picked it up and slowly raised it to his face, holding his breath against the smell. He opened his mouth.

CHAPTER SIX

An explosion of glass hurled toward his face. Clouds of black smoke obscured his vision. A man with long, dark hair and frenzied eyes clad in a dirty pair of ragged shorts and robe charged through the smoke. The man raised his fist and sent it flying into Colin's face…

Colin jerked awake, then groaned at his splitting headache. *That was understandable,* he thought, c*onsidering I just survived a crash a few…a few… How long ago had the ship crashed?*

He looked up and his eyes met the floor. He blinked, and realized he hung upside down from the high ceiling of a large room. He guessed he hung at least six feet from the floor. He turned his head and saw a gray brick wall behind him. And out of the corner of his eye saw Diane hanging next to him, still unconscious. Kelly, Blair, and Trevor were nowhere in sight. He closed his eyes and ground his teeth to try and cope with the throbbing pain in his head.

I need to turn right side up, or my blood is going to make my head explode.

The room itself was an enormous warehouse. A musty odor filled the air. Six feet away from where Colin and Diane hung were stacks of large, metal, cube-shaped containers, with long black handles on their sides. At the right was a group of round, blue plastic, gallon-sized containers. Further into the warehouse sat a row of seven tables holding large displays of weapons. The first two tables held a collection of laser pistols and several guns Colin recognized as projectile firing weapons. The next two had dozens of long-barreled laser rifles. The last three had a large assortment of hand weapons: daggers, hunting knives, axes, hatchets, and swords. At the left and right of the tables were short walls of large cardboard boxes stacked four high. To the far end of the warehouse was a short flight of metal steps leading up to a huge metal door.

And possibly to the outside.

Colin tried to move his arms, but they were tightly bound at the wrists by a thick leather strap. A much longer strap bound his legs at the ankles and connected to a length of rope. He twisted his neck and his eyes followed the rope up through two metal hooks affixed to the ceiling, then down to where it was firmly tied to another hook in the concrete floor. Near the hook were several cardboard boxes filled with scrap metal and rusting tools. Just a few feet away from the hook stood two scowling men.

One was a muscular man wearing a pair of shorts and a hooded cape both made from reptile skins. The other man was a seven-foot-tall giant with a massive build and dressed in dark blue, tight-fitting coveralls, and black boots studded with metal spikes. A black leather mask lined with spikes hid the left side of his face, and large ashen pockmarks heavily scarred the exposed right side.

There was a moan to Colin's right. Diane stirred as she regained consciousness.

"Where the hell are we?" she demanded.

The huge man in the coveralls looked over, appearing almost bored. "Glad to see that you're finally awake," his baritone voice boomed.

The man sounds friendly enough, Colin thought. "Is it possible for you to let us down from here?"

"I went through all the trouble of hanging you up there for a reason. It makes it easier for me if I have to kill you."

Guess I was wrong.

Colin made a quick study of these men and their savage appearance. He remembered hearing of tribes of feral sociopaths on several outlying planets considered to be outlaws within the Protectorate, and who frowned at the notion of integrating back into society. It was possible that he and Diane were the prisoners of two such individuals, and if so, he didn't think their intentions could be pleasant.

"Look, you'd better do yourself a big favor and cut us down from here right now." Diane jerked at her restraints. "You'll avoid a hell of a lot of trouble. We're both very important members of the Protectorate military. And they're bound to come looking for us."

"Threats from the Protectorate don't impress me," the man snorted. "There wasn't much salvage on your ship. But since you ladies are such important members of the high and mighty military, then I think I'll see how much they're willing to pay to get your asses back."

"You're holding us for ransom?" Colin shouted. "Our superiors will never go for that."

"Damn right they won't!" Diane snarled. "Listen up. I'm Captain Diane Christy. I'm a fighter pilot. The military is gonna want me back at any cost. And they'll most likely use force to do it. Now unless you want to find yourself buried under all this junk I advise you to cut us down now."

The two men laughed. The giant stepped menacingly closer to Diane.

"Well, *Captain* Diane Christy. I'm Vic De Boer. I may be just a lowly merchant but my boys and I control this region. And I've got enough firepower stored here to hold off any army—even your precious Protectorate. But just keep in mind that if your pals want to pick a fight then you'll both be the first ones to die."

"What about our friends?" Colin cut in. "Are they still alive?"

"Don't worry about them," Vic said with the wave of a hand. "They're already sold."

"Sold?"

Vic did not answer. He turned away to his minion. "Harper, I've got some business to take care of. Finish cataloging the instruments that we pulled from their ship. Then get started on the scrap metal dumpsters. They're both full so you'll have to wheel them out and empty them." He took a final look back at his two prisoners. "Take the girl to help you. She should be easy enough to manage. Just don't be all day. We've got a lot of other things to do."

Vic left, his hulking body disappearing behind a tall stack of boxes.

Harper pulled out a long dagger from a pocket in his shorts. With a single stroke the blade sliced through one of the straps. Diane screamed as she dropped to the floor. Her arms hit the concrete first, and then the rest of her weight painfully slammed her onto her back. Harper reached down and cut the straps from around her ankles and wrists, then slid the dagger back into his pocket. He scanned Diane from head to foot, giving an approving nod.

"Scrap metal dumpsters are a big job. We got a lotta work ahead of us."

"Look, I'm a fighter pilot," she shot back. "Not a laborer, and I don't plan on staying here. So why don't you cut my friend down and show us the way out?"

Harper grabbed Diane by her hair and lifted her up off the floor. Colin was surprised at how easily Harper was able to wield Diane. His strength matched the beefy appearance of his thickly muscled arms.

"Let her go!" Colin protested, not really expecting Harper to comply.

Harper addressed Diane more forcefully, his voice raising an octave. "You're gonna have to learn to show a little respect and remember who's in charge. Vic's my boss. I'm yours. When he barks you jump first. Now if you want to stay in one piece then you'll behave yourself. You do want to behave yourself, don't you?"

Diane simply cried out in pain, her face tight and eyes closed.

"I knew you'd see things my way," Harper said gleefully. He released his hold on Diane's hair and let her drop to the floor. He kneeled down and gently ran his fingers across her cheek. "You be a good girl and maybe I won't have to chain you. Not like they do at the slave market. That's where you're headed if we don't get a ransom from the Protectorate. Of course, I'd like for us to spend a little time alone before that."

Diane rubbed her scalp to soothe the pain. She leaned back against one of the boxes filled with small rusty hammers, screwdrivers, and wrenches. Harper looked down at her. He had a smug look on his face that Colin wanted to bash away with a heavy rock.

"If you hurt her then consider yourself a marked man," Colin said slowly. "There won't be a planet within the Protectorate that you'll be able to hide on."

Harper twisted and delivered a solid fist into Colin's chest. Colin's body swung back and slammed into the wall behind him, the back of his head bouncing against the hard bricks. Colin coughed to regain his breath while his chest burned in agony. His body swung forward, spinning, then back and the left side of his body collided with the wall. Still spinning, he swung back a third time, but with less momentum.

Harper turned back to Diane, who now stood on unsteady feet. She held a long screwdriver in her right hand. Harper laughed and stepped toward her, just as Diane swung her arm around and thrust the tool at his head to stab into his ear. He let out a howl that reverberated throughout the warehouse and collapsed to his knees, clutching the wound.

"Quick," Colin hissed through clenched teeth, still trying to breathe. "Get me down before he recovers."

Diane hurried over and tried to loosen Colin's strap from the hook. She growled at the intricate knot, her fingers working furiously.

Diane looked up. "This damn knot won't come loose. I'm gonna find something to cut it off."

"Sometime today would be nice," Colin said, his vision starting to blur from the rush of blood to his head.

Diane reached into one of the boxes on the floor. She picked up a large pipe wrench nearly two feet long. Colin struggled against the wrist straps.

"Are you going to beat it into submission? Get something to cut the strap. Something sharp. Hurry!"

An angry snarl came from behind Diane. They turned and saw Harper slowly rising to his feet. A look of rage radiated from his face. He grabbed the screwdriver and yanked it out of his ear. He pressed his hand against the left side of his head. Blood bubbled through his fingers. He pointed the screwdriver menacingly toward Diane.

"You are gonna die slow and painful!" Harper growled through clenched teeth.

"What the hell's going on?" Vic's blaring voice echoed from across the room. He darted from behind a stack of crates and came charging to investigate.

"Run!" Colin yelled. He knew the game of cat and mouse would become more complicated with the appearance of a second cat.

Diane turned and ran, managing to get twenty feet away before a third captor, an obese, six-foot-tall man wearing a badly tattered, dark hooded robe, leaped out from behind a stack of cardboard boxes to bar her way.

Diane turned back to where Colin hung. Vic and Harper charged toward her. She spied a pile of rusted garden tools laying on the floor, among them an axe with a badly splintered wooden handle. She quickly grabbed the handle, but the blade slipped off when she lifted it and clattered to the concrete floor. She dodged around the third man to one of the tables displaying the collection of laser pistols and quickly grabbed one, her hands shaking.

Harper stopped in his tracks at the sight of Diane holding the gun. The obese man pulled his own laser pistol from within a fold in his robe. He took aim at

Diane and fired just as she yipped and dove behind a wall of stacked boxes.

Colin struggled desperately to get free of his straps. He had to get out to help Diane. His eyes followed her progress as he worked. She was still crouched down behind a wall of boxes. The obese man stood several feet away, taking wild shots to try to either hit Diane or flush her out into the open. Harper was crouched down behind a table at Diane's left. Colin scanned the area to locate Vic, and finally caught sight of him stooped down behind a stack of metal containers a few feet away from Diane's right, and was steadily creeping closer. Diane's attention was focused on the obese man firing at her, and her back was turned to Vic.

"Diane!" Colin shouted. "Look out!"

Vic bolted forward and pounced down on Diane. Diane tried to fire two shots at Vic but the shots went wild toward the ceiling. He grabbed her gun hand and threw a swift blow to her face. She dropped the gun and slumped back to the floor. Vic grabbed her by the neck in a tight grip and lifted her off the floor, then hurled her through the air. Diane landed on one of the tables holding knives and swords, the table collapsing beneath the impact. Diane did not move. If she was stunned, then Colin hoped that she would get back to her feet very quickly, as it seemed their enemies would give her no respite.

Vic walked over and picked her up as though she were a limp rag and wrapped her body in his bulky arms, and slowly constricted his arms to crush her. Diane finally came to and struggled wildly against him, but Vic's strength was unyielding.

"You're too much trouble to keep around and wait for a ransom," Vic grunted. "And you're not gonna live to see the slave market."

Colin squirmed harder than ever against the straps, hard enough that he felt his skin being torn by them. Colin yelled, not wanting to let a few small wounds stop him. He continued to struggle with added intensity. He doubted that he could do anything to help Diane, but his own life depended on him getting free. He poured every bit of strength that he could summon into the task of struggling out of these straps. After a minute of this, Colin's head pounded with a nearly intolerable pain, but he tried to ignore it and continued his efforts to break free.

A strange tingling sensation suddenly washed over Colin's entire body. It overwhelmed him so much that he had to stop struggling just to keep breathing. His stomach contracted, making him twitch sporadically, as a sudden blinding blue flash and a hail of sparks exploded about him. For a moment Colin felt weightless, then he cried out at the painful impact of his body slamming onto the floor.

Colin felt an intense pain on his wrists. He glanced down to see smoking fragments of the straps burning his skin. He quickly tore them off and was surprised when sparks flew out of his hands. He stared at his hands, and his eyes widened in amazement. Then he was blanched in fear.

What the hell is this?

He knelt, shaking, afraid to move, unsure if he should sit still. He stared at his wrists, trying to see if his skin had burned away along with the straps. He frowned and inspected them closer. Not even a single hair had been singed. His heartbeat gradually slowed.

I'm alright. But how in hell's name is this possible? Is this dangerous?

It suddenly occurred to him that this might be a manifestation of the power that Blair said he was supposed to possess. Evidently this power had generated a surge of energy that burned through the straps. Colin wondered if this power was dangerous enough to burn through his frail flesh as well.

Well, this could not have happened at a better time, he thought.

But the image of his skin bursting into blue flames made him bite his lip, and he wondered if he dared to try and use this power again. He blinked at the sudden silence. He glanced up open mouthed at the others, remembering where he was.

Vic and his two thugs were staring dumbfounded at him, so amazed that they were almost ignoring Diane's weak attempt to break free of Vic's hold.

Colin shakily rose to his feet. He swallowed. "Back off and let the lady go," he said, his voice shaking. "Or…or I might have to get rough." He received only confused stares from the three men. "I think it's time to show you just how much trouble you're getting into," Colin said with a more confident swagger.

Colin raised his hands toward the obese man, his heart pounding. He smiled and tried to release enough energy to transform the man into charred bones.

"Burn in hell then," he muttered, opening his hands wide.

A single blue spark jumped from Colin's fingers, and then faded away as it sizzled on the floor. This paltry effect fell short of the deadly power that he had summoned seconds ago. Colin's mouth moved twice, but no words came.

The obese man aimed his weapon at Colin. Colin dropped to the floor just dodging the shots as the man opened fire, and swiftly crawled behind a crate for cover. He peered around the crate and saw Harper charging toward him, still wielding the bloody screwdriver. He glanced over to the tables holding laser guns, and knew it was too far away for him to reach safely. Colin jerked back behind his cover and closed his eyes.

Dammit, what now?

Harper leapt on top of Colin, easily wrestling him to the ground, then lifted Colin up by the neck and tossed him into the air. Colin yelled as he crashed into a stack of boxes, the cardboard collapsing and burying him under dusty electronic components.

Dazed and sore, Colin barely had a chance to stand before Harper was on him again. Harper roughly lifted Colin to his feet, and jerked Colin's arm behind his back before shoving him back to the ground. As Colin's head cleared, he found himself being shoved to the ground at Vic's feet, the ominous form of the huge man towering over him. Colin raised his hands defensively.

"The military won't be too happy if any harm comes to us."

Vic scowled at Colin. "Throw him in the pit with the rejects! They aren't worth this shit."

In the pit with the rejects?

Colin did not know whether that meant life or death, and was not looking forward to finding out on Vic's terms. He scuttled away slowly. Nervously, he looked to his left and right to see that Vic's two henchmen were closing in on him. Colin stared back at Vic's enraged face. He raised his trembling hands.

The obese man grabbed Colin's arm to drag him away. A blue flash and a burst of sparks erupted upon contact, and the brute quickly recoiled. Harper dove on top of Colin and forced him to the floor. Colin was able to grab hold of Harper's wrist before he was slashed across the face with the screwdriver. Colin cried out and a powerful surge of energy whipped out from his skin to course through Harper's body. Harper's cape suddenly became a shroud of fire.

Colin screamed as fire surrounded him on both sides. He gagged under the sickening, sweet odor of burnt flesh. He pushed the man's burning body aside and saw that the obese man was taking aim at him with the laser gun. Colin froze.

Vic stared at them wide-eyed. He still had Diane held securely in his embrace, but did not seem to be paying attention. Diane intensified her effort to free herself from his tight hug. She shrieked loudly and pried Vic's arm open with an ease that belied her earlier struggles.

Still holding onto Vic's arm, Diane used it to lift him off of his feet. She swung him around and sent him flying several feet across the warehouse and into a brick wall. Vic crashed face first into the wall with a loud, moist thud, the impact cracking the wall's surface and leaving a splash of blood against the paint. Vic slumped to the floor and lay still. A pool of blood slowly expanded under his head.

Colin turned to see the last man turning to aim his pistol at Diane. "Look out!" he yelled.

Diane dove behind a dumpster holding chunks of scrap metal. Colin dove down behind a dark metal crate when he saw the man whirl about, the man's gun spitting out a volley of bolts that bored through the crate, coming dangerously close to passing through Colin as well.

The man turned to see Diane take cover behind a large wall of metal and plastic containers. He opened fire and shot everything in that area. While the man's back was turned Colin saw this chance to make a counterattack.

I need to use this power as quickly as this guy pulls that trigger.

He took a deep breath, then sprang up from behind the crate and thrust his right hand out. He visualized himself releasing the power to strike the man down. Colin was startled at the bolt of energy that discharged from his hand. With a burst of white sparks the man was lifted off of his feet and swiftly hurled into a stack of boxes several feet away. Colin stood shaking as Diane ran over to him. She smiled.

"We did it. We won!"

"So we did," he whispered. His skin tingled. He glanced over at Vic's unmoving body. "How the hell did you do that?"

Diane looked at her right hand. She clenched it tightly into a fist. Colin could tell by the broad smile on her face that she had a different reaction to this newly found power.

At least she did not carry a power that could be potentially lethal to herself.

"I don't know, really," Diane said, still smiling. "I just needed to fight back. It was him or me, and it just sorta…happened. But nevermind me. What about you? Firing the lightning bolts?"

"When I was trying to break free of those straps I felt this weird sensation. Then somehow I generated this energy surge that burned off the straps. At first I thought that I was going to get fried. I still don't know much about this power, or if I should even keep using it. Who knows what effects this will have on me."

Diane curled her lips and scrunched her nose. "What are you, insane? The only effect that I saw was that it saved your ass. Just like this weird strength saved my life. That Vic character was crushing me. Then all of a sudden I felt like something exploded inside me, like I had all this energy and nothing to do with it. That's when I had the strength to pull his arm away."

"I guess Blair was right about these abilities of ours," Colin said. "We couldn't have dealt with these clowns without them... Diane! We need to find the others."

The obese man moaned. Tendrils of smoke rose from his body, but he was alive and slowly regaining consciousness. Diane displayed no compassion for the injured man. She grabbed him by the back of his neck and lifted him up over her head.

"We need him alive," Colin said quickly, almost reaching for her. "He can lead us right to where the others are being held."

Diane rolled her eyes and reluctantly complied. She allowed the man to drop roughly to his knees on the hard floor but kept a firm grip on his neck.

"Where are the other members of our group?" Colin demanded, his nerves settling slightly.

The man gave an animalistic grunt as he grabbed for Diane's hand, and she yanked him to his feet.

"Let's try that again," she said, her fingers tightened.

"Over there," he managed, pointing toward an area to the right.

Diane released her hold on the man and shoved him in the direction he had pointed. She and Colin followed him closely. He brought them to a wide metal plate mounted onto the floor with several small slits cut into the face and secured by a large rusty lock fastened to a metal latch firmly attached to the floor.

"Can you open it?" Colin asked Diane, pointing to the plate.

Diane grinned and hit the wounded man over the head and then shoved him aside before kneeling down to grab hold of the plate. The metal bent quickly under her grip. She ripped out the plate and threw it across the warehouse just as easily. They all stepped back as a gust of air reeking of oil and urine wafted up to them, then covered their noses and peered down into the darkness.

Four dirty and ragged troopers blinked awkwardly up at them from a deep square pit laying among heaps of animal bones, soiled rags, scrap paper and rusted metal debris. Strangers, with no sign of Blair, Trevor, or Kelly. Colin wondered how long these men had been here. From what he could see they had not bathed in quite a while, and by the looks of their thin frames and pale sunken cheeks were probably not fed regularly either.

"Don't be alarmed," Colin said quickly. "We're here to help you."

Diane bent down and offered a hand, then pulled the troopers up from the pit one by one while Colin continued to explain.

"I'm Sergeant Colin McKenzie. This is Captain Diane Christy. We're looking for our friends. Blair Van Doren, Doctor Arnold Trevor, and a real young guy, Kelly Lytton."

One of the troopers, a tall and slim-figured individual with his left eye swollen shut from an obvious beating, frowned.

"No use worrying about your friends. If you're here to rescue them then it's too late. Too late for all of them."

CHAPTER SEVEN

Colin knew that he would regret jumping into the dark metal chute to the disposal pit below. As he plummeted feet first his boots and hands failed to miss every protruding bump and strip of metal. Dusty sheets of cobwebs collided with his face and clung to his skin. Diane's screams echoed above him, as she followed closely behind. It had been her idea for them to jump down into the chute and stage a dramatic rescue.

This might be a drastic method of reaching the chamber below, Colin thought. *But the troopers said there is little time to spare. Kelly's life depends on how quickly we move.*

Colin's long, bumpy ride came to an abrupt end as he landed on top of a large pile of trash. He cried out as Diane's legs slammed onto his back. Colin was thankful the pile of refuse was soft enough to break their fall. He tried to stand but his legs would not cooperate. A brief struggle sent a series of painful spasms through his legs, and he looked down to discover his legs were tangled in a large mass of barbed wire. He credited the wire for helping to break his fall, despite the painful process it would be to free himself.

A muffled cry brought his attention about, and he twisted under Diane's deadweight onto his side. Kelly lay next to him, his hands tightly bound behind his back by a dark adhesive tape and a strip of tape across his mouth. Kelly squirmed frantically about. His muffled cries burst through the tape as he motioned with his chin to something behind Colin.

Colin looked up at the rocky ceiling to the opening they had dropped through. The ceiling seemed low enough for him to reach up and touch with his fingertips. They were sprawled on top of a twenty-foot-wide pile of garbage that had an unbearably rancid smell. He wrinkled his nose and looked beyond the trash heap to the many lights mounted on the rough, sandy walls that illuminated their surroundings. The trash heap sat directly below the garbage chute in the middle of a large chamber that stretched nearly forty feet in all directions. The edges of the chamber were lined with large groups of tall cacti, the green spiny trunks pulsating as though they were breathing.

Colin blinked. The cacti were slowly moving toward the trash heap, pulling themselves along by the mass of thick roots and long snaking tendrils at their base.

Colin reached over and tried to tear the barbed wire free from around his legs. He looked over at one group of cacti getting dangerously close, their probing tendrils giving them a reach extending almost twenty feet. An opening formed at the top of the nearest cacti's trunks. Hungry jaws extended to display rows of gleaming white fangs. The trunks bent forward, slowly writhing like snakes as their jaws repeatedly snapped open and closed.

Colin desperately tried to pull away the barbed wire and free his legs. It was a painful endeavor as the wire stuck to his legs with each careful jerk. The sharp barbs jabbed his hands with each grip, and the metal became slippery under his reddening hands. Something touched his foot, and Colin fought all the harder.

This is not how I want to die. I'm a soldier, I'm supposed to die in battle, with a weapon in my hand, taking several Brelac enemies with me. I didn't sign on to die as plant food!

"Captain Christy!" Colin shouted, struggling under Diane's weight. "Wake up!"

Kelly squirmed violently against his bonds, and small flashes of red light suddenly shot out from his face. Colin lurched back when red, pulsating waves of energy emanated from Kelly's head.

It's happening again, Colin thought. *First with me, now with Kelly. Whatever this energy is, it is hot enough to ignite the soiled waste of a trash heap.*

Dozens of small fires began to burn all around them and slowly grew into a large inferno. Kelly let out a muffled cry through the tape on his mouth, his frustration evident. Diane finally managed to move, and slowly sat up on Kelly's chest.

"Oh, man," Diane groaned. "My back."

"You think you have problems?" Colin yelled. His bleeding hands fought to unravel the barbed wire from his legs. He coughed on the thickening smoke.

Kelly screamed through the tape to get Diane's attention, and she finally looked down at the flames licking at her feet. She jumped and began to kick at the fire, only to see more flames surrounding her. Then she finally noticed Kelly lying under her. She ripped the strip of tape from his mouth.

"Get off me!" Kelly roared.

Diane jumped up. "Sorry kid."

"Untie me! Hurry!"

"I could use a little help too," Colin said.

Diane easily ripped the tape from around Kelly's wrists.

"Damnit!" he yelled. "That hurt!"

"The fire!" Colin yelled, coughing.

Diane leaped over to Colin and stamped out a nearing fire. She coughed on the smoke and waved at the air in front of her face.

"Watch the cacti," Kelly warned.

"Some help here?" Colin impatiently reminded Diane.

Diane looked about at the horde of plants surrounding them. Their tendrils crept forward toward them, displacing barrels and wood to reach them. Coughing, Diane searched through the debris until she found the laser pistol she had dropped during the fall.

"Give me a hand here," Kelly demanded. He was having difficulty trying to pull the tape from his ankles.

Diane growled, "Give me a break, kid. I still haven't dealt with the fires yet."

"Don't call me kid!"

Diane ignored Kelly's protest and immediately put the pistol to use. She pumped several laser bolts into a cactus, blowing large green fragments away from its trunk. White liquid gushed out from each burn hole. The cactus stopped moving and drooped over to the ground. She took aim and killed two more cacti. Kelly was still ripping at the tape around his ankles when two tendrils wrapped themselves around his legs. He screamed and Diane spun around and severed the tendrils with laser fire.

Diane stamped out fires to her left and right. She spun back to her left and shot at tendrils reaching for her feet. She put out a fire near Kelly, who was still having trouble removing the tape.

"Pathetic," Diane grumbled. She kneeled down and casually ripped the tape with her fingers.

Diane reached down to Colin's legs. Instead of trying to unravel the tangle of barbed wire she carefully ripped it apart.

Two tendrils snaked their way around Colin's neck, tightened, and pulled. He was drug on his back through the trash toward the open mouth. Kelly moved to grab hold of Colin's ankles, but hesitated when a sudden burst of sparks leapt out from Colin's body. A charge of electricity surged through the tendrils and into the cactus, and the plant exploded on contact. Warm, white cactus fluid rained down on them and Kelly raised his hands defensively and turned his head while small spiny chunks of the plant peppered the area.

"What the hell was that?"

"No time for explanations," Colin gasped.

Colin unwrapped the quivering tendrils from around his neck just as others were reaching for him. He jumped to his feet and raised his hands. A flash of twin electrical bolts sprung from his hands, surprising a nearby Kelly. Dozens of cacti exploded with a huge spray of white liquid when the energy touched them. The surviving cacti in the area were pelted by a hail of plant fragments, their green bodies now milky-white after being soaked by the juices of their brethren. Colin shot two more bolts at a thick wall of cacti, and the ground became a lake of white and green chunks. Colin spun around and swept the area, front and back, exploding more cacti than he hoped to count.

Colin fired two bolts at another group of cacti and exploded four of them. Behind the group of plants Colin saw a trooper standing twenty feet away, waving a hand in the air. The trooper stood near a thick metal door. He had a laser pistol in hand and started shooting at the cacti in the area that began to swarm toward him.

"There's a way out of here!" Colin shouted.

Diane and Kelly followed Colin toward the door, but the multitude of items that composed this foul smelling collection of garbage effectively slowed their pace. They had to stumble over large cardboard boxes filled with paper trash and bones, large tree branches, and long rusted beams of scrap metal hidden among the smaller refuse. Diane lost her footing twice and nearly fell as she stumbled forward.

Up ahead the trooper continued shooting at the mob of cacti that were converging toward him, but his progress was slow. One by one the plants slumped over and fell to the ground under his assault. Kelly picked up a thick branch and began to swat at the tendrils at his right as he moved ahead. Colin and Diane stopped to clear away some of the cacti that were barring their path to the door. Diane shrieked fearfully and jumped away from the blue flash of electrical blasts released from Colin's hands. She took aim and pulled the trigger of her gun. Nothing happened. She shook the weapon and slapped her hand against its side, then tried to shoot again.

"I'm out!" Diane cried. She dropped the weapon and shrieked again, jumping back to avoid tendrils that were moving close to her ankles.

Colin spun to his left and his hands sent a bolt of electricity that severed a cactus in half. Another blast destroyed the cactus standing next to it.

"Keep moving!" he shouted.

They were just twelve feet away from getting out of this trash pile and reaching the cacti barring their way to the door. Colin's hands fired an electrical bolt that shattered the bodies of two cacti up ahead. He blasted away at them, reducing them into scattered chunks until he created a six-foot opening between them. He could see the trooper stepping back to the door as he shot at cacti and the tendrils whipping across the ground toward him.

"Let's move it!" Colin yelled to Diane and Kelly. He stepped over a box filled with broken glass and bolted forward, dozens of tendrils reaching for his legs. "Don't stop!"

Finally out of the sea of trash Colin charged ahead over the sand with Diane and Kelly running close behind. Up ahead, several cacti turned their snapping jaws to face them. Their swarm of tendrils, once moving toward the trooper, now rose into the air to curl around and change direction to their new targets. The cacti themselves began to move, closing the space between them. Colin did not stop running; his feet crushed chunks of cacti and nearly slipped on the white juices that stained the ground. He dashed past the moving wall of cacti on his left and right, his exposed arms brushed up against their hard trunks, covered by small white spines. Colin briefly felt the pain stab through his palms, forearms, and elbows. But he did not slow his stride until he emerged through the wall of plants.

Colin quickly turned and saw Diane running just a foot behind him. Several tendrils tried to wrap themselves around her legs but her momentum was too fast and strong. She almost crashed into Colin as she made her escape. Kelly ran screaming through the now closing pathway, arms forward and eyes wide. The tendrils were entwining themselves around his legs. Tendrils wrapped themselves around his waist. He screamed for help, his right arm reaching out. Behind him, two cacti bent toward him with their jaws open wide. Laser shots from the trooper's gun blew the jaws of the plants apart, and Kelly's body was showered by white cactus juice. Diane charged forward and grabbed Kelly's hand. Kelly cried out in pain as Diane pulled him free of the tendrils embrace and away, the squirming ends of severed tendrils still wrapped around his ankles.

The trooper ushered them through the door, though they needed no urging to rush through the doorway and up a flight of concrete steps. The trooper swiftly pulled the door shut behind him, and slid the thick metal bolt into a large hasp mounted on the wall, securely locked. They quickly followed the trooper to the warehouse above.

Kelly spun on Diane, his face dripping with the white juice. "What the hell's wrong with you?" he shouted. "You almost killed me back there! You almost ripped me apart while I was tied up by those things!" He pointed down at the twitching tendrils still clinging around his legs.

"Sorry, I didn't have a chance to rehearse your rescue," Diane snapped, glaring back at him.

Colin turned to the trooper. "Thank you for showing us the way out of there."

"We could have told you that there was an easier way down but you didn't wait," the trooper explained, shrugging. "And we needed time to find the key. Vic likes to keep the door locked so that the cacti won't get up here. They're his waste disposal system. They would have appreciated some fresh meat instead of the usual bones and food scraps."

Kelly shuddered. "Maybe this Vic should consider recycling." He started pulling the tendrils off of his legs.

"We appreciate your help," Colin said, holding out his hand. "We haven't been properly introduced. I'm Sergeant Colin McKenzie. This is Captain Diane Christy."

"Captain Diane Christy, Ace Pilot," Diane added proudly. "You've probably heard of me."

The trooper stared back at her, silent.

Colin hurriedly continued. "This is Kelly Lytton. We're part of a special unit. Silencers Squad."

The trooper stood up straight. "I'm Sergeant Cyrus Mandell. My comrades are troopers Ron Jarret, Bret Regis, and John Hild. We're with Paladin Squad, Third Combat Division."

Colin noticed that the other troopers that Mandell named were not present. "How long were you guys here?"

"Seven or eight months. I lost track of the exact time. We were riding our cycles on patrol, and the four of us separated from the rest of the squad. That's when Vic and his crew jumped us and brought us here. Vic was going to sell us to the Brelac, but then he changed his mind. He wanted to keep us around for slave labor. He probably had the same idea for some of you people. We tried to escape, but Vic and his men were always armed and watched us closely. Especially when they took us outside to work."

From the far corner of the warehouse near the steps the other three troopers approached the group, followed by Blair and Trevor.

"I thought we'd never see you guys alive again!" Blair exclaimed. "Those thugs had us locked up in a dusty pit. These troopers let us out and told us that you both just liberated the place by yourselves. But how?"

"It can only mean that their powers are functioning," Trevor said, smiling.

Blair looked ecstatic. "This means that the project is a success. I'm sorry that we weren't here to see how you handled these maniacs."

"I almost set myself on fire down there," Kelly cheerlessly told Blair. "Thanks for warning me about this ahead of time."

"You almost set *yourself* on fire?" Diane said in disbelief. "Just *yourself*?"

"Fire?" Blair inquired. "If you say that you started a fire then my theory is that you may be projecting a form of pure psionic energy. Energy amplified to a highly destructive level. It's the same basic power that fuels all of your abilities."

"I'm not worried about the technical part," replied Kelly. "I'm worried about the setting my bed on fire when I go to sleep part. How do I turn this power off before I accidentally cremate myself?"

"How did your power become active?" Blair asked.

Kelly shrugged his shoulders. "I don't know. I was tied up. Those cactus things were almost all over us. I had this bruiser sitting on top of me," he explained, jutting a thumb at Diane, "I just wanted to get free. Then I felt this burning sensation flowing inside of me. The next thing I knew I'm surrounded by fire."

Colin stepped closer. "It seemed that stress was the key to triggering these abilities. But now we need to gain a better control over them."

"Are these powers dangerous?" Kelly asked. "I mean, dangerous to *us*?"

Blair thought for a moment. "There's no way to tell. We barely had the time to evaluate your abilities. There's always the possibility that something could go wrong somewhere."

Colin frowned. "That's not a very comforting fact, Blair."

A loud, deep voice slowly echoed throughout the warehouse. "Vic! This is Danton! Come in!"

All eyes scanned the area to locate the source of the sound. Mandell pointed to a small black box sitting on top of a table. An intercom.

"Vic! This is Danton! Where the hell are you?"

"Sounds like Major Danton," Mandell said.

"Who is Danton?" Colin asked.

"Clive Danton. He's a Brelac major, stationed at some place called Rantraven. He's supposed to be some kind of science officer. He's also one evil son of a bitch. He comes here quite often with a gang of troops. Likes to throw his weight around with the locals in order to keep them in line. He's real pals with Vic, and Danton has done a lot of business with him."

"Vic!" Danton's voice boomed. He sounded more irritable. "We'll be arriving in three minutes. Have the merchandise ready for immediate transport. Danton out."

"What was that all about?" Kelly asked nervously, wringing his hands.

"The hell if I know, but I don't like it," Diane groused. "I'm gonna go above and see what's going on." She turned and ran upstairs.

"I already told you that it's too late for your two friends," Mandell said. "Vic made a deal to sell them to Danton."

"He sold us?" Blair exclaimed.

"Vic often sells prisoners to the Brelac and back to our side if the price is right. He was planning to sell you and the old guy for now. Hang on to Colin and Diane until he decided what to do with them later. He thought that the young one, Kelly, was just another kid. Vic had no use for Kelly so he dumped him into the disposal pit."

"Nobody's going to be sold off anywhere," Colin declared. "We've got to find a way out of here."

Diane dashed back down the stairs. "Two attack shuttles are about to land outside. They'll be here any second."

"Kelly, you're with me. Everybody else take cover," Colin ordered.

"There's a second way out of here," Mandell offered. "It's a tunnel in the back."

"Then let's hope that the Brelac aren't using it. Get these bodies out of sight and follow Mandell. Kelly and I will try to hold them off."

Colin made a hurried inspection of several cardboard boxes filled with stacks of papers yellowed with age, empty bottles, and dust-covered books. After a few moments he finally found the box he was looking for. It contained old clothing and shoes. They were dirty and smelled strongly of mildew. Colin quickly took off his coveralls and boots, motioning for Kelly to do the same. Colin picked out their new attire from the box: two pairs of ragged blue denim shorts and dirty white sneakers. He gave Kelly a sleeveless black shirt while he selected a blue shirt that was heavily marred by reddish stains.

Meanwhile, Diane and Blair assisted the four troopers in the job of removing the bodies from view. Getting rid of them was easy. They simply dropped the bodies into the disposal pit and let the cacti below do the rest. Diane glanced at the wounded obese man, afraid he would create a huge problem if he remained in the warehouse. Her quick solution was to drag him over to the disposal pit and dump him in.

"Vic!" a deep throated voice blared out from behind the door at the top of the stairs.

Colin grabbed a push broom that was propped against a table and thrust it at Kelly.

"What if we have to fight?" Kelly asked, his knuckles white around the broom handle.

"We'll have to fight if we want to live," Colin told him. "Can you still use your power? We're definitely going to need it."

"I'll try," Kelly said. He began to casually sweep the area while awaiting the arrival of their visitors.

Mandell led the others to the rear of the warehouse. They moved around a large stack of wooden crates to reach the escape tunnel. Kelly and Colin strode silent as a heavily armed Brelac force headed down the stairs, their claws clicking against the metal plates as they descended.

The first one that caught Colin's attention was the leader. He was wearing silver armbands that prominently displayed his rank insignia: a black oak leaf symbol above three black stripes, and below the stripes a small black star.

Major Danton, Colin thought, his heartbeat raising a notch.

A dozen Brelac soldiers accompanied Danton, all clutching heavy plasma rifles.

"Who the hell are you?" Danton demanded when his face turned toward them, scaled lips curling back.

Kelly quickly put his head down and kept sweeping. Colin smiled cheerfully and extended his hand in greeting.

"I'm McKenzie. The kid here is Lytton. We're both new here. Vic just put us on today."

For a minute Danton stood before Colin, only the sound of his heavy breathing breaking the thick silence. He flipped his tail and tilted his head slightly to the left. Then he stepped closer to Colin until their faces were only inches apart. He sniffed Colin's face twice, nostrils flaring, then stepped away and walked past Colin and Kelly and began to scan the area. Kelly managed a weak "hello" but was ignored.

"Where's Vic?" Danton grunted.

Danton's troops slowly surrounded Colin and Kelly.

"Vic?" Colin said with a smile. "He went back to the crash site."

Danton's eyeless face looked confused. "The crash site? Why the hell did he do that?"

"He said that there was still some equipment he wanted to take out of that Protectorate ship. There's no telling how long he'll be gone. Maybe you can come back later."

"I'm not leaving without the two prisoners Vic told me about," Danton said slowly, his gruff voice even. "Bring them out!"

"Vic took the prisoners with him," Colin stammered. "He said that he'd need some labor to help carry the equipment back. Perhaps we can interest you in something else?"

Colin pointed to Kelly. Kelly nervously looked about at the cardboard boxes near his feet. He quickly reached down for the first item that he saw. A long wooden stick with a dusty rubber suction cup mounted on the end. Kelly's face blanched.

"How about this 'deadly little weapon' here?" Kelly asked, quietly.

Danton slapped the instrument out of Kelly's hand, the old wood cracking as it slapped the floor. He growled showing off an impressive display of exceptionally white teeth.

"I don't want a damn plunger! Where are Vic's other guys? Where's Harper? Scab?"

Scab? thought Colin. *That was probably the big man…* "Vic took them along. He said that he needed somebody to keep an eye on the prisoners."

This was all that Danton could tolerate. He let out an enraged snarl and lunged at Colin. He grabbed Colin by his throat and shoved him back against a table, knocking several boxes over. An empty can clinked and rolled across the floor.

Colin stared back into the eyeless reptilian face. He could not see the slightest shred of humanity or compassion. There was just rage and intolerance.

Dear God, this guy is intense. Colin told himself. *I wonder if all Brelac were like this? What do they do to lighten up? Trade jokes or sing while torturing prisoners?*

Colin shook his head to clear his thoughts. He would ponder the issue at a later time, providing that he survived this encounter.

"I don't like wasting my time coming out here to listen to a bunch of crap!" Danton shouted in Colin's face. "Something stinks! I'm not leaving until I find out what it is!"

It's a pity Danton can't smell his own breath, Colin thought. *I wonder what kind of rotting carrion he just ate.*

Danton shoved Colin to the floor, then walked away. "Four of you keep these morons covered. If either of them tries anything, shoot them both. The rest of you search this building."

Two Brelac kept their plasma rifles aimed at Kelly's head. Two others charged over to Colin and trained their weapons on him as he slowly sat up. The other eight spread out and began to search through the warehouse.

Danton jumped back after his foot stepped into a pool of liquid. Danton dipped his fingers into the liquid. He brought his fingers to his nostrils and sniffed.

"Blood!"

Colin raised his hands at the two soldiers standing in front of him. They were caught off guard when Colin fired twin bolts of electricity that hurled them across the warehouse. Kelly yelled and raised his hands at his twin targets. Nothing happened.

The two soldiers guarding Kelly had been momentarily distracted by Colin's assault. They quickly turned their attention back to Kelly and raised their weapons to fire. Kelly screamed and raised his hands defensively in front of his face. The plasma rifles blazed crimson just as a panel of shimmering red energy appeared in front of Kelly. The multiple plasma bolts instantly bounced off the panel and were reflected back at the two Brelac. They quickly collapsed to the floor after the plasma bolts penetrated their bodies.

Kelly's face quickly transformed to an image of wide-eyed fear. "Look out!" he shouted. He dove to the floor.

Colin turned to see Danton draw his pistol from its holster. His hand discharged an electrical bolt, and Danton quickly ducked and returned fire. Two plasma bolts zipped past Colin's head. He had no time to make a second attack against Danton, as the other Brelac were quickly converging on his and Kelly's position.

Colin grabbed Kelly's arm and led him to the back of the warehouse. They dove down between two tables holding computer keyboards. Kelly stayed close to Colin as they crawled forward. A trio of Brelac opened fire, shredding the tables and keyboards. Colin stood up from behind the tables and hurled two bolts that knocked all three Brelac to the floor. He spun right and struck down another Brelac who had his weapon trained on the boxes where Kelly hid.

Colin ducked down. "We have to get out of here now. There's just too many of them!"

Colin crawled to the back wall of the warehouse to reach the tunnel and Kelly followed close behind. Sparks flew as plasma bolts burned into boxes and hardware around them as the Brelac's flanks moved closer. One bolt hit a wall of metal containers and the stack toppled noisily into a barricade before Colin and Kelly, cutting off their projected exit. They were trapped.

The containers suddenly lifted and flew out toward the Brelac as Diane burst through and gunned down four surprised Brelac with her laser pistol.

What the hell is she doing here? Colin thought. *She was supposed to be outside with the others.*

"Let's go!" Diane shouted to them.

Colin and Kelly stood and ran to follow Diane, leaving the safety of the boxes. They dashed into the tunnel where the others anxiously waited. They found themselves running through a small, brick passage, the low ceiling illuminated by a row of small bulbs, spaced six feet apart. They ran thirty feet before they came to a short flight of steps. They hurried down the steps and continued running through the passage toward a square of light in the darkness ahead, not bothering to look back to see if any Brelac were following.

Within seconds they reached the light, finding that it was an open doorway to the outside and emerged from the base of a large building, the upper floors gutted by past bombings. Blair and the others stood just outside the door, eagerly waiting for them. They clasped hands and stepped away from the building, then stopped in their tracks at the sound of clicking pistols. Colin looked up to see a small group of Protectorate troopers circled around them, their weapons ready.

"My God." Blair smiled and moved toward the troopers with open arms. "Am I ever glad to see you guys. There's a gang of Brelac inside—"

"Freeze!" the nearest trooper ordered. He raised his rifle. "Stay where you are. Move an inch and I'll take your head off."

"It's fine," Blair assured, stepping back. "No need to get hostile. We're on your side. We can identify ourselves."

"Shut the hell up!" the trooper snapped. "Say another word and I'll burn a hole through your face. Don't any of you move. Keep your hands where I can see them. Do it now!"

That belligerent attitude seemed familiar. Colin wondered if this trooper was somehow related to Diane. He joined the others as they slowly raised their hands and knelt down in the dusty ruins of an ancient street.

CHAPTER EIGHT

The Morthos star system was once a prime industrial, mining, and agricultural center that provided large supplies of food and manufactured goods for a majority of the Protectorate's colony worlds. Today, the five inhabited planets had been converted into temporary headquarters for Brelac operations in this sector of the quadrant. The bulk of the Brelac space fleet rested at the seven gargantuan spherical starbases stationed at the outer rim of the system. Hundreds of the Brelac's large conical battle cruisers, their manta ray shaped attack carriers, and larger battleships were docked along the outer hulls of the star bases. Fleets of ships departed the system daily only to be immediately replaced by other ships returning from combat for repairs and fresh supplies. Multiple divisions of ground units were housed in the expansive military bases that were established on the planet Morthos Three.

In an underground level of Rantraven base Doctor Fenlow worked diligently in the Brelac provided laboratory, examining the bio monitor on an incubation tube.

Ninety-eight degrees. Fenlow nodded, confident that there would be no complications with the organism that was growing inside.

In dealing with the Brelac, Fenlow found that they were actually quite generous. They'd given him a huge laboratory loaded with an abundance of supplies, and never failed to produce at his every request. Behind him, a powerful computer sat in the middle of a metal workbench, a small rack holding six test tubes filled with a clear liquid to the left of the monitor. On the right rested a small metal tray holding two pairs of surgical forceps, a scalpel, and six clear plastic envelopes containing shiny, dime-sized disks.

Fenlow had no qualms about being there. He was not haunted by the specters of the men that he killed. It did not matter if he was branded as a traitor. He and Carp Technologies were working to save the future of humankind, and some small sacrifices would have to be made in working to insure that the race survived this war and continued to flourish. Then he knew he and Carp Technologies would be hailed as the saviors of their people.

The door behind Fenlow clicked and slid open as someone entered the laboratory. Fenlow spared a glance back. Major Clive Danton, Fenlow's official guardian, or guard, as the case may be. Danton personally saw that Fenlow received everything he needed, while keeping a close eye on the doctor. In Fenlow's opinion, Danton was a non-intellectual animal whose only solution to any problem was to shoot it repeatedly and burn the remains. He tolerated Danton, knowing that this particular Brelac would not be around forever.

"Hello, Major," Fenlow greeted in a cold voice, not bothering to face Danton.

"I'm just checking to see if there's anything you might need," Danton said. "I also have an unusual report to relay. I got into a fight on Voran with two strange humans. They called themselves Colin McKenzie and Kelly Lytton."

Fenlow slowly turned from the incubation tube and faced Danton.

Danton clicked his claws together. "It seemed that these two possessed some kind of strange abilities. One of them had the ability to shoot bolts of energy from his fingertips. The other produced a defensive shield that reflected our firepower. I tried to bring them both back with me for examination. Dead or alive, I didn't care, but an unexpected attack by Protectorate troopers forced me and my men to back off." He paused. "What do you make of this?"

Fenlow spat out a brief burst of laughter. "The beings that you described were not human, they're Reploids. Two of the three advanced Reploids that my government captured. They were supposed to be out in space aboard Lodestar."

"They're not at Lodestar, they're back on Voran," Danton countered. "Possibly planning to retaliate against you for defecting. And what if your people should somehow create more of them?"

"Impossible. We hold all the proper resources to create Reploids. Especially the advanced class. I have nothing to fear from this matter."

"Just the same, as a precaution I've asked General Lagar to place the entire system under alert and increased security."

"Sounds like you're afraid," Fenlow said, a small grin tugging at his lips.

"Nonsense," Danton smiled, baring teeth. "Only a fool relaxes his guard in the face of an unknown threat."

Fenlow laughed. "I was right. You are afraid."

Danton gave a faint, hoarse snarl. "In war, you keep your guard up at all times and never let your enemy off the hook. That's why we've been able to handle you humans so well. Wouldn't you agree?"

Fenlow glared at Danton, his eyes narrowed. Danton was clearly trying to provoke him, but Fenlow was not about to waste his time on any petty arguments. He simply stared for a moment, and then addressed him quietly.

"I agree that you Brelac have the upper hand in this war. That's why I'm here. To make sure you keep it. As for the Reploids, I don't consider them a threat. They're obsolete when compared to my current projects. But if it will make you feel any better I'll handle them. After all, they are my creations. Take me to the base's robotics research lab. I have a plan that's guaranteed to put the Reploids out of action."

CHAPTER NINE

Once they arrived at the heavily fortified military base of Nocturne on the planet Trillion, Colin, Diane, and Kelly were immediately placed in separate secured detainment cells. Diane was put in a cell directly across the corridor from Colin and Kelly. For three days they waited in the small, white brick cells illuminated by a bright light shining from a foot-long tube on the ceiling, and were forced to sleep on crude bunks that consisted of metal slabs protruding from the walls topped with thin mattresses. Their bathroom facilities consisted of a shiny metal sink and toilet at the right. Three times a day they were fed meals on small plastic trays through a thin rectangular slot that slid open in the middle of the white, reinforced metal door.

Colin leaned up against the door, peering through a thin open slot at his eye level. He looked across the corridor at Diane's cell. He saw the top of her head moving back and forth through the slot in her cell door. The rapid click-clack of her racing footsteps was occasionally accompanied by shouts of profanities. Kelly sat on the lower bunk brooding, slouched over with his arms propped up on his knees, his head resting against his clenched fists. During this time they had not seen or heard anything from Blair or Trevor. Colin was just as upset as they were at the thought of being locked up like prisoners of war, especially by their own side. He knew that with their powers the three of them could easily break free of this frail prison, but such a drastic action would only make matters worse, and he had no urge to be in a more depressing place than this.

At least we're not sitting here idle, Colin thought.

Colin had taken the time to coach Kelly in trying to gain control over his power. Kelly became less fearful, and eventually learned how to manipulate the energy that he generated. At first, under Colin's direction, he had experimented in mimicking Colin with trying to project energy from his hands. The initial results had scorched a large circle in the middle of the floor and set part of the mattress of the upper bunk on fire, much to the irritation of their guards. After a little practice Kelly could a point a finger and send a beam of fiery energy to melt pin-sized holes through the metal door with little effort.

Kelly also learned he could summon a blue shield of defensive energy at will, and in any shape or size he desired, the panels of glowing blue energy ranging from small enough to shield his hand to large enough to cover an entire wall. Kelly's first try with this shield had been less than stellar. Trying to create and maintain a small square shield to stand up against Colin's rushing fist had resulted in Kelly gaining a punch in the nose. With better concentration, he was proud to find that his energy shields were quite durable, withstanding an assault against Colin's fists and powerful electrical bursts.

Kelly gave an impatient sigh. "So, I guess we're going to spend another day here."

"Possibly," Colin said. "But hopefully this will all be cleared up and we won't be here much longer. Somebody will come for us."

"You said that two days ago." Kelly sat up straight. "Being locked up here is driving me insane. Maybe we can experiment with my powers again. I think I can create some bigger effects than I did the last time."

Colin frowned when he looked at the scorched area near Kelly's feet. "Maybe we should wait until we get out into open spaces before we try something more advanced. It'll be a little safer."

The door to the cell suddenly slid open revealing Blair, Trevor, and General Larkin. In the presence of a high-ranking general Kelly jumped up from the bunk and stood rigidly at attention next to Colin, who had already assumed the same position. Diane was there as well, standing at attention in the doorway.

"At ease," Larkin said. "You're the ones that deserve the respect after all you've been through. If it weren't for the three of you, Doren and Trevor would be in the hands of the Brelac. And you also rescued those four troopers in the process."

Colin silently agreed, but he thought that it would be best to appear modest. "We were just doing a soldier's duty, sir. Fighting the enemy and protecting our comrades' lives."

"Duty or not, you saved us from those thugs back on Voran," Blair stated. "And ultimately the Brelac. You guys are heroes in my book. We should go to President Drennen and recommend you all for medals. I'm sure that Doctor Fenlow would agree."

"Doctor Fenlow?" Colin inquired.

Trevor stepped forward. "He's the head of the project that gave you three your powers. I'm quite sure he would be happy to meet you and see that you are all alive and functioning properly."

"Assuming that we can find him." Larkin frowned. "The man vanished shortly after you left. We contacted Lodestar but they told us that they haven't seen him. No one at Carp has seen him either."

"He's probably off hiding someplace working where he can't be disturbed," Trevor mused. "He's probably working on some special project. I wouldn't worry. In time he'll show up."

"I hope so. His insight on this project could be vital," Larkin explained. "But in the meantime we're finally letting you out of here and reassigning the three of you to other duties within the base."

Diane smiled, nodding in approval. "About time, sir. I was starting to go nuts in here. I'm ready to get back to my squadron."

Larkin hesitated before responding. "For the moment we have other plans for you, Captain."

"The three of you are an experimental unit," Trevor said. "There are still many aspects of your abilities that you haven't explored. Until we can consult with Doctor Fenlow and develop you to your full potentials I've suggested to General Larkin that we should hold off deploying you for any missions."

Kelly gave an impatient gasp and a frown appeared on Diane's face as she turned her gaze down to the floor. Colin quietly gave a sigh in disappointment and wondered how much longer they would be kept in the dark as to what they would do next with their lives.

"It makes sense," Blair added, almost sympathetically. "You'll want the full range of your powers working when the time comes to deal with the Brelac."

"Escort them to the command center," Larkin ordered. "Captain Roberts will give them their new assignments. In the meantime, I have several pressing matters to deal with. It's been a pleasure meeting you all. I'll check up on you from time to time."

Larkin left the cell and disappeared down the corridor. Colin felt apprehensive about the idea of a general making surprise visits, but not as apprehensive as he felt about his new assignment. He stared at the end of the corridor where the general had left, trying to imagine what their future would hold.

"I wonder what kind of new jobs they're gonna give us," Diane said. "We've got all these fancy powers and I'm ready to see some action."

"You won't see any action for a while," Blair said. "Chances are you'll be given jobs within the base."

Diane scoffed. "Not any damn grunt work I hope. I'm a fighter pilot and an officer."

Kelly let out an irritated grunt. "We're soldiers. We go where we're told."

"You look a little young to be calling yourself a soldier, kid," Diane chided, sarcastically.

"For the last time, I'm not a kid!" Kelly snapped.

Colin was not in the mood to listen to Diane and Kelly argue. "I feel a lot better knowing that you two will be separated."

"And I feel a lot better knowing that the three of you are staying here," Blair stated. "You're not ready to take on any dangerous missions."

"We already took on those guys back on Voran." Diane shook her head. "And the Brelac."

"We were lucky and they were taken by surprise," Colin scolded. "I don't want to gamble my life on it happening again. Maybe we can take the time to learn

98

more about our powers. Kelly's been making progress. There still might be things that Blair and Trevor can tell us about our own."

"The three of you have specially designed psionic implants within your brains," Blair said. "They amplify the brain's level of psychic activity. Your powers are psychic in nature and each power manifests itself differently. It's my theory that this is how each of you developed different abilities. Diane's power manifested itself in the form of increased strength. Colin gained a form of increased electro chemical activity. And we've already established that Kelly manipulates psionic energy in its pure form. There could be several other applications for each of your abilities, we just have to be patient and train you to find them. That time will come, but just not right now."

"And how long will that take?" Diane grumbled. "The Brelac won't wait for us to complete any training sessions."

"What about this Fenlow?" Kelly asked. "You said that he could help us."

"If he ever decides to show up," Blair replied. "He knows far more about the implants than we do. We could certainly use his knowledge."

"But until then you three have new jobs to go to," Trevor reminded them. "You'd better not keep Captain Roberts waiting."

Captain Roberts awaits, Colin thought. *As soldiers we have to go where we're told. Following orders is the main creed of a soldier's life, but I'm not happy with the idea of taking on a new assignment while there were several gaping holes exposed in my life. The memories of my past are as unclear as my future. I can't help feeling incomplete, and Blair and Trevor are doing very little to help.*

Colin could not conjure any logical reason why Blair and Trevor would withhold any vital information if they were all a part of a project that was supposed to be so important. Whatever answers were waiting, Colin knew that he had no choice but to be patient. He knew that it was only a matter of time before he uncovered the truth about his life.

CHAPTER TEN

"Another damn leak."

Colin kneeled down and placed the blue plastic bucket on the floor under the spot where water slowly dripped from the ceiling. Colin intended for the bucket to serve the dual purpose of catching the drip and hiding the two-inch puddle that had already formed on the floor. For a final touch he took out a white rag hanging from the back pocket of his gray camouflage trousers, balled it up, and placed it inside the bucket to muffle the annoying sound of the constant *tap, tap, tap* that each drop of water made as it hit the hard plastic.

For the last week, life at Nocturne had been uneventful, and Colin was terribly bored with his new job in the quartermaster's corps. He'd been assigned to work alone in a small storeroom. Wearing his usual fitting gray fatigues and shiny black boots, Colin spent his time standing in front of a sturdy metal Dutch door handing out supplies, taking inventory and positioning buckets to catch the regular leaks. Colin had put his best efforts into his job and gained compliments from his immediate superior, Captain Roberts, and was even advanced a week's pay. But regardless of his performance Colin still felt that his efforts could be devoted toward something that was less mundane.

Colin knew he was not the only one assigned to an undesirable job. Blair occasionally stopped by to chat and give him reports about Kelly and Diane, who also seemed unhappy with their new functions.

Diane was eager for a combat mission, and as a last resort would even settle for guard duty. Instead of getting either position, she'd been thrown a curve and assigned to an excavation crew within the subterranean levels of the base—just one of several crews that worked to dig out tunnels and expand chambers.

Diane reported that her coworkers were amazed at her inhuman strength. She could move large rocks far easier and faster than any machine, and she could carry heavy loads of equipment and supplies without strain. With her help, her crew was days ahead of schedule. Her coworkers considered her to be invaluable, although there were a few who felt uneasy being around a person with her strength.

Colin had heard that rumors were circulating throughout the tunnels that Diane was not really human. One story said she was an advanced prototype robot being tested by the military. Another stated she was some sort of mutant grown in a laboratory. Colin felt sorry for the person starting these wild rumors. Diane was already irritated about her job, and Colin thought she would relish the opportunity to vent her frustrations out on the troublemaker.

Kelly had been assigned to the maintenance corps. Blair recalled the bitterness in Kelly's voice when he described how much he disliked mopping floors, emptying trash containers and cleaning latrines.

Poor Kelly, Colin thought. *The kid started out being so compliant to follow orders.*

Two days ago Blair told Colin that Kelly had been reassigned to help expand the base's command center by installing new computer systems and communications equipment. Kelly started out as an aide to one of the older technicians. A much better job than cleaning bathrooms and emptying trash. Kelly realized that he possessed extensive technical knowledge, and in no time was reading electrical schematics and installing instruments on his own. Then Kelly had made the mistake of offering his own improvements to a senior technician's schematics. Now, Kelly was forced to work silently in fear of being sent back to bathroom duty.

Colin glared at the slowly filling drip bucket.

Though I can't say I blame him.

While Colin, Diane, and Kelly were pursuing their unappealing jobs, Blair was putting his medical skills to good use by treating wounded troopers in the base's infirmary. Colin did not envy Blair's daily twelve-hour shifts. But after listening to Blair describe his activities, Colin sensed that the young man was gaining a great feeling of accomplishment by helping to save lives. And Blair even got to work in his civilian clothes instead of the gray camouflage uniform Colin was required to wear.

With his ability to generate electricity, Colin imagined himself receiving many accolades as a legendary hero, performing many dangerous missions against the Brelac to bring the war to a victorious conclusion. But the cold, hard fist of reality punched holes through his frail daydreams as fast as the accumulating water dripped from the saturated ceiling.

Colin was fortunate that he at least had the opportunity to leave the base and travel to Lenora when he was off duty. Lenora was the largest city near the base, just five miles away. Colin had made two trips there to ease his boredom, spending hours walking the streets while marveling at the sight of the tall cylindrical and rectangular buildings with their metallic blue surfaces, glossy black windows, and bright lights glowing around their top floors. Jet-styled ships with short bodies flew overhead and would occasionally land or take off from the top of these buildings. He admired the different styles of four-wheeled, fusion-powered cars driving along the road and parked at the curbsides.

Among the multitude of humans that Colin passed by he saw robotic maintenance workers. Machines constructed in human form, their plastic covered bodies coming in different colors of red, blue, green. Their faces were human-like, with unblinking eyes, no hair, and thin, horizontal slits for ears. The robots mingled about, carrying vacuum canisters with long accordion hoses, sucking up litter from the streets and sidewalks.

Colin would spend hours walking the streets and browsing through some of the different shops. While exploring, Colin often came across macronet terminals. Rectangular, five-foot-tall plastic slabs standing close to the outside wall of a building. The terminals had computer keypads at the middle and a large monitor above it that held a vast amount of information and served as a communications network spanning every planet in the United Protectorate. When the macronet was not in use, the monitors usually displayed news reports that featured clear video and audio of

Protectorate troops and ships in action on the war front.

Colin briefly considered visiting Lenora that night after his shift but he was hungry and tired, and planned to visit the base cafeteria for a quick meal before returning to his room at the barracks to crash on his simple cot.

Colin glanced at the computer on the desk near the metal Dutch door. The computer was used to keep inventory of military hardware and track shipments, but it was also connected to the macronet. Normally his shift was busy enough to keep him off the computer for more than a minute, but no one had come to his window in over an hour, and it was close to closing time. He glared at the window, found that he was alone, and sat down at the desk.

His eyes focused on the flat monitor in front of the keyboard. At the right of the monitor was the shoebox-sized computer with the heavy coating of dust that he regularly neglected to clean off. The small printer next to the computer was also quite dusty. On the monitor was a page with the image of the United Protectorate flag at the top: a circle of small white stars on a background of red and blue stripes. Below the flag was the inventory page, with a long list of military hardware. Scrolling his wireless mouse across the desk, Colin clicked to enter the main macronet page. A large array of small, colorful windows and photographs advertising countless items and services appeared. Colin had no interest in any of it; his only concern was the thin box at the top of the screen.

Colin clicked on the empty search bar, typed *ID and Records*, and then clicked on the small search button. The result came up faster than he expected. A long list of websites appeared that dealt with personal data available to the public. Having no patience to read the list of every website Colin clicked on the very first one: *Universal Eye.*

The site's home page appeared on screen, the logo of a wide, red eye in the top center. Below displayed several columns listing different options and links related to information compiled on individuals and businesses. Colin noted a box with a disclaimer stating that some information may not be available and by law cannot be displayed or will be under restricted access. Colin skipped the full read, acknowledged this and went on to the next screen. A list of options in a small gray box appeared on the left. He clicked on the info-citizen option. A small window appeared asking for the name and central identification number of the person to be searched. Colin typed in his name and the lengthy identification number that had been assigned to him at birth. *BX873-226W-513S-836P-52051.* He clicked search.

It took several moments for the information to appear. An entire page devoted to Colin McKenzie. His photo floated at the top left of the screen. His hair was longer, and there was a smile on his face. Colin thought that this must have been taken when he was younger. Next to his picture was a small white bar with a message in red lettering.

Military personnel. Restricted data. Status: missing in action.

After being gravely injured in combat and being a part of a grand military experiment Colin understood why he was given these classifications. But he wondered how long he would be listed by the military as missing.

Below Colin's picture was a list of his available personal data. His age, twenty-five, born July 11, 2407.

106

His last civilian address was listed as 622 Alcove Street. In the city of Hosea, on the planet Viola Three. Colin blinked at the names of his parents. Alice and Jacob McKenzie. Both deceased. Until now Colin had given no thought about his parents, and he sat back, disturbed at how his mind could not produce any memories about them. Or even their faces. Colin clicked on the name of his mother. Her picture appeared, showing the image of a dark-skinned, middle-aged woman with brown eyes and a broad smile on her chubby face. Her long black hair with streaks of gray near the roots was tied into a ponytail, visible behind the thick collar of a purple turtleneck sweater.

Colin wasn't sure why he suddenly felt sad after seeing his mother's face. He could not remember the last time he saw her in person. Or even spoke to her. He did not know the sound of her voice. With his memory being so blurry he had no idea how long he had been away from home since joining the military, as it seemed like forever.

Colin went back to the previous page and clicked on his father's name. His father had a lighter complexion than his mother. He was bald, with a thick moustache intermingled with black and grey hairs, and wore thin glasses with gold wire frames over dark eyes. He smiled in the photo, but not as brightly as his wife.

Colin closed his eyes and tried to dig within his memory to find any recollection of any activity with his parents: holidays, birthdays, family gatherings. There was nothing.

How serious had this injury been to wipe my mind so thoroughly?

Both his parents were deceased, killed during a Brelac assault on Viola Three. He had no siblings, but he saw under his parents' information that they both had surviving relatives located on other planets within the Protectorate. He clicked on the name of his mother's brother. John Duggan. He had no picture, but there was contact information listed. An address at 118 Union Avenue, in North Marriot, located on the planet Narcos, and an e-mail address. Colin copied the e-mail link and typed a message to the man who he believed to be his uncle. A man whose face was a complete blank in his mind.

His message was not long or eloquent, just a simple hello and an assurance that he was still alive and well. He clicked send and wondered how long he would have to wait for a reply. If he ever received one. Colin retrieved the names and contact information for another uncle, two aunts, and two cousins, sending each person the same message. He was hoping that his efforts would not be a waste of time. And that at least one of these people that he was reaching out to would reach back. From any of them he was certain to learn more about his past.

Colin went back to the pages with his parents' photos and clicked on the computer's print command. He heard footsteps approaching out in the corridor. He took both printed pages and neatly folded them in order to fit in his back pocket as a female trooper with short red hair appeared at the Dutch door, a yellow requisition form in her hand.

Colin stood and smiled to greet her. "Another customer," he said. "What can I get you?"

"I need a new pair of boots, Sarge." The trooper handed Colin the form. "Size nine."

Colin took the form and examined it briefly. It was in proper order, with the trooper's and her immediate commanding officer's signatures both at the bottom. Colin went to one of the shelves in the back where military footwear was stored and retrieved a cardboard box containing the boots.

"I see they have you stuck down here by yourself, Sarge," the trooper said upon his return. "How do you like it?"

"Gets a little boring at times," Colin said, handing her the box.

"I imagine that you have a lot of mopping to keep you busy," she said. She pointed at two buckets sitting on the floor just a few feet behind Colin, catching water still dripping from the ceiling.

Colin turned and shook his head, his upper lip curled in disgust. "Those. I'm thinking about raising goldfish."

"Working around all this water dripping on your head all day would drive me up the wall. This is worse than serving a tour back on Meridan."

Meridan.

An image formed in Colin's mind of a planet with chilly air and constant rain.

The memory of himself diving to the wet ground was still vivid. Cold water and mud oozing into his boots. The cold clammy feeling he got when the knees of his uniform would get soaked with water. Dead bodies lying in the mud. Protectorate troopers gunned down during a furious battle.

Colin wanted to ask when she was stationed on the planet Meridan. But when he looked back she was gone. He'd been so absorbed by his memories that he'd failed to notice her leave. He leaned over the Dutch door to look out into the corridor, but no one was there, only the quiet sound of footsteps, growing fainter as she left the storeroom.

Colin wondered who this mysterious woman was, and how much she knew about the past events back on Meridan.

And, more importantly, how much she knew about him.

CHAPTER ELEVEN

Another week.

Colin was low on enthusiasm as he unlocked the Dutch door to the storeroom and entered for another boring and uneventful day at this job that he was growing to hate. As with every morning, the storeroom was dark. He blindly felt along the wall near the door to press the light switch. His mood grew darker when the lights came on and he looked at the rows of shelves of countless supplies that he was sole guardian over, in addition to the numerous buckets spaced along the floor in every other aisle, each one collecting the dripping water from the ceiling.

Colin approached one of the buckets, and saw that it was nearly filled. He looked up at the white ceiling panel, to a large area with a light brown stain. In the middle of this spot a tiny pool of water slowly built up in size, growing and stretching until it formed a drop heavy enough to fall with a plop into the bucket.

Colin had appealed to Captain Roberts about these leaks several times, but no action was ever taken. No one had even been dispatched to take a look at the ceiling, and he began to suspect that his complaints were being ignored on purpose. After all, he was considered an outcast. Like Diane and Kelly, he was probably given this menial job to keep him busy and out of the way.

Why spend the time and expense to make life easier for an alien?

That notion nearly made Colin angry enough to kick the bucket of water across the room. Then he calmed himself, concluding that venting his frustration on the bucket would accomplish nothing except create more work for himself. And he wasn't in the mood to do any unnecessary mopping.

Colin blamed his gloominess on the fact he'd gotten little sleep last night. Every night he had vivid dreams about the seemingly simple activities he performed during the day—dreams of himself in the storeroom.

He saw himself picking up one of the water filled buckets on the floor and carrying it to a large white sink that was kept in a small janitor's closet in the far back of the storeroom. It took Colin several minutes to reach the closet while carrying the bucket, while hoping that he would not have a mishap and spill it.

Colin would wake in the middle of the night but go back to sleep, only to experience the same dream again. Colin remembered his previous nights the same way: repeating scenes of whatever he did while he was awake. He failed to understand the significance of these dreams, and doubted whether there was any. Regardless, it made nights rough and the days seem to stretch on forever.

Colin sat at his desk and faced the computer, then opened up the macronet to check his e-mail for any messages—the only activity he looked forward to in his job. He'd sent e-mails to a total of eight relatives. It had taken his Uncle John four days to send a response, and it was less than friendly, as his uncle firmly believed he had been killed in action by the Brelac. He'd said that whoever sent the e-mail was only trying to pull off a sick prank, and warned Colin not to send any more or he would notify the authorities. Colin decided to hold off contacting his uncle again until he could find a way to reason with the man and convince him that this was no hoax.

Colin had also received replies from his Aunt Liz and a cousin, Rose. They both expressed shock over the news of his survival, but were glad to hear that he was well. He checked his e-mail twice a day for any more replies, but beyond those three he received nothing else.

The screen lit up and Colin was greeted by the usual image of the inventory page. On the task bar at the bottom of the screen he clicked on the e-mail icon. A small window appeared in the middle of the screen bearing a single e-mail.

Greetings from Cousin Keith.

Colin clicked on the title to open the message and was intrigued by what he read. His cousin, Keith Berry, actually lived nearby on Trillion, in the City of Lenora. Keith stated that he was glad to hear that Colin was still alive, and invited him to come over to his apartment building on Kirk Street, number 206.

Family members only. Visit anytime. Come alone.

Colin became so excited about meeting his cousin that he lost his grip on his mouse and dropped it on the floor with a clatter. He picked it up, hoping it was not broken. He did not recall the last time he'd smiled but he enjoyed it today. He hated the thought of being confined in the storeroom for the next eight hours and would have caught a shuttle into the city immediately if it weren't for his being on duty. At least he knew that while handing out supplies and keeping the buckets of water from overflowing he had something to truly look forward to.

*****

At 5:00 P.M. Colin closed the storeroom and rushed to his quarters. He quickly showered in the multi-stalled facility he shared with the dozens of other men in his barracks, then changed into the civilian clothes that he bought at the base's post exchange: a pair of white sneakers, jeans, and a gray, hooded sweatshirt. Colin walked out the base's front gate with several other off-duty troopers who were on their way off base. Looking to the sky he saw the bright orange glare of the sunset. He inhaled a breath of the cool air. Colin hoped that this sweatshirt would keep him warm as the night grew colder.

A few yards away on the small landing pad the public shuttle landed right on schedule, male and female passengers in civilian clothes and gray and black camouflage uniforms started boarding immediately. The oblong vessel had a blue paint job on its body and broad wings, had a heavy coating of dirt, and was marred by scattered rust spots. Colin walked up a small ramp at the front of the shuttle to board, his sneakers shuffling against the metal tread. He passed the pilot sitting in the front seat of a small instrument panel with a glowing display flanked by three rows of buttons. Dressed in brown trousers, jacket, cap, and dark glasses the pilot kept his hands on the twin control sticks and gave each passenger a nod as they deposited their fare into the gray, three-foot-tall column-shaped fare machine at the right side of the pilot's seat.

Colin already had the money in his hand. Two light blue certificates with the aged face of Leon Maseklos printed on the left side, and on the right the numerical symbol of 'one' displayed within a circle surrounded by ivy vines. Colin slid his money into a slot at the top of the machine. A small numerical display above the slot read the amount of fare that it received for the transaction, and beeped twice before a little green light clicked on.

Colin sat two rows on the left behind the pilot, and strapped himself in firmly. As with his last trip he looked down at the usual grimy floor and ripped seats, cigarette butts scattered about on the floor, and the occasional empty beverage can on the floor that would roll around noisily during the motion of the flight. This mode of public transportation may not have been the most glamorous, but Colin knew it was much better than walking into town. He settled lower in his seat and folded his hands. When all passengers had boarded and were secure, the ramp retracted, the door slid shut, and the shuttle lifted itself smoothly into the air by the power of nearly-silent engines.

It took only a few minutes for the shuttle to reach the city and arrive at the Second Street landing pad. Colin had limited knowledge of the city's streets, and asked the shuttle pilot for directions to Kirk Street.

"Two blocks away, take a left at Fourth and follow the road till you hit Kirk," the pilot answered, readying the engine for takeoff. "'Bout a half-mile long that street is, might be a walk."

Colin nodded and departed the shuttle to begin his long trek on foot. He took a left at Fourth and studied every street sign until he came upon his destination. Kirk Street.

Colin had never ventured to this section of the city before. This area seemed to have a seedier atmosphere.

And the streets were busy this evening, with human traffic on the sidewalks heavy. The rows of streetlights placed near the curb on both sides of the street were alive; the tall, metal poles with brightly glowing cylinders on top enhanced the festive atmosphere of the busy nightlife. He saw groups of men and women in civilian clothes congregating in front of the bars on both sides of the street, uniformed troopers in gray fatigues among them. The sounds of laughter and rowdy outcries floated down through darkened alleys.

A red vehicle with broad white stripes painted along its sides and a red and blue bar light mounted on its roof passed by as Colin crossed the street. A Lenora police cruiser. Colin passed a few fast food restaurants that he had heard about but never eaten in. A restaurant that was a part of the Frytag's burger chain, Airwaves Pizza, and Marshal's Ice Cream and Pastries. He passed two pawnshops across the street from each other on the way to locate the address where his cousin resided.

Colin continued walking until he caught sight of gold metallic numbers attached to the wall of a yellow, four-story brick apartment building. 1810. Colin wondered if this was a security building. He went to the entrance and grabbed the metal bar to open the glass door. The door swung open freely. There was a small lobby inside the building, and Colin was repulsed at the thought of having to clean the yellow and black checkered carpeting here. It had a trail of dirty footmarks and black splotches that he did not even want to guess what had made the marks. The shiny twin elevator doors loomed straight ahead, just to the right of a flight of stairs leading up to the next floor.

Colin walked to the right wall to examine the rows of small, gold mailbox doors. Each had paper labels with the tenant's names and apartment numbers taped above their keyholes. Colin quickly scanned each box until he came across number 206 and the name, Berry. He took a quick ride in the elevator to the second floor. There was no one else in the corridor when he got off of the elevator. The carpeting on this floor was of the same checkered design as in the lobby, and just as dirty and stained. The blue painted walls had black smudge marks and oily handprints, and the air reeked of oily fried foods similar to what he would expect back in the base cafeteria. The grating and thumping sound of heavy metal music blared out from the walls of an apartment on the next floor. Between the odor and the noise, Colin felt blessed that he did not live in this building.

There was a black door directly in front of him with a small white plastic tag engraved with the black numbers 203. Colin looked both ways then headed down the right corridor. He followed the doors until he finally located apartment 206. On the wall at the left was a doorbell button. He lifted a hand to press it when he noticed the door was ajar. He hesitated, then pressed the button and heard a loud chime ring twice. He waited, but no one came to the door. He rang the bell again. Still no response. He took a deep breath, patted down the front of his sweatshirt, and then pushed the door open and stepped inside.

The apartment was small with meager furnishings. Brown shag carpeting kept spotlessly clean covered the floor, and in the center of the room was a dark wooden table with stacks of papers and books. At the left of the table against the wall sat a small bookcase with three

117

shelves loaded with more books. Above the bookcase was a dartboard, several darts stabbing into it. Against the back wall were two more bookcases standing side by side, both also filled with a large collection of books. At the left and right of the bookcases were closed doors.

A reclining chair with a brown plaid covering and a small table with an extremely thin, flat screen television mounted on a tripod sat at the right side of the room. Colin enjoyed watching the television sets back at the base cafeteria while he ate his meals, and looked forward to the day when he could own one himself. There was an open doorway near the television.

"Hello!" Colin called out. "Keith?" He stepped further into the room. "It's me, Colin!"

There were no sounds in the apartment other than the noise of the music filtering in from the corridor. He drew closer to the table. Some of the papers that he saw piled there were actually maps, marked with the names of areas and cities he failed to recognize. There were also piles of photographs. He picked up a stack and flipped through them. They were photographs of troopers and civilians, people that he had never seen before.

Colin walked toward the doorway by the television, and found it led to a small kitchen. On the left was a counter with a sink full of unwashed dishes. On the right was an electric stove with greasy smears on its surface, a black tea kettle resting on one of the front burners. Next to the stove was a small white refrigerator. Something black scuttled under the fridge as Colin turned on the light.

Maybe the guy stepped out to get some takeout from one of the fast food places I passed, Colin thought. *That would explain why he is not here. Something from Frytag's would be great…*

Colin left the kitchen and returned to the living room. He needed to use the toilet. There were the two doors flanking the bookcases. He turned the knob to the door on the right and sighed when he saw it was the bathroom. A typical small bathroom with white ceramic floor tiles, a white sink mounted on a brown wooden cabinet. On the right an ordinary toilet next to a white, rectangular bathtub.

Colin jumped back, slamming into the small sink. The body of a young black male was lying in the tub filled with bloody water. The head was tilted back, both eyes wide open and directing an empty stare toward the ceiling. The man's white sweatshirt was as bloodstained as the water. His left arm hung out of the tub, and blood dripped down from his fingertip to leave a widening pool of blood on the otherwise clean floor.

Colin hesitated, and then slowly moved forward. His heart beat faster as he fearfully glanced over the dead man. There was a long, thin slash along the man's throat, cut deeply from one ear to the other. Colin had no photograph of his cousin but he surmised that since this was Keith's apartment, then this was also probably his corpse. Regardless, he knew he needed to inform the police.

Colin turned quickly and left the bathroom, holding his mouth. He was surprised by the presence of another man. Dressed in dark clothes, the black male appeared to be older than the dead man in the bathroom. He matched Colin's six foot stature, but his build was huskier. He had one hand hidden in the pocket of his black trench coat, the other held a dark, thin beverage bottle. The long fingers partially covered the bottle's silver logo of a crescent moon overlapping a pair of outstretched bird's wings. Colin recognized this as the logo for Acheena Beer from a sign he'd read on the Airwave's window.

"Sergeant McKenzie," the man greeted Colin and smiled. "Glad you could make it."

"Who are you?"

"Keith Berry. Thanks for coming."

"You're Keith Berry? Then who is that back there?"

"Him? Don't worry about him. He's just a bit of unfinished business. If you want to use the bathroom then go right ahead. He won't give you any trouble. Unless you're a little shy."

"I can throw a towel over his head."

Keith took a slow sip from the bottle. "Sorry that I didn't greet you at the door. I was in the bedroom collecting a few things when you dropped in. During all the excitement I forgot to lock the door. Our friend in there put up a bit of a fight and I was in a hurry." He grinned. "And I hate to break the news to you like this, but, we're not related."

Colin was not disappointed to hear that information. If Colin were forced to defend himself then he would feel less sad and guilty killing this man after knowing that he was not a relative. But not just yet. He still needed answers.

"If you're not my cousin then why the ruse?"

"My ruse was the best way to get you out here," Keith said. "And I needed you here because you and I have unfinished business."

"Unfinished business?" Colin did not like where this conversation was going. He glanced back at the body

120

through the bathroom doorway. "So, who was that guy?"

"If it makes you feel any better you weren't related to him either," Keith said. "He didn't even live here. He was just an operative who worked in our network. And this place was a safe house."

"A safe house?"

"A safe house for Vendetta operatives." Keith shrugged. "We have a few others on this planet. If I recall correctly, you were here once."

"*I* was here?"

"Yeah. You and Eddie Driscoll. You were here a while back. That was early in your tour of duty."

"What?" That was the only word that Colin was able to gasp out. He focused on the name, Eddie Driscoll. The man who seemed to shadow him at all times.

Driscoll in his full combat uniform. Driscoll without his helmet, his blond hair shaved down to a crew cut. He was laughing. He drank from a small dark bottle in his hand. The same type of bottle that Keith was holding now. Colin saw himself here with Driscoll.

"*Was* I here?" Colin asked himself in a hushed voice.

Colin turned and looked at the dartboard mounted on the wall.

His hand holding a dart, throwing at his intended target. He missed. The scenery switched to a wooded area. It was dark. Two men and a woman in civilian clothes on their knees with their hands tied behind their backs. One of the men was tearfully pleading for his life with a tirade of obscene curses. Driscoll stood over the man. A laser pistol in his hand. He quickly took aim at the man's face and fired. Colin was also in this scene. Also with a gun in his hand. Taking aim at the next victim.

"Sarge," Keith's voice called out.

Colin's memory was broken. He turned his eyes back on Keith.

"You were out there for a minute," Keith told him. "Reminiscing?"

Colin thought that he was indeed reminiscing. About details on his life that he was still in the dark about, and things that were disturbing to him. Colin knew that Vendetta was a criminal organization currently at war with the United Protectorate. He had no idea what this Keith's connection was to Vendetta, the dead man in the bathroom, or himself. He wanted no part of what was going on here, and suspected that there would be increasing danger if he remained.

"I...I have to get back to the base," Colin said quietly, shifting from one foot to another, his eyes darting toward the front door.

"Can't let you do that, Sarge," Keith said. The smile faded from his face. "My job here is to shut this site down and dispose of any connections that have been compromised. That's one thing you have in common with our friend in the bathroom."

Colin took that remark as a cue to go on the offensive against this man. As he lifted his hands to use his power Keith drew his hand out of the pocket of his trench coat, revealing a laser pistol. He took aim at Colin's head. Colin's right hand discharged a burst of electrical energy into Keith's chest. The force of the shock pushed Keith back across the table. Books and papers scattered about as Keith tumbled to the floor with a grunt as the gun flew out of his hand. Colin stepped back as Keith recovered from the attack almost instantly, jumping to his feet and lifting his hands. Keith moved too fast for Colin to react and hurled a table at him. The table slammed into Colin, knocking him to the floor.

The hard wood struck him in his face. His nose throbbed painfully. He watched Keith look around for the gun. Colin spotted it on the floor near the reclining chair. Colin struggled to rise with the table lying on top of him. Keith saw it as well and rushed to retrieve the weapon. Colin reached out his left arm out from beneath the table and fired a surge of energy from his hand. Keith dove to the floor behind the recliner just in time to avoid a stream of electricity that burned through the air over his head.

Colin fired at the recliner, and the energy burned through the chair. He was not sure if he hit Keith in the process. He spied the top of Keith's head near the table with the television set. Colin aimed his hand and discharged a stream of sparks that struck the television instead of his human target, and the screen exploded with a burst of sparks and glass. Keith shouted like an enraged animal and leapt to his feet. He lifted the smoking television in his hands and hurled it at Colin. Colin crouched down and turned his back defensively. But he moved too slowly. The television struck him in his back, and he dropped to one knee.

Pain burned through his back and seemed to flow to the rest of his body. Keith was on top of him in a second. He grabbed Colin by the back of his sweatshirt and picked him up with no difficulty. With a vicious roar Keith threw Colin back into the bookcase against the wall. Colin's body struck the bookcase with a force that sent a few books flying from their shelves. Colin hit the floor. The pain in his back had overridden all other senses.

With a brutish growl Keith shoved Colin into the bookcase beneath the dartboard. The collision knocked three books off the shelf and onto the floor, and cracked the peeling drywall. The impact on Colin's chest knocked the breath from his lungs. He felt himself falling back. He struggled to grab hold of anything to stay on his feet. His hand scraped at the dartboard and ripped it from the wall as he fell. The bookcase fell along with him, landing on his legs.

Keith grabbed Colin by the neck again and dragged him out from under the bookcase. He thrust Colin's head against the now broken television set lying on the floor. Keith leaned down and pointed at the television. "This was a good damn set, you son of a bitch!" he shouted. "I was going to take that home!"

Colin's slightest move seemed to increase every painful sensation in his body. He feared his ribs were broken because it hurt to even breathe. He looked over at the dartboard lying on the floor, the darts still stuck to it. Colin summoned a burst of strength, reached over and grabbed a handful of darts and rammed their points deep into Keith's right thigh. The man screamed loudly and jumped back. Colin rolled away and struggled to get back to his feet.

Keith was not giving Colin the chance to act. Keith grabbed Colin by the shoulders and pulled back, then spun him around and hurled him into the bathroom toward the tub.

Colin cried out and raised his arms to absorb the impact and managed to protect his head from the fall. His body dropped onto the corpse in the bathtub and sunk into the warm, red water. Both his forearms ached, making his fingers numb to the soft, bloating flesh of the dead man below him.

I've got to get out of here!

Colin turned to see Keith limping into the bathroom, the darts still penetrating his leg. He was breathing heavily. Keith reached into the pocket of his trench coat and brought out a long-bladed knife.

Keith grabbed the darts with his free hand and yanked them out of his leg. He held them up. "So it's going to be this kind of a fight." He threw the darts down. They bounced against the ceramic flooring and rolled away. He held up the knife. "I like to use the up close and personal approach anyway. Just ask your buddy there."

Keith took a step forward. He grimaced in pain as his weight shifted to his wounded leg. Colin knew he had to act now. He jumped to his feet, grasped Keith's knife hand and swung him around to send him crashing into the bathtub. His head hit the wall as a deluge of water splashed onto the floor. The dead man's head dunked under the water as Keith struggled and sputtered to get off him. Colin charged forward and delivered a quick punch to the side of Keith's head. Keith twisted and swung his knife and slashed Colin's left arm.

Colin yelled and caught Keith's hand as his other hand continued to hammer the side of Keith's head with punches. Colin's mind raced as he realized his punches were not as potent as he desired. He struck Keith repeatedly but the man showed no sign of weakening. Colin gritted his teeth, he needed to use more power if he was going to end this fight.

Colin's fist took on a bluish glow, the electrical power pulsating from his hand. There was a large burst of sparks as Colin's fist connected with Keith's face. The tub water erupted and splashed back on Colin's face and sweatshirt. Keith jerked and then stopped moving. His head slowly submerged under the bloody water and his hand wielding the knife grew limp, and the blade dropped into the water. Colin stepped back, breathing heavily. He watched and waited to see if Keith was going to recover and continue the fight. Keith's arm hung out of the bathtub, parallel with the arm of the man that he had murdered earlier.

Was the fight over? Colin thought. He watched Keith's hand jerk back to life. Keith pushed himself out of the water and gasped loudly for air.

"You want up close and personal?" Colin shouted. Colin rushed toward the bathtub and thrust his electrically charged hands into the water. The water bubbled and smoked and Keith's body convulsed violently. Keith uttered a series of incoherent grunts, and then sank back under the water and remained still. The open-eyed stare from bloody eyes told Colin he would stay that way.

Now Colin could step back and enjoy a respite. His heart still beat rapidly, his breathing heavy. For a moment he stared at the two dead bodies crumpled together in the bathtub. And his breathing quickened as his mind recalled the moments of Keith's electrocution, and suddenly realized he had enjoyed it.

"Was that up close and personal enough for you?" Colin shouted.

He blinked and inspected his wounded arm. A sharp spasm of pain stung his arm as he lifted it. Keith's knife had performed an efficient job of cutting the sleeve of his new sweatshirt. Pulling the cut fabric apart revealed a slice across his skin that did not appear to be as deep as he feared, but it was still bleeding. Colin found it unsettling to feel his own warm blood flowing down his arm. He snatched a stained washcloth from off of a towel bar mounted on the wall near the bathtub. He wrapped the cloth around his arm and pressed hard to try and stop the bleeding.

Colin stalked out of the bathroom. His body ached. He stopped and took a seat in the reclining chair that he had burned a large blackened hole through. Though sore, Colin felt that his real hurt came from his wasted effort in coming here. He'd come with the hope of meeting a relative face to face.

Instead, all he found were more dark questions about his life and disturbing memories. In addition to a man who lied to lure him here, and then tried to kill him. Colin just wanted to leave this place without being noticed and return to the base. But not in his current state. His left sleeve was cut and stained with blood, and the front of his sweatshirt was soaking wet with bloody water from the bathtub. Not being noticed would not be an option.

Colin stood and entered the small bedroom. At the right side of the room was a nightstand with a lamp and a waist-high bed covered by a white blanket. The nightstand drawer had been removed and lay on the bed, several documents dumped across the floor. Colin looked longingly at the bed thinking it looked far more comfortable than the hard cot that he was forced to sleep on back at the base. Over to his left was a sliding door that revealed a small clothes closet. He pushed aside the doors to rummage through the few items of clothing. He found a black sweater with long sleeves that would perfectly hide his wounded arm.

Colin grimaced at the pain shooting through his arm as he gingerly removed his sweatshirt. He used it to wipe the blood from his arm and hand. He inspected the cut on his arm. The bleeding seemed to be slowing. The way that his arm hurt when he moved it Colin feared that he might have a broken bone. He wrapped the cloth back around the cut and donned the clean sweater.

Back at the base he could go into the storeroom and use the medical supplies there to better treat and bandage his wound. But for now, there was a man he had killed floating above an unidentified murder victim soaking in the bathtub. Then, there were Keith's allegations of Vendetta's involvement with this 'safe house' to think about. There were so many dark questions for him to think about. And behind the questions would be even darker answers.

The events of this evening created huge complications that Colin just wanted to leave behind as he closed the apartment door.

CHAPTER TWELVE

Sitting at his desk, Colin looked back at the clock on the wall. 4:56 P.M. Close enough to his usual 5:00 P.M. closing time. Two days after his run-in with his fake cousin, Keith Berry, parts of his body still ached. He was thankful that he had such a boring job where he sat at this desk and rarely performed strenuous labor. He'd had only eight people to wait on today, and enjoyed the restful breaks in between, even though the day was slow and uneasy for him.

For the last two days Colin sat in his chair all day and waited in fear that someone was going to come and question him about his activities. Or even outright arrest him, not only for Keith's murder, but the other man's death that he had nothing to do with. Colin meditated on the charges of double homicide, conspiring with known terrorists, and treason. Not to mention what other past crimes he might have been involved in. Until he uncovered more answers, he thought that it would be in his own best interests to keep the events of the other night to himself. Providing, of course, that he successfully got away with it.

Colin was about to close the top half of the Dutch door when a female trooper appeared. She had a shoebox in her hands.

"How's it going, Sarge?" she said. "Almost five o'clock. I caught you just in time."

"I've got time to serve one more customer. What can I do for you?"

The woman put her finger on the shoebox. "These boots are a little too tight around the toe."

"Size nine," Colin remembered. "I might have something a little wider,"

Colin reached for the box, grimacing as he picked it up. It was the pain in his arm again.

"So, how was your night, Sarge?" the woman asked.

Colin's mind brought up the image of Keith Berry lying dead in the bathtub at that Lenora apartment. "It was a washout," he told her. He headed to the shelves in the back.

"Sorry to hear that. Too bad you couldn't have had a little fun. Maybe gotten together with a relative or something."

Colin froze and turned back to the unnamed woman. "Relatives?" he breathed, his mind racing. "No. I don't have any family on this planet."

"Really? My mistake," she said, twirling a lock of her hair between two fingers. "Too bad. I could have sworn that you had at least one relative living close by. A cousin maybe."

Colin moved closer to the woman. "Just who are you?"

"Think of me as a friend."

"A friend? That's not much of an answer."

The woman nodded. "Okay then. Think of me as a better friend than the one you met last night."

Colin's eyes widened. His lips parted but uttered no sound. He managed to clear his throat. "What do you know about last night?"

"I know that you left a hell of a mess back at apartment 206."

"I...I don't..."

"Don't try to deny anything," the woman snapped in a stern voice. "We kept you under surveillance when you left the base last night. We went into that apartment after you left and found your two friends in the bathtub. And both in a very compromising position, I might add."

"You followed me?" Colin said, taking a step back from the window. "Who the hell are you?"

The woman brought out a black billfold from her pocket. She opened it toward Colin. The top half contained an identification card with her small photo at the bottom right corner. At the top of the card were the bright red letters C.I.D. On the bottom half of the billfold was a shiny gold badge in the shape of a star imposed on an oval shield.

"Captain Melony Carter, Central Intelligence Division. And yes, you were being followed. We've been keeping tabs on you, Diane Christy, and Kelly Lytton since you three arrived." Melony went on. "You didn't seriously think that you and your friends would be allowed to just run free without any kind of supervision, did you? You guys aren't your average troopers."

She has a good point, Colin thought. *But it doesn't make me feel any better.*

"So what now? Am I under arrest?"

For a moment she did not answer. Her eyes flicked up at him, studying. "No. All I can tell you is that you and your friends are a part of an important military project. And that makes you valuable. At least for now. And as far as the mess you left behind in that apartment, we don't have the full story on the big guy that you fried in the bathtub. But the one with his throat cut was a suspected Vendetta operative. So in light of the many other problems facing the Protectorate I'm personally classifying his death as one less. And we'll leave it at that."

"Thanks for cutting me a break," he mumbled, still cautious.

Melony sent back an expressionless gaze. "Just don't create any more messes for me to clean up," she advised, and then backed away from the Dutch door. "Keep the boots, Sarge. I don't need them. Never did."

Colin watched as she stepped out of view. He followed the sound of her footsteps as they faded down the corridor. He dropped the box with the boots on his desk, turned out the lights, and exited the storeroom, locking both halves of the Dutch doors.

So what do I do now? Colin thought. *All this time I was being watched by the C.I.D. How far were they going in order to keep an eye on me? No doubt they had me under surveillance during my previous trips to Lenora. But were they looking into my Public Eye searches on the macronet? And how will Diane and Kelly react when I tell them this news?* Colin began to wonder if it would be wiser to keep this knowledge to himself.

Colin made no definite plans for later. For now he was only concentrating on the biting hunger that began to taunt him. He stepped out of the building and into the chilly night air. Faint puffs of fog became plumed with each breath. Again, he was thankful for his indoor job where he could remain comfortable and warm.

It was a short walk across the base for Colin to reach the building that served as the cafeteria. He swung open the pair of large wooden doors, and was instantly met by the strong aroma of hot food. Walking across the spotless, white-tiled floor he passed by four rows of long tables lined up end to end. Each filled with male and female troopers seated and eating their meals. He approached the three long black counters lined up close to the back wall. The line at the counters was short. Colin was glad that he had arrived after the majority of the dinner crowd had gathered.

He picked up a blue plastic tray from the top of four tall stacks. At the left of the trays he took a white ceramic plate from one of the two stacks, and loaded up supplies of white plastic forks, knives, and spoons, all neatly arranged in their separate rows.

He glanced to the second and third counters where a large selection of food items sat in wide metal pans. The menu of the day featured piles of milky white mashed potatoes, macaroni and cheese with a bright golden color, string beans, kernels of yellow corn, slices of boiled carrots sitting in a pan filled with cloudy water, chipped beef, and a large pan of dark brown gravy that was half-covered by an even darker, lumpy film. Behind the counters four female servers dressed in white trousers, shirts, aprons and caps waited with large metal spoons in hand to serve the hungry troopers.

Colin shuffled along the line and reached the servers. He closed his eyes and savored the aroma of chipped beef with gravy. The female server winked at him and issued him a large helping, as well as mashed potatoes with gravy, boiled carrots, and string beans. The server went to a table against the wall to the gray, square coffee dispenser. She took one of the small, white Styrofoam cups stacked on both sides of the dispenser. Pressing a button on the spout at the lower side of the machine she filled the cup with hot, black coffee, then handed it to Colin. Colin smiled, moved away from the line and headed for an empty table near the end counter.

Colin sat and reached over to one of the many glass sugar and powdered creamer dispensers that were placed on the middle of every table. Black coffee was not to his liking. Colin used his fork to scrape away the hardened strands of dried gravy from his mashed potatoes. He ate a sample. It was still warm, but lacked the salty flavor he enjoyed on his food. Colin reached for the tiny saltshaker and sprinkled a liberal amount onto the mashed potatoes. He took a bite of chipped beef, then doused it in a heavy layer of salt.

Colin chewed hungrily and silently studied the camaraderie taking place around him. At the other tables groups of troopers sat and ate together. The sounds of laughter boomed out from joyful faces. Others were engaged in less boisterous conversation. At one table he even spied a card game being played among a group of four troopers.

Colin frowned. It appeared as if he was one of the few persons sitting alone. Since arriving at Nocturne, Colin was used to eating alone, and right now he had no desire to mingle with anyone. He was too submerged in his personal thoughts to concentrate on making friends. He stared into his tray, brooding about his identity. Why his past memories were incomplete, and where his future would take him. He still had no memories of his childhood or of any relatives. Nor of any friends, save for the intrusive trooper Ed Driscoll.

To this day Colin could still express little love for the man.

Colin glanced up when he noticed a small group of men enter the cafeteria and step in line. He was about to disregard their presence when he noticed a certain lieutenant among the group. Colin focused on the tall white male's face, searching for recognition. A name popped into Colin's head.

Yates. Lieutenant Paul Yates.

Colin cracked a smile and fought to restrain a burst of laughter. The last thing that he expected to see here was his former commanding officer. As well as a few other men from his old squad. Colin recognized some of their faces. In the past he had never acted friendly toward these men. Now being out of the squad after all this time Colin wondered if this would be a perfect time to get reacquainted. There was also the chance that the lieutenant or some of these other men could reveal a few vital facts about his past life.

Colin's gaze never left sight of Yates. The man steadily moved down the line, as servers dispensed his meal onto his tray. Colin grew nervous while wondering when he should get up and approach these men. Colin was startled out of his musings when a person roughly pulled out the chair at his right and plopped down, slamming their tray onto the table. It was Diane, the last person that Colin expected, or even wanted to see at this moment. She was dressed in civilian clothes. Black shoes, black pinstripe trousers and jacket over a bright pink shirt.

"Well, Sergeant McKenzie," she said in a jocular tone. "What a surprise to see you here. I haven't heard from you for nearly two weeks."

"I know."

"I'm off duty. Got a few bills in my pocket, so I'm headed to Lenora for a night on the town. What have you been up to?" Diane asked. She jabbed her fork into her beef and loaded it into her mouth.

Colin never broke his gaze from Yates. "Nothing special. Just doing my job."

"Your job? I assume that you're still working in that leaky storeroom?"

"What else am I going to do? I just follow orders until something better comes along."

Diane gave a short laugh. "I've got news for you, Sarge. You're never gonna get ahead by just sitting on your ass and waiting for someone to notice you. You've got to take what you want. Like myself. I'm a captain. I'm not gonna keep doing this hard labor crap for the rest of the war. Yesterday I put in for a transfer to a fighter squadron. I should hear about it any time now."

"Maybe you should be packing," Colin suggested grimly.

Colin's eyes followed the lieutenant as he and the other men sat at a table at the far end of the cafeteria. Diane noticed that Colin was doggedly staring at the group. She elbowed him softly.

"Friends of yours?"

"That depends," Colin said. He rose from his seat, deciding to act.

Colin slowly strode over to the table where the lieutenant and the other men were seated. In his mind he held the vision of Lieutenant Yates expressing surprise over his unexpected appearance, giving him a firm handshake and welcoming him to sit down among the others so that they could grill him on his activities these past weeks. The sitting men ate, drank, and laughed to humorous tales that they exchanged to themselves. Their festive mood evaporated and the men grew silent as Colin drew near to their table.

Colin waved a hand in greeting. "Lieutenant Yates. How have you been?"

For a moment the lieutenant quietly glared back at Colin.

"This is a dream," Yates stated, frowning at Colin, "no, make that a nightmare. I took a shot to the head and right now I'm in a coma having a bad dream. In that nightmare I'm seeing that murdering son of a bitch, Sergeant Colin McKenzie."

Colin stepped back, shocked and confused by the lieutenant's words. His mouth opened slightly to gasp out the word, *what?* But nothing came out.

"You're the last person that I've ever expected to see here. Here in a Protectorate military base. Just strolling along like you're one of us."

"I am," Colin corrected. "At least…I was, until I left your command."

"You *left* my command?" the man laughed. "That's an interesting way to put it. But I think I like my version a hell of a lot better. You remember, don't you? When I nearly caved your face in back at Meridan."

"I don't understand," Colin said. "I…"

"You don't understand?" Yates snarled back, his anger mounting. "Maybe I beat you in the head a little too hard. That's the only way you could have forgotten about the two men you killed."

"The men that I killed?"

"Yeah. Troopers Lance and Meyers. You shot Lance. And Meyers, I don't know how you did it but you burned him to a crisp. Couldn't recognize his body after you were done with him. And I'll never understand what Driscoll did to trooper Craven."

Killing fellow troopers in cold blood?

Colin was skeptical of the charge. Until he began to scan through his past memories when he served under the lieutenant's command. There was that mission on Meridan, the cold and rainy planet.

He was in the forest. Being wet. There was a downed Brelac shuttlecraft. Trooper Driscoll was shadowing him, as usual. He saw several white cylinders. There was a firefight. Trooper Driscoll was dead, his body armor penetrated by several laser bolts. The weapons fire was furious. He saw himself using his powers to fatally electrocute a Protectorate trooper. The acrid smell of burning flesh penetrated his nostrils...

As Colin looked into the lieutenant's enraged face he recalled the nightmares that he was having. Of lying on a wet ground during a heavy rain. The unknown person hovering above him, mercilessly beating him while spitting out an intense verbal assault. The face of that man started to become clearer. It was Lieutenant Yates who relentlessly pummeled him in his nightmares.

But now it was not just a simple bad dream. It was one of the past memories that Colin sought. A sick feeling overwhelmed him, like a cold metal spike being rammed into the center of his stomach.

"Oh, that," Colin meekly replied.

"Oh, that?" the lieutenant shouted. "You sound like you're talking about a couple of overdue library books, asshole!"

Colin felt like crawling under a table and hiding his face. But he thought that he could still salvage his attempt to establish a friendly dialog with the lieutenant.

"I'm sorry," Colin said in a soft voice.

The lieutenant sprang up from his seat and knocked his tray off of the table with a swift backhand swipe. His plate shattered as it hit the floor, leaving a smear of food in the process. His tray bounced off the wall and landed on the floor. He stormed from around the table and approached Colin, stopping just a few inches away from his face. The lieutenant's voice exploded into a fiery rage.

"And you think that a petty little 'I'm *sorry*' is gonna fix things? I'm sorry too. Sorry that we didn't put your ass down back on Meridan the way we did Driscoll. I'm sorry that I listened to Trooper Jones, telling me that you might be a useful prisoner. So I cut you a break and turned your ass over to covert intelligence. But apparently they didn't consider you to be too valuable, or a threat. So they turned you loose. Now here you are, back in my face."

Colin took a step back. "This was a mistake. I just thought that we could have a friendly conversation and discuss old times. I don't want any trouble so I'll just leave."

Colin turned to walk away from the lieutenant when a sudden, sharp impact struck him on the back of his head. He helplessly watched the floor rise to meet his face. His forehead pounded against the hard surface, leaving him dazed.

He tried to rise and grunted at the sharp pain in his left arm.

"You want to talk about old times?" Yates yelled. "What the hell do you want to talk about? Two trusted soldiers under my command turned on the entire squad to kill their own. How stupid I felt having traitorous murderers hanging under my nose. The memory of how you shot me four times. The reaction I got from those troopers' families when I told them the bad news. And now here you show up wanting us to be old buddies?"

An unidentified trooper shouted out from the gathering mob surrounding the lieutenant. "Maybe we should finish the job you started back on Meridan."

A chorus of voices within the group echoed the trooper's sentiment. Colin saw hatred in every face. He was already attacked once. Would they allow him to leave in peace? Or would he be attacked again and severely injured?

Colin held up his hands defensively. "Listen guys. I'm leaving. I didn't come here to fight anybody."

"You might not leave until you do," the lieutenant replied. "Driscoll's dead. Now we've got you to deal with."

The group of men was becoming more agitated. One of them roughly shoved the table aside. Plates fell on the floor and shattered as trays were knocked about. People sitting at nearby tables quickly abandoned their trays and scurried away from the area. Colin did not expect to receive help from anyone here.

"I still owe you for trying to kill me," the lieutenant said.

His fist flew into Colin's face. The impact and the searing pain between his eyes caused his vision to temporarily black out. He stumbled back and fell against two chairs as he hit the floor.

"Those men that you and Driscoll killed had friends here!" Yates yelled. "Everyone's gonna want a piece of your ass."

Colin tried to stand as several pairs of hands grabbed him from behind and pulled him up. The men held his arms firmly behind his back. Colin imagined his enemies felt that he was helpless as they closed in though he knew he could use his power to easily free himself. But he was adamant on his position; in spite of his impending fate, after what he'd supposedly done, these were men that he could not harm.

One trooper raised his arm and sent a burly fist rushing toward Colin's head. A hand suddenly reached out and grabbed it in time to halt the connection. Diane had stepped in to prevent Colin from being lynched by these men.

"Step back," Diane warned the men.

The trooper struggled desperately against Diane's unyielding grip, only to submit to her power, his hand firmly locked in place.

"Sergeant McKenzie is with me," she continued. "You have a problem with him then maybe you can include me in your little discussion."

"Oh yeah?" the lieutenant demanded. "And just who the hell are you?"

"Diane Christy," Diane stated with an air of pride.

There was silence among the men.

"That's Captain Diane Christy," Diane added, "Ace pilot. You might have heard of me. I've scored 230 confirmed enemy kills."

Colin was in no mood to suffer through another session of ego polishing with Diane. "They don't know you, Diane. Just drop it."

"Captain Christy?" the lieutenant skeptically inquired. "And just what are you to this freak?"

"Like I said, he's with me." She shoved the trooper's arm away, easily sending him to the floor in the process.

"Maybe the captain would want to watch who she associates with. Unless you already know that he's a murderer."

"All this is new to me," Diane said. "You might have the wrong person, so maybe you should let him go."

"Trust me. We have the right man. I was up close and personal when I saw him kill two of my men. I was even closer when he tried to kill me."

Diane turned her eyes to Colin. "Is this true?"

Colin hesitated for several seconds, ashamed to incriminate himself in this room full of silent people who were now focused on him. "I just now remembered. So I suppose it is."

For a minute Diane joined the silence in the room and stared at Colin. Colin was at least thankful that there was no anger on her face. No look of disgust. Nothing.

"Let him go," Diane ordered the men.

"No way in hell!" the lieutenant shouted. "No goddamn way! Maybe you didn't hear me. This man killed two of my men. He's a murderer and a traitor. We're taking him down."

"Maybe you made a mistake."

"It's no mistake, lady!" Yates wailed, eyes wide and face red. "You think I imagined him shooting me four times?"

Diane continued staring at Colin. Colin felt as though her eyes were slicing away layers of his face in order to fully expose his cowering soul to every hostile person in the room.

"I'll deal with Sergeant McKenzie," she said slowly. "Let him go."

"No way, lady." Yates shook his head. "He's not walking out of here—"

142

Diane shifted her eyes to the lieutenant. "I'm giving you men a direct order to let the sergeant go. If not, then I'll have all of you charged with insubordination, assault and battery, inciting a riot, and whatever else I can find in the book. Or maybe you guys would like to take your little problem and deal directly with me?"

Diane took a step toward the lieutenant. Her tall stature with both fists tightly clenched was an imposing sight that even gave Colin cause to shudder.

Yates stared back into Diane's determined, unsmiling face. He glanced down at the fallen trooper. His shoulders slumped. "Let him go."

The other men were slow to comply, but they released their hold on Colin and backed away.

The lieutenant pointed his finger at Colin's face. "This is the second time you got your ass saved by the top brass, McKenzie. You must be leading a charmed life. But don't think that this is over."

With that warning the lieutenant and his entourage stormed out of the cafeteria. All eyes in the cafeteria were still fixed on Colin. He could endure no more of their judgmental stares. He quickly headed for the door.

"Hey Sarge, wait up!" Diane called.

Colin ignored her. He shoved his way out of the door and walked toward the barracks. So much for a perfect evening, he thought. But at least he did not leave any bodies behind like he did that past night. He now planned to lie on his cot and brood.

"Sarge." Diane's voice called out from behind. "Sergeant!"

Colin continued walking.

"Colin!" Diane shouted.

Colin decided to stop.

"You wanna tell me what the hell's going on?" Diane demanded.

"Were you taking a nap back there and missed everything?" Colin admonished bitterly. "I killed a couple of their pals so now they're pissed off at me. Happens all the time."

"Did you really kill those guys?"

Colin spun to face Diane, his eyes burning. "If I remember it, then it's true."

"Maybe you had a good reason. I don't know. I wasn't there. But, what I meant was, why did you take all that shit from those goons?"

"What are you talking about?" Colin growled.

"I'm talking about the way that they swatted you around. Hell, they knocked you on your ass twice. They would have taken you apart if I hadn't stepped in. And you didn't do one damn thing to stop them."

"How was I supposed to stop them?" Colin held out his hands. "You want me to use my power against men on our own side? It's obvious that I've already done enough damage."

"I'm not saying that you should become some kind of serial killer. I'm saying that you should have done something to defend yourself," Diane exclaimed. "I don't understand you. You snub me to rush over to those knuckleheads. Then you let them walk all over you. Are you stupid or something?"

"No, I'm not," Colin snapped back. "I did what I did because those guys were part of my old squad and I don't have any friends. I was hoping to hook up with them and find out a little more about myself. Looks like I found a little more than I bargained for."

Colin noticed an immediate change in Diane's demeanor. Her mood switched from stern to disheartened. "That's very interesting. You don't have any friends. I don't have any friends either. That's why I sat at your table. I haven't seen you in a while. I was hoping that we could open the curtain between us, just a little, and try to be friends."

Colin stared back at Diane's unblinking gaze, surprised at the tears welling up in her eyes. A frown formed on her face and she turned her gaze to the ground.

"I can see that I was just wasting my time," Diane muttered. "Just as well. I'm an officer. A captain. It doesn't look right for an officer to fraternize with the *grunts*."

"I didn't mean any harm by what I said," Colin said softly. "It's just that I feel like there's this huge void in my life. I'm trying to regain my past. I'm trying to link up with old friends. Relatives. What about you? Have you contacted your family? Your parents?"

Diane did not answer. She continued to stare at the ground. Colin watched as her eyes, now red, narrowed. He hesitated to say anything else in fear of hurting her even further, or worse gaining an angry response.

Diane's eyes shifted back to Colin. "My parents are dead, Sarge," she said softly. "Both of them. There's nobody else. Just me. All that I have left is my career as a pilot. And as it looks, I might not even have that."

Looking behind Diane, Colin spotted Blair Van Doren heading their way. After enduring a horrendous evening like this, Blair was the last person that Colin wanted to see now, if ever.

"Colin, Diane!" Blair called to them. He smiled brightly. "I was trying to contact you both earlier. What's going on?"

"Nothing, Doctor," Diane said with a cold tone, "I was just leaving. The sergeant here can do whatever he wants."

Diane walked away, leaving Colin feeling even guiltier.

Stupid move, Colin scolded himself. Now the wedge between him and Diane would certainly be driven deeper.

"What was that all about?" Blair asked.

"Just a little disagreement. Nothing that would concern you."

"Maybe we should get her back and try to smooth things out."

Colin balked at that idea. "Let her go. She wants to be alone. So do I."

Colin turned his back to Blair and began to walk away.

"Hold on. Maybe we can sit and chat for a while."

Another idea Colin quickly found distasteful. "I don't think so. Just leave me the hell alone."

"Colin, wait!" Blair called. "If I've done anything to offend you then you can't keep it to yourself. Join me for dinner and we'll talk."

Colin ignored Blair and continued walking.

"I can answer a lot of questions. There are several important things that you should know."

Colin stopped. He turned around. "You better make this good."

Colin followed Blair back into the cafeteria. Blair entered the line and picked up a tray. Colin returned to the table where he previously sat. His tray was still there. His food had gotten cold. No matter, he was not hungry anymore. He was here to gain information from Blair. It took Blair a few minutes to get a full tray and sit down next to Colin.

"You're not hungry?" Blair asked.

"I already ate."

Blair looked over at Colin's food tray, then his bandaged arm. "What happened there?"

"Had an accident," Colin muttered in a glum tone. "Don't worry about it."

Colin noticed that a few people were picking up their trays and walking over to a large video screen in the far corner.

"Looks like it's time for the floor show," Blair commented, taking a bite of corn.

The Brelac regularly transmitted scenes of mutilated bodies scattered across a desolate landscape: stacks of dead troopers being incinerated on a mass pyre, the smoldering ruins of cities and military bases, scenes narrated by the slow-speaking, gravelly voice of an unnamed Brelac, his snarling face occasionally appearing on screen to predict that all humans would soon die for the glory of the Brelac Empire.

Most troopers were unimpressed by the Brelac's threats. A few considered these videos to be more entertaining than demoralizing. Colin began watching them when he first started working here at Nocturne. In the beginning he had been highly disturbed. But after gradually getting used to them he regarded them as pure propaganda. At the moment, he was more interested in what Blair had to say. The transmission would be nothing that he had not seen and heard before.

Blair nearly choked on a mouthful of beef as his attention turned from Colin to the screen. Blair dropped his fork and bolted from his seat and rushed over to the small crowd gathered in front of the video screen. Colin thought that this broadcast must be serious if it could pull Blair away from his meal so quickly, so he followed.

The man on screen cheerfully introduced himself. "My name is Doctor Howard Fenlow. I'll be replacing your regular host for tonight's episode of total obliteration, courtesy of the Brelac Empire. For those of you who aren't familiar with me I used to work with the military on various projects. I stress the term, *used to*. I've recently decided to broaden my horizons and work with the Brelac to help bring an end to this pointless war."

"Fenlow, working with the Brelac?" Blair said in a barely audible voice. "This has to be a ruse."

"I'm not going to waste your time showing you any scenes of charred bodies or bloodied torture victims strapped to chairs," Fenlow continued. "Instead, I'm going to make this message as brief as possible. At this very moment the Brelac and I are on the verge of completing a weapon of devastating power. A weapon for which there will be no defense. It is not my wish to cause any unnecessary bloodshed. Therefore, on behalf of the Brelac Empire I am issuing an ultimatum. The United Protectorate has three days to order all military forces to disarm and surrender. I will personally guarantee the safety of any person who decides to cooperate."

A trooper standing at Colin's right scoffed. "A traitor guaranteeing our safety?"

"Three days should be enough time for you to contact all forces stationed throughout the quadrant," Fenlow went on. "For everyone's sake, I hope that President Drennen will have the courage to do the right thing and put an end to this war. There will be no other broadcasts made after this. Remember, three days."

The screen went dark.

Colin turned to Blair. "Doctor Howard Fenlow? Isn't he the man that you said can help us?"

"It looks like Doctor Fenlow isn't planning to help anybody," Blair stated to his chagrin.

Colin had heard enough. He turned and walked away from the screen. Blair said nothing and made no attempt to stop him. So far this was the second time that Colin would go to sleep after having a bad evening. But sleeping was the only thing that he was looking forward to now. He figured at least no harm would come from that.

*****

Colin returned to the barracks and his small room, the room so small that he did not bother to turn on the light in order to find his way to the cot. He simply shuffled forward a few feet and sat down on the thin, stiff surface that barely passed as a mattress.

Colin sat in the dark for a moment. Then he lay on his back. He intended to rest for a moment before he changed out of his uniform and into the t-shirt and shorts he always slept in. But right now all he wanted to do was forget about the hard life that awaited him outside of this shield of darkness that he rested his tired body in. Colin closed his eyes.

He was back in the cafeteria, being confronted by a group of angry, shouting troopers, Lieutenant Yates among them. Two men held his arms while a man standing in front of him raised his fist to send a damaging blow to his face. Before the man's fist could strike Colin another hand reached out and grabbed his arm. Diane had stepped in to save him from getting a severe beating. The men that were binding Colin's arms quickly released him. They did not want to confront Diane's inhuman strength. Harsh words were shouted between Diane and Lieutenant Yates. Diane still had the trooper held tightly in her grip. With little effort she shoved him to the floor and he slid back across the room.

Diane turned and approached Colin, their eyes locked together in an unblinking stare.

"We showed them who's really in charge around here," she said. "Didn't we, Sarge?"

She wrapped her arms around him in a tight embrace. Her face moved in closer to his, their lips were inches from meeting.

Colin opened his eyes and sat up quickly. He glanced around at the dark walls of his room. His breathing slowed. "What the hell was that?" he gasped out.

Over the past few days Diane was the last thing that was on his mind. And now here she was in his dream, about to kiss him.

None of this made any sense.

He'd been disturbed by his dreams before; now he had to worry about them becoming creative. Dreading the prospect of falling asleep again, Colin knew that he was in for a very long and restless night.

CHAPTER THIRTEEN

Carp Technologies' enormous disk-shaped starbase rested peacefully on the far outer fringes of Protectorate space, sparse traffic coming to and from the structure. Huge rectangular cargo vessels delivered their payloads collected from the mining operations on distant moons. Small, oval shuttlecrafts transported work crews to and from Carp's lunar-based research laboratories scattered throughout the region.

Since the start of the war, Carp's starbase remained relatively safe, thanks to the graciousness of the Brelac. The starbase not only served as a corporate headquarters, but it also housed over a dozen heavy manufacturing operations, as well as research and development laboratories. The starbase was also a safe haven for five hundred of the company's technicians, scientists, and executives, including Carp's Chief Executive Officer, Walter Carnaby.

Carnaby walked alone through the brightly lit corridor, his dark suit standing out against the lights and white-paneled walls. This entire section of the starbase was restricted to executive level personnel. The other members of Carp's executive board had called a special meeting, and Carnaby expected the others to already be assembled in the main conference room. But he was in no hurry. One of the many small perks of his position was the ability to invoke patience in others. His subordinates could wait; no one was going anywhere. Not when he had the answers to all their questions.

Carnaby was a man capable of being an alluring, smooth talker. He considered himself to be highly skilled in the art of selling unpopular concepts, or sidestepping unpleasant issues. When necessary, he could easily adopt a more aggressive mode of behavior. He was known, by many individuals, to be like a swarm of boulders in an avalanche, not stopping for any smaller force until he reached his goal, the smaller force often crushed and forgotten.

The conference room door quietly slid open upon Carnaby's approach. Carnaby grinned at the sight of the seven executives seated at the round wooden table with its polished surface. The grim frowns on the faces of middle-aged men seemed to be an extension of the dark suits and ties that they wore.

"Good afternoon, gentlemen," Carnaby greeted light-heartedly. He sat down in his usual reserved seat.

Rodger Bannister sat at Carnaby's left, Carp's director of security. A bespectacled man with receding black hair, he wore a black suit coat over his white shirt and red tie. His right arm rested on the table while he impatiently drummed his fingers on its polished surface. At his right was a chubby man with curly brown hair. John Steiner, Carp's director of operations.

"I don't have to imagine why this meeting was requested," Carnaby stated. "No doubt everyone here heard Fenlow's little message to the government."

"We couldn't help hearing. It was on every damn wavelength. Video and audio. Who the hell does that idiot think he is? Shooting his mouth off, making such a demand. And with our preparations for Operation Broad Axe. He's sure to expose us."

"Not if we're careful," Carnaby said. "Fenlow is probably acting on my orders. I instructed him to do whatever he could to advance our plan. Remember, we all mutually agreed that it would be prudent to move as quickly as possible. With the increased Brelac aggression and the gradual deterioration of the Protectorate military, this ultimatum could work in our favor."

"Have you had any contact with Fenlow?" Bannister asked.

"It's been a few days since I've personally spoken with him. And if he is working with the Brelac then I imagine that he'll be more difficult to reach. But I can afford to be patient. However, if it makes any of you feel a little better, I'll try to contact him to get an update."

"And just what happens when the three days are up and the government doesn't surrender?" Steiner asked

Carnaby gave serious thought to that question. He knew that Fenlow would not make such a threat without the power to back it up. "Then that could be the opportunity for the final phase of our plan to finally get underway. When that opening comes, we'll take it."

"You sound so confident," Bannister said. "That this small group can accomplish what thousands of heavily armed Vendetta troops failed to do, and overthrow the central government."

Carnaby laughed. "The fearsome hordes of Vendetta. Without our guidance and material support they would quickly revert back to splintered groups of right-wing extremists venting their spleen at any suitable target. A more technically conceived plan is sure to succeed where lowbrow aggression has failed."

"Speaking of technical concepts, what about the three second-generation Reploids that were lost?" Steiner asked.

"They pose no threat," Carnaby simply stated. "My intelligence reports that the Reploids are now currently stationed at Nocturne Base on the planet Trillion. They spend their time serving in menial tasks."

"And if the military decides to send them against us?" Bannister asked.

"The military doesn't know about our activities or where to find us," Carnaby replied impatiently. "And if they were to pose a threat to us and our plans, then I'm placing my trust in Fenlow to deal with them."

"Fenlow and the Brelac."

"Do you still think that we can trust the Brelac?" Steiner said.

"I don't confidently trust the Brelac," Carnaby said. "But we need them. We need them on our side in order to accomplish our goal. They are a powerful force that will eventually crush the United Protectorate and move on to their next target. Their goal is the total annihilation of the human race. In order for Carp Technologies to survive, we have to convince them that it's in their best interests to allow the human race to live, under a joint supervision between them and us. This way the war comes to an end, the bulk of their time and resources moves on, and the entire United Protectorate will at last be under our rightful control."

CHAPTER FOURTEEN

Deep within Rantraven base, Mariner was enjoying a little rest and recreation in his study. A dim light from the ceiling illuminated the small room and reflected off the brown linoleum floor and polished dark wood wall panels. Mariner was seated at a small dark wood table at the back of the room with his faithful confidant, Senior General Owen Lagar. They both sat on thickly cushioned ottomans. At the left and right walls were small, rectangular wooden tables with long thin legs. Mounted on both walls above the tables were large star maps in gold frames, their black backgrounds peppered with dozens of tiny white dots representing star systems. Beneath each one was a thin label baring the system's name.

In the middle of the room were three more wooden tables side by side. Wide computer monitors stood on each table displaying dozens of small pop-up windows, each containing relayed information from the warfront. On the middle table was a computer keyboard with glowing red keys, where Mariner received incoming messages and any data concerning the war effort, as well as issued orders to his commanders in the field. In the middle of the wall behind the tables was a dark wooden door with a curved gold handle.

Mariner and Lagar were absorbed in a centuries old game that consisted of a multicolored board with cards, dice, and tiny plastic houses. It was an economic game involving the principles of buying and selling. Two forces working to amass wealth and resources until one gained sufficient power to ruin the other. It was a game that Mariner's Brelac mind could perfectly relate to.

Monopoly.

Lagar often joined Mariner for these gaming sessions. Since Mariner handpicked Lagar as his second in command, the two were rarely far apart. Mariner valued Lagar's military mind. They shared a mutual brilliance and a love of warfare. Together they executed many successful military campaigns to expand the power of the Brelac Empire. Mariner demanded no less than total efficiency from his subordinates. Like Mariner, Lagar was a strict disciplinarian and a rigid perfectionist. Overseeing all military operations it was Lagar's job to see that Mariner's directives were carried out without any deviation.

Mariner held the dice in his scaled hand. He shook them then lifted his arm to roll when a series of loud beeps came from a small monitor on the middle table. Mariner hissed, then cursed aloud. There was a transmission coming in. Fenlow's face appeared on screen.

"Have you heard any word from my government?" he inquired.

Mariner ignored Fenlow for the moment. Lagar also remained silent. Mariner rolled the dice across the game board that was faded yellow with age. Doubles, two fives. Mariner's clawed fingers clumsily pushed a small metal thimble figurine ten spaces across the board. He landed on Baltic Avenue, a space he had already owned and had a green house on.

With his roll completed, Mariner diverted his attention to Fenlow's remarks. "No word yet," he croaked in his deep and gruff voice.

"I didn't think so," Fenlow said. "Perhaps I've underestimated their tenacity when I issued that ultimatum. It would appear that they're not going to lie down and surrender because of just another transmitted threat. Even if the format suddenly changed and it featured a human face."

"They've still got two days left," Mariner replied, reaching for the dice. "I'm in a good enough mood to give your people the benefit of the doubt."

"Patience and restraint from a Brelac? You really must be light-hearted right now. Perhaps at the start of the war we could have ordered Protectorate troopers to play polka music and juggle knives to keep you Brelacs amused. It might have saved a lot of bloodshed. But it the meantime I have work to get back to. I'll leave you to your recreation."

Mariner's head jerked up. "I'm glad that you mentioned your work, Doctor. I'm anxious to receive a status report on this grand project Viperhawk that I'm helping to support."

"I'm running a series of final checks on the Viperhawk's systems. My ultimatum transmission was simply one test that I've conducted. I estimate that it will be another few days before I can execute a final test run. I'll keep you posted as things develop."

"If you need anything, then don't hesitate to ask."

Fenlow hesitated. "What is that? On the table?"

"Just a game. Monopoly," Mariner said. "It's a simple diversion that involves the use of strategy and elements that one can appreciate. You should try it."

"Some other time," Fenlow replied. His image blinked out and the pop-up windows returned to the screen.

Now that Fenlow was gone, Mariner's display of patience faded. "I look forward to the day when Fenlow has outlived his usefulness. Then he can be eliminated"

"I can't wait to be rid of him either," Lagar said in agreement. "And his masters at Carp. Who the hell does he think he is making an ultimatum like that without consulting us first? And it continuously irks me that this human was able to make such a quantum improvement on our technology."

"The advanced second generation Reploids," Mariner nodded. "His work is highly impressive. Our experiments in giving our soldiers advanced psionic powers through their implants have had little success. The huge surge of psionic energy always destroyed the subjects' nervous systems, and was one hundred percent fatal to the test subjects. But Fenlow has found a way around that problem. His subjects have an engineered gene that enables their nervous tissue to rapidly regenerate. Rather than have our own technicians try to duplicate Fenlow's work I think that it's better to bide our time and get everything we can out of him and Carp. Then they will both become expendable."

"I can hardly wait," Lagar added, "for that moment to come. I suppose I'll just have to wait until this project Viperhawk of his is completed before I can act."

"It's fortunate that he's sharing his data. Adding Fenlow's regenerative gene enhancement will allow us to finally go forward with our own advanced psionic augmentation program. We have the superior technology to cut a path of conquest wherever we go. But there's only one problem that we have to face."

"The manpower," Lagar quickly replied. "There's only a few million of us. If we want to take on the entire universe we'd be stretched out pretty thin."

"Exactly. We need a hell of a lot more personnel if we want to move on and engage the next quadrant. Having soldiers with advanced psionic abilities will give us a huge edge against our opposition."

"With an army of super soldiers our military power will increase a hundred fold," Lagar said. "After we get the United Protectorate worlds under control we can start a mass cloning and construction program. We can turn entire star systems into massive factories. Cranking out enhanced troops, ships, and equipment. Then when we're ready to make our move, nothing can stand against us."

"Carp," Mariner said with a snort. "The big fish in the lake, as they like to refer to themselves. To think they expect us to grant them governorship over the United Protectorate. They will do us the favor of maintaining order. The fools fail to realize that I see no distinction between them and any other human. We will crush the United Protectorate and exterminate them all. That is our mission. To cleanse the entire universe of the human species. Wherever we find them. And they will provide us with the tools to help bring about their own destruction."

CHAPTER FIFTEEN

Starbase Twelve, a circle of six gigantic, white pillars penetrating through a huge orb drifted in a silent orbit high above the planet Morthos Three. Its entire surface was aglow with thousands of bright lights. Dozens of manta-ray shaped attack carriers and enormous battleships with their long, cone-shaped hulls and huge triangular wings mounted both horizontally and vertically at the rear section of these ships, were docked at the lower pillars of the base. Among the many Brelac ships docked there was one that Fenlow had converted into his immediate base of operations. The Viperhawk.

Viperhawk was a dark, oval-shaped battle cruiser with broad, swept-forward wings folded against its side to allow the ship to dock. At the ship's nose dozens of spider-like construction drones floated about like a swarm of bees, each drone equipped with eight telescoping arms with dexterous pinchers. Several drones carried panels of transparent crystal while other drones assisted them as they interlocked these panels of crystal together on the nose of the ship. Molecular bonding tools at the end of their arms fused each panel seamlessly together.

Inside the ship the dimly lit corridors were empty. There were no Brelac crewmen manning their stations. Fenlow sat at a metal table in a large circular room with gray paneled walls, jotting down data on a small notepad. He rose up and headed for a white, six-foot-tall, column-shaped device in the center of the room in the middle of a black, circular area on the floor. There was a multicolored keypad installed on its side. Above the keypad was a red light, constantly glowing like an unblinking eye.

This device was a specially designed computer system that Fenlow had created. A powerful computer enhanced by living brain tissue that Fenlow had cloned and rapidly grew in the incubation tube back at the laboratory in Rantraven. The tissue itself was enhanced by larger versions of Fenlow's psionic implants. Within the computer's housing, the large mass of cerebral matter rested inside a life support container. Through a network of plastic tubes it was constantly fed oxygen and a nutrient fluid while it was connected to the computer hardware below by a thick cable.

All of the Viperhawk's functions were maintained by this computer, so no crew was needed. Instead of the bridge, this circular room was the ship's nerve center, and Fenlow was confident that this computer could operate every function within this ship far more quickly and efficiently than any living crew. For a personal touch, Fenlow could not resist granting the computer a name—Succubus.

Fenlow pressed a sequence of keys on the keyboard to summon data on the ship's status. The crisp holographic image of the ship's schematics was projected above the keypad. Fenlow smiled. Succubus' control of the ship's entire propulsion system was now flawless. Fenlow nodded in silent approval.

The door behind Fenlow slid open. Major Danton entered the room. "Still no reply from your people?"

"Not even an invitation to go to hell," Fenlow replied. "I don't expect them to send an answer tomorrow either. But still, it was a perfect way to test Succubus' communications capability. President Drennen and the others would be amazed to know that they had received a message transmitted telepathically over the gulf of space."

Danton scoffed. "I still think that it was a waste of energy. And an unauthorized waste of energy at that. You should have cleared it with Mariner or General Lagar first."

"I saw no need," Fenlow calmly rebuked, "considering the fact that Mariner himself placed me in full charge of this project."

"If you say so," Danton ceded. "But I am curious to know what you intend to do if your people refuse to surrender. Do you intend to take on the entire Protectorate military by yourself?"

A sinister grin appeared on Fenlow's face. "In a way, yes." He turned back to the computer. "Succubus."

Above the computer's column form the holographic image of a large, red eye surrounded by yellow, pulsating cerebral matter appeared. This self-image was another personalizing touch that Fenlow had given the computer.

"Contact Captain Stergis at Rantraven's robotics research lab. Tell him that I need the Deltans transported here at once."

"Deltans?" Danton asked.

"Yes. While I was building Succubus, I came up with the idea to conduct a scaled-down experiment with a few of your robotic assault units. Your Delta Nova Three Series. Deltans for short. The Deltans will carry out my retaliation. Now would be the perfect time to use them."

"I hope that you're planning to seek Mariner's approval for this," Danton said.

"You're free to consult Mariner and tell him whatever you want. My only concern is the success of this experiment."

"An expensive experiment," Danton returned, showing skepticism over the idea. "If you send these Deltans out to find the Reploids then they might wind up fighting an army of Protectorate troopers at the same time. I would be more confident if you had built more than just three of them. They won't be able to stand up to any sizable force."

Fenlow laughed. "You'll change your mind about my Deltans after they win their first battle. Have you forgotten that I've incorporated my psionic technology into their construction? They're part machine, part living organisms. Their psionically-based weapons systems make them more powerful than a battle cruiser. Their sensors are twice as powerful and accurate than anything you currently possess. The success or failure of these three prototypes in the field will determine whether I'll create more like them."

"I hope you're right," Danton sighed. "But if they should find where the Reploids are stationed then they must report their position to central command. We'll send out a strike force to aid them in dealing with any enemy resistance."

Fenlow suspected that Danton wanted to barge in on the operation and claim some credit for himself if there was a successful attack. That was of no consequence. *Let the fool join in on the fun and games if he wants to*, thought Fenlow. "If you feel that it's necessary to send in some troops then I won't argue with you. But I'm confident that the Deltans will easily handle any resistance."

"If you say so."

"I'm glad that you agree," Fenlow said flatly. "And since you're in such an agreeable mood perhaps you can tell me something. What exactly is Monopoly?"

"A game. Rarely used," Danton said. "We hardly have time for such distractions."

"Curious," Fenlow replied, "I never heard of such a thing. And I have trouble picturing you Brelac as game players."

"There are a lot of things you don't know about us."

"I can imagine," Fenlow mused with a nod. "There's another thing that I'd like to ask. Earlier on, Mariner made a comment to me about being kissed by Pandora. Can you tell me what he meant by that?"

Danton hissed softly. "He made reference to an affliction from a bygone era. A weakness that we have been bred to resist."

"Bred?" Fenlow smiled, surprised. "What I know about you Brelac is that you creatures are not bred. You're made. And I'd like to know a little more about that."

Danton shook his head. "You already have knowledge of how we are produced."

"I know. Brelac units are cloned en-masse from the same genetic stockpile. You're all grown to maturity through an in-vitro process at spawning facilities." He paused, looking up. "Where were you produced?"

"I came from a spawning facility located in the Mediterranean Sector."

"I would like to see one of these facilities. I'd find it fascinating."

"You would find it fatal," Danton growled. "Such facilities are high security areas. An alien like yourself would never be able to get within sight of them."

An alien like myself? Fenlow thought. *A curious statement coming from an eyeless, scale-covered monster.*

"Where is this Mediterranean Sector? I never heard of it."

"That is because such knowledge is not a part of our agreement with your company," Danton explained. "We maintain our security just as you maintain yours."

It was clear to Fenlow that Danton would not give any further information on the subject of the Brelac's origins.

No matter, Fenlow thought. *At his command there were other ways and means to get information.*

"Perhaps we'll talk again later. Right now I have a ton of things to do."

"So do I," Danton returned. "But I also came to report that the Viperhawk's forward lens array will be completed in two hours. We're going through a lot of trouble to make everything to your specifications. That lens installation, the computer hardware. We even donated this ship to your project. It's fairly new. Only saw two battles since it left the shipyard. I hope that this project of yours is worth all the hype that you gave us."

Fenlow grinned. "I've already bet my life on its success. Since the lens array will be completed soon then perhaps we can drop another unexpected surprise on our friends."

CHAPTER SIXTEEN

Colin, Kelly, and Blair sat at a dark, oval table in a small conference room. Colin sat nervously with both hands lying on the table, slowly tapping his fingers while he shifted his gaze from the four empty black chairs on the left side of the table to the smooth, white-paneled walls of the room. There was another black chair at the head of the table. Behind it a gray metal door. Colin's eyes moved to the door while imagining several reasons why he and the others were assembled here. Diane was also summoned but had yet to arrive. Kelly, sitting at Colin's right, remained quiet while nervously biting his thumbnail. An equally silent Blair sat at Colin's left. All they'd been told was that General Larkin needed to speak to them about an urgent matter.

"How have you been sleeping?" Kelly asked Colin.

Colin turned. "Why are you asking?"

"Just wondering. I have these dreams. They're pretty vivid. I find myself replaying my day's activities. What I've done and who I've talked to. It's the same thing every night."

"I know what you mean!" Colin exclaimed with surprise. He turned to Blair. "Does this mean anything?"

"It could be stress connected with your jobs," Blair calmly explained. "It's possible that you've been concentrating too much on displeasure of your work. Your subconscious minds are replaying your activities in your sleep."

Colin felt that Blair's reasoning was highly dubious. The format of these dreams was too systematic to be just a vexation over work. He wondered if Diane was having the same dreams as well. And then there was the question concerning the strange dream that he had about Diane last night.

The door to the conference room slid open and Diane strode in.

"Hello Diane," Blair cheerfully greeted.

"Doctor," Diane returned. She walked around the table and sat down next to Blair. She said nothing to Colin or Kelly and simply stared down at the table.

The conference room door slid open again. This time General Larkin entered. Colin joined the others in unison as they jumped to their feet and stood at attention.

"Please be seated," Larkin told the group. "I'm glad to see you all here. Sorry that we couldn't meet under happier circumstances. But as you know we have an urgent situation on our hands. Undoubtedly you've heard that one of our top scientists, Doctor Howard Fenlow, has apparently defected to the Brclac and issued an ultimatum on their behalf. He claims that he can give them the power to win the war overnight."

"What does that have to do with us, sir?" Colin asked.

"I was hoping you could tell me," Larkin returned. "It's likely that Fenlow is working on some new weapons project with the Brelac. The three of you are Fenlow's creations. You might have some knowledge of what he's doing. And with your powers you might be able to find some way to stop him."

Colin felt that Larkin was grasping at straws. There was little that he, Diane, and Kelly could do against such an unknown menace. But still, Colin did not want to disappoint Larkin. "We'll be glad to help out in any way we can, sir."

Diane raised her hand. "Excuse me, Sarge. Any idea how we're gonna pull this off?" she asked, a heavy tone of sarcasm in her voice. "Maybe you can share your game plan with the rest of us."

To Colin's chagrin he almost felt guilty about voicing a commitment without consulting the others. "Undoubtedly Fenlow is now under the protection of the Brelac. He won't be easy to reach. Were you able to trace his transmission?"

"The previous ultimatums were sub-space transmissions traced to an unknown source in the Dione system." Larkin explained. "That's deep within Brelac territory. Now Fenlow's transmission is a total mystery. The previous transmissions were received on a specific frequency. Fenlow's transmission was received on every frequency imaginable, video and audio. Military and civilian. It broke into every channel all the way back to Maseklos Prime. Even though it was such a powerful transmission all attempts to trace it have failed. It was as if the transmission came from nowhere."

"Maybe it's possible to retrace Fenlow's steps," Colin suggested. "We can search his home and his workplace to get a clue on what he was working on. Possibly find out how he was able to contact the Brelac."

"That will be easier said than done," Larkin replied. "His apartment and lab back on Maseklos Prime were already searched. There was nothing out of the ordinary. And his associates and superiors at Carp Technologies offered very little information."

A sudden high pitched wail filled the room. Colin saw worried looks appear on Larkin and Blair's faces.

"The emergency alarm," Blair said. "The base must be under attack."

A shrill beep sounded out from Larkin's coat. "What now?" he muttered in frustration. He took a cellular communicator—a small black, oval-shaped device with a keypad and a thin display—out of his hip pocket. He pressed a button. The display began to glow. "Larkin here. What's going on?"

The look on Larkin's face changed from distress to confusion as he listened to the report. "The command center reports that we are indeed under attack. So far we've suffered heavy casualties. We've lost a full battalion of troopers and a dozen hover tanks."

"The Brelac must have a couple of divisions out there." Blair stood wringing his hands.

"It's just three," Larkin said.

"Three divisions?" Blair asked

"Three units," Larkin corrected. "Sounds incredible, but that's what all reports have stated. Three robots of some sort. I'm told that they're extremely powerful and there's a large force of Brelac air and ground units heading this way. They'll be here in twenty minutes."

For a moment Larkin was silent. "Silencers Squad has been inactive for far too long. I'm putting the three of you back in action. I want you to go out, assess this robotic threat, and deal with it as needed. I'll be in the command center monitoring the situation."

Colin joined Diane and Kelly in an enthusiastic, "Yes sir."

Colin could not help noticing the broad smile that illuminated Diane's face. He wondered if she could see past her zeal for combat to appreciate the seriousness of what was going on. *Is she out of her mind? She looks eager to go rushing headlong into this fight and she doesn't even know what the hell is out there.* It was a different matter for Kelly and Blair. The worried frowns on their faces revealed their apprehension at the idea of facing an unknown enemy. Colin was also fearful of confronting whatever was waiting outside. Moments from now he would be in combat against an enemy that had decimated a battalion of troopers and twelve hover tanks. And it was possible that he and the others could only end up as their next victims. His heart pounded so heavily that he could not distinguish his excitement from fear.

Colin and the others rose from their seats and followed Larkin out of the room.

CHAPTER SEVENTEEN

Troopers fired every weapon from laser and plasma arms to portable missile launchers at their attackers. Several troopers already lay dead on the ground. Dozens of imposing hover tanks floated over the scene: vehicles with dark oval bodies and large bulb-shaped turrets on top with long cannons pointed toward the enemy. Mounted on the sides of their bodies were large cylinder thrusters, blowing out short plumes of flame as they pushed the tanks forward.

From out of a wall of fire and a cloud of dust and smoke emerged a trio of tall, silver robotic creatures. They marched through powerful explosions while countless energy bolts bounced off of their bodies without causing so much as the slightest blemish to their reflective surface. They towered seven feet tall with rough humanoid bodies. Their heads were large and oval shaped, their only facial feature a thin, red horizontal lens serving as an eye. Below the eye lens were two metallic accordion hoses that ran down to a disk-shaped unit on their broad chests. Projecting out from the sides of their heads were long, sharp metallic horns pointing upward. On their backs were large, triangular wings with long cylindrical thrusters mounted on their tips.

The massive left arms on these metallic creatures ended in large hands with three clawed fingers. Their right forearms came in the form of long cylinders with four wide fins mounted vertically and horizontally. The creatures slowly marched forward on thick, reverse jointed legs. The three toes of their feet were armed with curved metal talons that dug into the ground as they walked.

They continued to advance with impunity through the human assault without slowing their pace. They were seemingly impervious to firepower from the smaller arms.

Colin wondered how these metallic creatures could stand up to a heavy barrage from the many hover tanks gathered around. As far as Colin could see, the robots' advance was a passive one. They were allowing the troopers to do all the shooting. The robots spread out, then stopped before the small army of troopers still blazing away at them with intense fury.

One of the robots raised its right arm toward a hover tank aiming to fire. There was a bright red flash and the sound of a brief, loud whoosh as the robot fired a crimson beam of plasma energy from the end of its arm that demolished the vehicle in a thundering blast. Chunks of the tank's ragged metal debris rained down over the area while its remains began to burn.

That explains the function of this peculiar looking arm, Colin thought. It was clearly a plasma weapon. But its power was beyond anything he had ever seen from a weapon of that size.

The other two robots followed suit; they fired their plasma beams at tanks and troopers alike, sending red flashes in the air. The troopers scattered as bodies were hurled through the air by the explosions. A group of ten fighters flew over Colin and the others and closed in on the robotic invaders for a frontal assault.

The fighters' plasma cannons blazed away at the robots. A large panel of energy that resembled smoky glass instantly appeared in front of each robot, and these shields easily absorbed the firepower from the fighters. As the fighters soared overhead, the shields disappeared. The robots quickly turned and sent out a hail of their potent plasma beams at the aircrafts. The robots' aim was as reliable as ever. In a single strike all but two of the fighters were blasted out of the sky.

Colin spotted a swarm of black stingray-shaped fighter crafts making a rapid approach. "Incoming!" he shouted. "Take cover!"

Before Colin and the others could run for cover the fighters soared overhead without strafing the area. They ignored the activity taking place on the ground and headed for the base.

A trooper approached Colin's group. "We've been ordered to retreat. We can't hold these things back, let alone the Brelac ground troops heading this way. The entire base is being evacuated."

Colin absorbed the grim report but was not prepared to accept defeat so soon. "Those things will reach the base before any Brelac troops. We're going to have to deal with them. Maybe help buy some time for the evacuation."

"Suit yourself," the trooper replied, then quickly ran off.

"Let him go," Diane said. She walked over to a dead trooper lying on his back. She commandeered his AR-20 rapid mortar rifle from his hands—a cumbersome weapon with a long barrel and a large magazine on the top.

Diane seemed to be just as eager to get into this fight as ever. Colin stared at Kelly's face. His skin was pale and his hands shook. Colin sympathized with Kelly's fears, but if they possessed these arcane abilities then they had to put them to use and try to defeat this trio of robotic monsters. At least Colin was thankful that Blair reluctantly agreed to remain in the base. This was a dangerous situation. Without the benefit of special abilities, Blair was certain to be the most vulnerable target and the first casualty.

The three of them advanced toward the robots, and split up to face their opponent. Diane charged in to attack one of the robots. Her rapid mortar rifle spat out a burst of four explosive shells with a loud boom. Each shell she fired exploded on the robot's body. It staggered back a few steps, but seemed unharmed. Diane fired a second burst, but was also ineffective. Finally she tossed the rifle aside and charged toward the robot, her hands outstretched. The robot thrust its hand out and smashed its palm into Diane's face. Diane was knocked senseless, her nose bloodied.

The robot's massive hand engulfed her head and prepared to crush it into a bloodied gel. Kelly moved quickly to intervene, sending a burst of fiery energy that struck the robot directly into its face. The attack caused no damage but did serve to distract it. The robot turned to face Kelly. Kelly fired another beam of energy at the robot, and the energy bounced harmlessly off of the robot's metallic skin. The robot responded by throwing Diane at Kelly. Her body sped through the air and slammed into Kelly with a force that rendered him unconscious.

Colin watched the robot approach their immobile bodies. The two other robots were steadily closing in on his position as well. Colin decided to see if these machines could withstand a few thousand volts of electric current. He raised his hands. He gnashed his teeth and groaned as a sharp pain flashed through his left arm. The pain distracted him from putting his plan into action. One of the robots fired a plasma beam that exploded ten feet in front of him. The power of the blast threw Colin into the air and onto his back. Pain burned through Colin's shoulders as he was showered by hot particles of soil and rock. His head started to throb. Sparks leaped up from his hands. Streams of current flowed across the ground. Then the ground beneath Colin quickly sank to form a gaping crevasse that threatened to swallow him.

Colin desperately bore his fingers into the ground and hung onto the very edge of the crevasse. A thick cloud of dust quickly enveloped him as the crevasse continued to expand. When the throbbing in Colin's head abruptly stopped the progression of the crevasse also halted. Colin was certain that this was a bizarre new manifestation of his power.

A power like this could come in handy, Colin told himself. *Especially within the next five seconds.*

Colin turned at the sound of a small band of troopers charging in from behind him to make another assault on the robots. Through the rising cloud of dust he saw the multiple flashes of their weapons blazing furiously. But the countless laser and plasma bolts that they fired caused no damage to the robots. Colin managed to pull himself out of the crevasse while the robot's attention was diverted as a wave of energy bolts flew through the air above him.

Colin stood, brushed the dust from his face and neck, and prepared to make another attack. He grunted as his hands glowed and charged with electricity, then he raised his arms to release it toward one of the robots. The intense blue flash of an electrical bolt filled the air. In an instant, a panel of the smoky energy appeared in front of the robot and absorbed the assault. Colin fired another blast. This one was also blocked, then the barrier wavered, vanished, and the energy struck the robot on its gun arm. The robot quickly aimed its left hand at Colin and discharged its own bolt of electricity into Colin's chest. The charge lifted Colin off his feet and hurled him to the ground.

What the hell happened? Colin asked himself, glancing around wildly at the sparks dancing in the sand beside him. *Did that thing just re-route my shot through itself and send it back to me?*

The robots fired a quick succession of plasma bolts that obliterated the troopers near Colin in violent explosions. The screams of dying men filled his ears. Dismembered arms and legs flew about the area, blood and ash raining down on him. One of the robots suddenly turned to face Colin. It slowly began to advance toward him and raised its gun arm. Looking up, Colin knew that he was at the total mercy of this creature. At this range, one of its powerful energy blasts would reduce him to burning shards. He closed his eyes and turned his head as he heard the robot's gears wind up for the assault.

A barrage of laser bolts suddenly pelted the robot's face. Colin twisted his head and ducked to catch a glimpse of the shooter. To his surprise, Blair stood several yards away with a laser rifle in his hands.

A group of hover tanks roared up and fired their laser cannons at the robots. The robots reacted quickly, erecting their panels of protective shielding to absorb the tank's firepower. The tanks fired repeatedly at their targets, but the robots' shields protected them, and their plasma beams quickly demolished the tanks one by one.

Colin struggled to withstand the searing pain in his chest and rise to his feet. He sprinted toward Blair, hoping to reach the young man before one of these hostile robots killed them both. A huge shadow suddenly fell over Colin. He skidded to a stop and looked up to see a large ship hovering in the sky above him. Two forward wings spread out from against the wide oval body and long, silver rod projections extended from the tips of the wings. Colin cringed when he saw multiple openings appear underneath the ship to reveal numerous gun turrets. All pointed in his direction.

Between the enemy ship above him and those robots he could not imagine any thoughts of survival. He closed his eyes and instinctively threw his hands in front of his face at the sound of rapid shooting. Screams rang out all around him, and dust and rock chips flew into the air. He opened his eyes and saw the gun turrets spitting out multiple laser bolts that dismembered dozens of troopers who were still in the area. Colin was shocked to learn that his life was spared. Whether this was a mistake or a stroke of blind luck, Colin knew that he would have limited time to capitalize on it.

A small group of fighters came soaring in to attack the large ship, their twin engines roaring and drowning out the gunfire. A thick barrage of fire from the enemy vessel accurately destroyed the fighters instantly. Colin had seen enough of this ship. He ran to join Blair.

"What the hell are you doing out here?" he screamed "I thought we agreed that you'd stay inside."

"And if I did you'd be dead by now," Blair countered in anger. "I'm more than capable of taking care of myself. I am a trained soldier, as well as a doctor."

"That will make one hell of an obituary." Colin saw several more stingray fighters flying overhead. The large ship simply hovered silently, its presence serving as a dreaded omen. "We'd better grab Diane and Kelly and get out of here. This fight is getting way over our heads."

Colin and Blair charged over to the spot where Diane and Kelly were laying, both still unmoving. Blair kneeled down to pick up Diane. He slung her across his back and proceeded to run clumsily toward the base. Colin was grateful that Blair was lugging the larger and heavier Diane. Kelly was smaller and would be easier to carry. He scooped up Kelly's limp body and held him with both arms, grunting at the tightness in his chest he sped off to catch up with Blair, dragging Kelly's feet across the ground.

Colin looked up and saw several more Protectorate fighters soaring overhead being closely pursued by a group of stingray fighters. He looked back toward the three robots. They had effectively destroyed the last of the hover tanks that were plaguing them. The idea of taking these creatures on again was out of the question. They were too powerful while he, Diane, and Kelly were far too disorganized. They'd been lucky to survive the first encounter against these machines. A second battle would be a death sentence. As much as Colin hated to turn and run, his sense of self-preservation prevailed. He conceded the victory of this battle to the far more powerful enemy. But he promised himself that in the future the situation would be reversed.

If they encountered this robotic threat a next time, Silencers Squad would not run.

CHAPTER EIGHTEEN

Colin quickly caught up to Blair as they merged with a large mass of troopers ordered to retreat. Kelly had regained consciousness and was moving on his own. Blair became fatigued after carrying Diane's unconscious body across his back. He now carried her by her arms while Colin led the way, holding onto her legs. The mob flowed through the open gate of the tall, chain link fence that surrounded Nocturne's large airbase. Every fighter had been launched to engage the invaders. The only ships remaining were small wedge-shaped shuttles and cargo vessels.

Panicking mobs fought tooth and nail to board the first ship. Troopers desperately tried to coordinate the evacuation in the smoother and faster way that they were trained, though terrified masses were employing a different procedure to remove themselves out of harm's way. The thundering sounds of explosions in the background prodded many in the mob to move faster and become more desperate. Some individuals grabbed others trying to board shuttles and yanked them off, resulting in several fistfights breaking out. Officers in the air traffic control tower were unable to direct the ship's orderly departure. They had no choice but to allow the ships to take off at will. A few ships flew too close to one another upon take off and nearly crashed into each other in the air.

"What do we do now?" Blair gasped.

Colin looked through the mad rush of people. "Follow me."

Shoving his way through the crowd of shouting people, he led them to a squadron of small ships being prepared for immediate departure by the flight crews. Colin spotted a small wedge-shaped craft that looked as though it was barely large enough to carry the four of them. It was a scout craft, and there was no crowd fighting to board it. The hatch on the side of the ship gaped wide open. Colin grinned. They now had a ship ready to fly as soon as they boarded it.

Two Brelac fighters soared over the heads of the mob launching plasma bolts down onto the chaotic scene. Explosions erupted among the scrambling troopers. Flames and dismembered bodies were thrown about, and the sounds of screaming grew louder and more panicked. The fighters split and flew off in different directions as two Protectorate fighters took up pursuit with their laser cannons. Two more Protectorate fighters flew overhead, chased by three wild firing Brelac fighters.

"This is getting worse," Colin said.

With Diane in tow he led the others up through the hatch and into the interior of the craft. He expected to find the pilot waiting inside the cockpit but the seat was empty. Colin sat down in the pilot's seat and strapped himself in. Blair gently pushed Diane into the tiny space. Colin felt a sharp pain in his left shoulder as Diane's elbow pressed firmly against him. Blair squeezed himself in next, lying on top of Diane. In order for Kelly to fit inside he was forced to lay his body across Blair; half of his torso came to rest in the cockpit, and over Colin's head his face was mashed against the window. Colin had to lean forward to try and provide more room for Kelly, at the expense of his own comfort.

Colin stared down at the intimidating instrument panel with twin control sticks in front of a small monitor that displayed a cross-hair figure and a glowing yellow light. At the left were two rows of small displays with buttons beneath them. He looked closer at the displays. He could barely make out their designated functions, stated by tiny black letters.

Blair's frustrated voice broke Colin's train of thought. "Colin, this is not going to work. Let's try and board one of the other ships."

Colin shook his head. "You saw those mobs out there. We'd never be able to board any of those ships. We were lucky to get this one to ourselves."

"At least the people out there will be getting seats," Kelly said. "And since when are you a pilot?"

"Since you two are lying on top of our real pilot, who happens to be out of it at the moment," Colin grumbled back. "Besides, it can't be all that hard."

The engines were already on. All he had to do was put them in drive and manipulate the twin control sticks. He hesitated, fearing what would happen if he toyed with the wrong controls. Then he pressed several buttons and switches but yielded no result.

Colin heard a faint muffling sound rising up from the pile of bodies behind him. "Sounds like Diane is waking up," he said.

"Where am I?" Diane's voice cried out. "I can't breathe!"

"We're all inside a coffin that's about to be launched into space," Kelly returned.

"We boarded a ship," Colin's said glaring back at Kelly. "We're getting out of here."

"We're leaving?" Diane asked. "What about the fight?"

"We lost, quick and embarrassing. Now we're getting out of here before it becomes lethal. I'm shutting the door."

Colin located and pressed the switch on the panel that operated the hatch. The thick metal door whined, and then slid itself shut and sealed.

"Excuse me," Colin politely asked Kelly. "Can you push those buttons over there at your left?"

"What buttons?" Kelly shouted.

"They're at your left. Just below your neck. I can't reach them with you in the way. Unless Blair can reach them."

"Reach them?" Blair cried in disbelief. "I can't even see them."

"Never mind," Colin moaned. He contorted his body under Kelly to reach the desired buttons. He hoped that pressing them blindly would cause no serious harm.

The ship suddenly lurched forward, scraping out of control against the ground. Colin was still crouched under Kelly and away from the control sticks. He twisted around and looked through the ship's window to see dozens of troopers diving in every direction to avoid being mowed down. The ship barreled forward on a collision course with a grounded shuttle. Colin grasped the control sticks and pulled them back. The ship jumped sharply into the air and passed over the

183

shuttle. With the control sticks in his unsteady hands he sent the ship spiraling wildly into the air.

The ship crashed into a light tower, easily sheared the tower in half, and then climbed into the sky. Colin wondered if he would unintentionally do the job of killing the group instead of the Brelac, as the ship entered the air war zone where Protectorate and Brelac fighters were engaged in furious dogfights. Colin surprised himself by slipping the shaking craft through the battle without suffering a scratch. The ship suddenly began to weave and spin and Colin panicked. He probed the instrument panel to find any control that would help him to stabilize the ship.

Colin felt as if his stomach was being turned inside out. In his nauseous and dizzy state he noticed the small monitor on the instrument panel—the ship's scanner. It showed a triangle being closed in on by three oval-shaped objects.

That triangle must be us, he thought bleakly. *Great.*

"Three enemy fighters are approaching from coordinates one, zero, one, two." The scanner's voice system stated. "They are rapidly closing in."

Colin's job as pilot was getting harder. "One, zero, one, two? Where the hell is that?" he screamed to the instrument panel.

"It's someplace we have to get away from!" Blair yelled back. "Far away."

"Give me a chance," Colin said. "As soon as I figure out these controls."

He was unable to hold the jerking control sticks steady and fly the ship on a straight course. Through the window he saw the ship was still ascending into space. Several plasma bolts blazed past the ship.

"Oh great, now they're shooting at us!" Colin shouted. He knew that if one of those bolts struck this small ship it would mean instantaneous obliteration for everyone.

"Are they still on us?" Diane asked.

Colin glanced at the monitor. "As far as I can tell, yes."

"Why don't you turn and fight?"

Colin let out a burst of laughter. "You want me to fight? I can't even fly this damn thing."

"Well then, flying lesson's over, Sarge," Diane firmly exclaimed. "I'm taking over before you get us all killed."

"Gladly." Colin released the control sticks to try and maneuver under Kelly, whose torso was taking up most of the space in the cockpit.

"Guys, this is too much," Kelly whined. "I gotta get out of here. I'm gonna be sick."

"There's not enough room in here for you to get sick!" Colin shouted. His mind conjured the image of a slimy mess spilled across the cockpit. "Just try to hold on a little longer. One way or another, this will all be over soon."

With painful difficulty Colin squeezed under Kelly while Diane hurried to pry her way into the pilot's seat. Colin contorted his body into a tight fetal position. He apologized to Blair after his head and elbows accidentally struck the young man's face. Diane crawled past Colin, thrusting her elbow and foot onto his leg and aching left arm. Finally she placed herself into the pilot's seat leaning under Kelly's intruding body, and firmly grasped the control sticks. Diane's head quickly swiveled from one section of the instrument panel to another. Colin frowned.

"Diane, anything wrong?"

"No," she said, staring aimlessly at the controls.

"Diane, is anything wrong?" he repeated.

"No. I mean, I don't think so. I mean...my mind is a blank."

"What?"

"My mind is blank!" Diane snapped back. "I don't know what any of these things do!"

Colin stared wide-eyed at her. "Diane, I was under the impression that you were the greatest pilot in the Protectorate. If that was a joke then you should have told us back when we were on the ground!"

"It wasn't a joke!" Diane roared back. "I'm the best damn pilot there is!" She turned menacingly to Blair. "What the hell did you people do to me?"

"You suffered brain damage when you were brought to us," Blair explained. "That could account for your memory loss. Don't panic. It might be temporary."

"It'll be permanent if we get shot out of space," Colin argued. "We need a competent pilot right now or we're dead."

"Try using the control sticks," Blair suggested. "Maybe everything will slowly come back to you."

Diane followed Blair's instructions, and pulled the control sticks sharply toward her chest. The ship suddenly lurched upward. She looked over the instrument panel again. "What the hell is all this junk? These little windows with all these stupid numbers. Engine status, thrust, power, speed—"

"Try to find something that we can use," Colin told her.

"I'm trying!" Diane shouted back. "You think it's easy trying to figure out how to fly this thing with you guys breathing down my neck?"

"Well, sorry! Forgive me for not putting up a tarp so that you can have a little privacy."

"Let's not argue now," Kelly pleaded. "Let's concentrate on getting away from those ships before they blast us."

"I'm working on it." Diane studied the controls for a moment. "At least I think I've got a fairly good idea of how these sticks work. With a little practice I think I can pick the asteroid we can crash into."

Diane continued to work the various controls at her fingertips. She desperately needed to make an instant breakthrough, and quickly pressed three buttons on the instrument panel. The ship thrust forward sharply and was swallowed into a brilliant burst of white light.

CHAPTER NINETEEN

"Did we just make a warp jump?" Colin asked, staring out at the now empty space around them.

"I think we did," Diane said. "Any idea where we are?"

"I'm pretty sure that we're in the middle of nowhere." Colin fumed. *As if I have to answer to such a stupid question. After all, Diane is the pilot.* "Take a big sheet of blank paper and put a dot in the middle. That's us."

Colin tried to squeeze his body forward to get a better view of the window. He yelped out in pain as a sudden pressure was thrust into his groin. "Whose foot is that?"

"Foot? Where?" Kelly asked.

"That might be my knee," Blair responded. "Sorry."

"Well move it off!" Colin felt three hard objects butting against his legs. "I said move it off! Not down!"

The pain in Colin's groin surged up into his abdomen. He ground his teeth and closed his eyes to try and endure the agony that was near the point of making him sick.

"Ouch, dammit! My fingers!" Kelly cried out. "Somebody's on my hand!"

The pain in Colin's groin slowly subsided. Then Kelly's torso squirmed against his body, his shifting weight bearing down on Colin's head.

"Is it too much to hope that there's a bathroom aboard this thing?" Kelly inquired.

"You'd better hold that thought," Diane said. "I see something ahead."

Looking past Kelly's shoulder, Colin saw a tiny blue spot suspended out in space. As the seconds passed the orb steadily grew larger, but its true form was still vague.

"That could be a planet," Blair stated.

"There's your bathroom," Diane told Kelly.

Whatever it was, the small group knew that at the speed the ship was traveling they would not have long to greet it. As the ship neared the orb its image rapidly grew larger.

"Diane, we're heading for that thing awfully fast," Colin said. "Is there any way you can stop before we have a disaster?"

"I'll just throw an anchor out of the window and maybe we'll snag onto a rock," she replied sarcastically.

"This is no time for jokes!" Colin yelled. "I want to know if we can walk out of this thing alive after you make a landing."

"I'll try my best. But I can't promise that we won't be spread out across this planet when we hit." She held a firm grip on the control sticks and attempted to guide the ship in slowly.

Without warning, a large shining object streaked past the ship's window. Diane screamed and let go of the control sticks, and the ship titled sharply to the left. Diane grabbed the controls before the ship turned upside down. The object appeared again—a silvery blur flashing in front of the ship.

"What was that?" Colin whispered.

The object flew in front of the ship a third time at a reduced speed. They were now able to get a better look at it. It was a spacecraft. Colin could not identify its silvery boomerang-shaped form as being either Protectorate or Brelac.

Another ship appeared, flying on a swift collision course with their scout craft. Just as it appeared that both ships would crash into each other the alien ship veered upward and flew out of sight. Another ship flew across the window, coming so close that Diane swerved the scout ship to the left to try and miss it.

"They're coming at us awfully fast, Diane," Colin warned. "Can't you do something?"

"I'll throw out a couple of speed bumps! Think that will slow them down?"

The ship's radio crackled—a female voice sounding humorless and firm. "This is Panther Squadron Leader, Dayson to scout craft. Please give the required identification and security code."

"Panther Squadron?" Diane said. A broad smile beamed across her face. "Those are Protectorate ships. We're saved!"

The voice on the radio repeated the request. "This is Panther Squadron Leader, Dayson to scout craft. Please give the required identification and security code. If not then we'll be forced to take the appropriate action against you."

"Appropriate action?" Diane asked.

"They're going to blast us out of space!" Blair exclaimed. "Give them some identification."

Diane nervously pressed the button on the instrument panel to activate the transmitter. "My name is Captain Diane Christy. I have black hair...I...well. I'm about six feet tall. I'm twenty-four. I was born on March third—"

Colin cut her off quickly. "Diane, try not to make it too personal," he snapped. "Just tell them who we are."

Diane nodded. "This is Captain Diane Christy of Silencers Squad."

For a minute there was silence. Colin feared that the ships would start firing.

"Silencers?" the radio hissed. "Never heard of you."

"We're a newly formed squad," Diane explained.

"What are you doing out here?"

"We were running from the Brelac. They just invaded Nocturne."

"We weren't alerted about Nocturne being invaded. Assuming that it has been."

"I can't give you any video clips as proof," Diane snapped. "You'll just have to take my word for it."

"So, you hopped into this ship and decided to head for Lodestar for safety. Without any proper identification and security code to make your approach."

"Lodestar?" Blair gasped. "We're finally going to make it to starbase Lodestar."

"If they don't shoot us at the doorstep," Colin commented grimly.

Diane continued her losing argument with Dayson. "We were in a desperate situation. My friends and I snatched the first ship we could find. We didn't know we would end up here."

What little credibility that Diane had established with Dayson seemed to be evaporating. "Do you expect me to believe any of this, lady? Assuming that you really are a lady."

Kelly could not resist adding in a comment of his own. "She's no lady."

Dayson issued a stern warning. "I'm going to give you the benefit of the doubt. I'll allow you to turn back or we will open fire and destroy you."

Diane twisted around to look at Colin. "This is getting me nowhere. You'd better talk to this idiot."

Colin hoped that he would have better luck in dealing with Dayson. He took a breath.

"My name is Sergeant Colin McKenzie. My friends and I were just barely able to escape the Brelac forces when they invaded Nocturne. I realize that you have to maintain your security measures. But I can assure you that this is not some Brelac trick. We're on your side and we really need to land."

"Sorry Sarge. Your word carries as much weight as your friend's," Dayson quickly chided. "Turn your ship around or we'll have no choice but to open fire."

"Hold on. We have Doctor Blair Van Doren. He knows General Larkin. Will you at least listen to him?"

Dayson's position remained firm. "I'm not listening to anybody who does not have the proper identification and security codes. Turn that ship around now."

"Look, pal. When the Brelac invaded Nocturne we almost got ourselves killed trying to defend it. We got our asses kicked and had to retreat. We got in this ship and evacuated like everyone else. We had a bumpy ride trying to outrun the Brelac fighters that were trying to blast us out of space. We don't have enough room in this ship because there's four of us crammed in here. Our pilot has had a memory lapse and couldn't fly a kite, I've got a guy lying on top of my head, and my legs are getting numb. And to make matters worse this same guy has to go to the bathroom. Would it really hurt that much to give us a break?"

Diane smiled at Colin's bold confrontation. "Way to go, Sarge. You really gave it to her."

Colin shouted one final plea into the radio. "Can you at least check with one of your superiors? What harm can that do?"

There was a pause. "Stand by," Dayson replied.

After a tense minute, the radio crackled again. "You're in luck. The invasion of Nocturne has just been confirmed. I've been instructed to have you follow me back to base."

Dayson's boomerang vessel slid in front of the scout ship. Colin hoped Diane would not have any trouble following behind it. All she had to do was maintain a firm and steady grip on the control sticks and move them slowly. With any luck, the ship should give them a slow and steady flight.

The group waited in silence for the next ten minutes as they followed behind Dayson's ship. Then they saw their destination appear through the ship's window; the blue orb that they saw turned out to be a tubular structure of immense size. Both outer and inner surfaces of the structure were aglow with thousands of brilliant white lights. A fleet composed of twenty triangular battle cruisers surrounded it defensively while a swarm of small, oval-shaped shuttles, triangular, and boomerang-shaped crafts flew constantly back and forth from the larger ships to the structure they were protecting. On the inside of the tube, three battlecruisers were docked at the left and right.

"It's starbase Lodestar," Blair said. "A trip to Lodestar is where our adventure began. Now we've finally made it back."

As the ships drew closer to the enormous starbase its image filled the scout craft's window. A message from Dayson came through on the scout craft's radio.

"Panther Squadron Leader, Dayson to Silencers. We are approaching landing bay six. Cut your speed and stay behind me. They have an area cleared for us to land."

Colin saw the yawning opening of the landing bay directly ahead. All Diane had to do was follow Dayson's ship inside.

How hard could that be?

"Take it nice and easy," Colin advised. "Just stay behind the squadron leader's ship."

Dayson's ship glided smoothly into the landing bay with the scout ship dogging close behind. Both ships flew above a wide runway with dozens of other fighters parked on both sides, heading for a spot prearranged for both ships to come to rest.

Dayson's ship reduced its speed in order to hover and descend to a landing. The scout ship held its current speed and course. It crashed into the rear of the fighter. Both ships hurtled down and slammed onto the runway. Their momentum caused them to skid until they reached the small flight control booth sitting at the end of the runway. The booth's two flight controllers burst through the doorway and escaped just before both ships plowed into the frail metal booth and ripped it apart. Then they came to a halt.

Colin was covered in shards of clear plastic. The impact of the crash had shattered the front window. After being rammed against the instrument panel his legs hurt worse than ever. He looked up and saw black smoke rising from the rear of Dayson's ship. The smoke flowed in through the broken window. Colin was sickened by the strong burning plastic odor. He heard the deep toned buzz of a warning siren echo throughout the landing bay. He glared over at Diane, slumped over the control sticks. He brushed the sharp, pointed fragments out of his hair, and then was instantly consumed by rage when he saw her move.

"When I said stay close to the other ship I didn't mean this damn close!" he screamed.

"It was an accident!" Diane shouted back at him.

"No sense in arguing about it now," Colin said. The only thing that mattered now was that he and his friends were still alive. "Is everyone okay?"

"My ribs are a little sore, but I'll live," Blair responded.

"My damn head hurts," Kelly whimpered feebly. "I think I busted the window."

Diane unstrapped herself and stretched. "This ain't so bad. I expected this crate to shatter like an egg but it held up. Thank God I was able to bring this thing down in one piece."

Kelly snorted. "If I were a crash test dummy I'd have a better appreciation for your skills."

"Go to hell, Lytton!" Diane yelled "I'm the best damn pilot in the stinkin' Protectorate. I've got 230 kills to prove it!"

"With all those kills you must have flown more passengers than combat missions."

"Let's not waste time bickering among ourselves," Colin told them. "We're all alive. That's what counts."

Colin shot a glance out of the broken window and saw flames dancing from the rear of Dayson's ship.

"We'd better get out of here before that fire gives us a major problem."

Diane pressed the button to open the hatch. Blair crawled back, allowing Kelly to follow. After he crawled over Colin's head Colin now had room to rise and move out of the cockpit. Colin took another look at the fire and became greatly concerned about the damage that the crash had caused.

"They're not going to be happy about the mess that we made here."

Diane displayed little concern about the consequences. "I already told you it was an accident. The ship just went out of control. What are they gonna do? Slap a fine on me?"

Diane and Colin emerged from the ship to be greeted by dozens of troopers aiming guns in their direction. The frowns on their faces indicated that they were unhappy about the damage to their landing bay. Their retaliation would be more than a mere fine.

A hatch on top of the crashed fighter opened with a loud hydraulic hiss. A young black female pilot, Panther Squadron Leader Dayson, climbed out of her ship and jumped onto the runway. She drew her laser pistol from her belt and headed toward the scout ship's occupants. Shouting out in anger she shoved her way through the mob and raised her gun.

Dayson looked over the startled group. "Alright. I wanna know which one of you idiots is the pilot of this piece of crap?"

Kelly and Blair both pointed at Diane. Diane raised her hand.

"I am. Captain Diane Christy," she confessed with pride.

"Then you die first," Dayson hissed. She returned a cold gaze into Diane's eyes and aimed her pistol at Diane's head.

CHAPTER TWENTY

Night had fallen across the western hemisphere of Trillion. Fenlow sat in the Viperhawk's control room watching the holographic images that Succubus provided. He observed waves of Protectorate troopers in full retreat as the Viperhawk assaulted Dragos, the last Protectorate base on the planet. Fenlow was in good spirits because the Viperhawk was functioning as perfectly as planned. Dozens of fighter squadrons were sent out to engage the Viperhawk, but its power overwhelmed them easily. Its multiple gun turrets, powered by pure psionic energy generated by Succubus, destroyed the fighters in waves, their blazing remnants leaving short trails of fire as they plummeted to the ground.

Dozens of fiery explosions went off across the base while it was under heavy fire by Brelac fighters that strafed hover tanks, buildings, and groups of fleeing troopers. Flames shot out from windows and wide holes blown into the rounded metal roofs of troopers' barracks. Many of the two-story administrative buildings were being consumed by fires. Some groups of persistent troopers tried desperately to make a stand and fight, firing their small arms into the air at the attacking fighters. The multiple red flashes of their weapons in the dark produced a stunning pyrotechnic display, but they were swiftly cut down by the firepower of the descending Brelac and Fenlow's three prototype creations: the robotic Deltans. The three robots slowly marched across the base, their powerful plasma cannons destroying the troopers with single explosive blasts.

Fenlow considered any attack against the Viperhawk to be a feeble waste of effort. Succubus also generated an impenetrable shield of psionic force that easily deflected the enemy firepower. And though the shield's stability appeared to be a success Fenlow was hoping to test it against a greater threat than a swarm of paltry fighters.

Fenlow was disappointed to learn that the Reploids had somehow escaped from Nocturne. A quick scan by Succubus revealed no traces of Colin, Diane, or Kelly on the entire planet. He shrugged off his failure to locate the Reploids. He was already executing a contingency plan to acquire them. As for Nocturne, he ordered Succubus to obliterate the base completely. After which he would divert the Viperhawk to other bases in different sectors. With Succubus' telepathic scanning it was an easy task for the computer to locate every Protectorate base on the planet. It would be just as easy to destroy them.

This was the fifth base that the Viperhawk had attacked. After Nocturne fell, the entire planet would be under the complete control of the Brelac. Fenlow and the Deltans arrived at each base before his Brelac allies, who would arrive just in time to find a deep smoking crater burned into the ground. Only a handful of fleeing troopers would be left behind for them to mop up.

In the distance, at the nearby city of Septimus, the red glow of several large burning buildings lit up the dark horizon. The Deltans were easily cutting a path of destruction through the city to reach Dragos, leaving a trail of rubble, flaming structures, and burning bodies lying on the ground behind them. Fenlow watched the spectacle as the Deltans' three plasma beams burned through the air. Brilliant flashes of fire erupted when their targeted two-story buildings exploded. The combined blasts created a deafening roar. There was a chorus of male and female screams as scores of troopers scrambled to escape the threat of these robots. Four Protectorate jets engaged in wild aerial looping above the base as they were pursued and fired upon by Brelac fighters. Red plasma bolts streaked through the air and struck three of the Protectorate ships, causing them to explode in midair with a burst of fire.

Succubus projected the image of six fighters approaching for another attack. Their laser cannons blazed away but were unable to penetrate the Viperhawk's shields. Succubus dealt with them automatically. The Viperhawk's multiple turrets targeted and destroyed all six ships in a rapid succession.

From his vantage point, Fenlow had little sympathy for the victims of the carnage that he created.

"The great Protectorate military," he said with contempt. He thought that these people were so effective when dealing with a few motley battalions of the Vendetta resistance, of which he supported.

"Where is their power now when facing an enemy of superior power?"

"Succubus," he said with a stretch, "order the Deltans to return to the ship. And instruct all Brelac forces to evacuate the area. They'll know what's going to come next."

Several laser cannons and rectangular missile turrets rose from their protective underground housings around the perimeter of the base. Fenlow dismissed the possibility of these weapons posing any viable threat to the ship. He would allow them to pelt the Viperhawk's shields, granting them the dignity of fighting back.

"Succubus, fire at will."

The crystal assembly that was installed at the ship's nose glowed red with an arcane power. Succubus provided Fenlow with a perfect view as the assault took place. Fenlow watched as the ship discharged a flaming torrent of energy down on Dragos. In an instant, Dragos' airfield, buildings, hover tanks, and personnel were enveloped in an enormous explosion and an expanding mushroom cloud of flame that billowed into the sky. There were no recognizable structures remaining. No occupants survived. Dragos was totally obliterated. Another successful display of the Viperhawk's power.

The deep voice of Succubus interrupted Fenlow's playtime. "There is an incoming message from Major Clive Danton."

"Send it through," Fenlow sighed.

Danton's scowling face appeared below the image of the carnage outside, transmitting from his personal shuttle craft. "Is this becoming a habit with you?" he growled in displeasure. "I was hoping to find any useful data or prisoners down there. Now there's not even so much as a paved spot for me to land."

"You should be grateful that I've saved you the trouble," Fenlow replied with a smile. "There was really nothing down there of any value. And besides, with this last base gone we now control the entire planet. Perhaps after this little display of power the government will jump at the chance to call for an immediate cease fire."

Succubus beeped again. "There is a message coming in from the Brelac Supreme Commander, Bane Mariner."

Fenlow was in no mood to speak to Mariner now. But he thought that it would be wise to at least hear what his benefactor wanted. "Send it through," Fenlow ordered in a dry voice. "And then put me through to Walter Carnaby's office."

Next to Danton's image a new window appeared with Mariner's toothy, grinning face.

"Greetings Doctor," Mariner greeted. "I just had to call when I heard the news. Major Danton informed me that you've got this Viperhawk up and running. And that you're making a big impression on Trillion."

Fenlow gazed at the towering billows of fire that rose from the deep and expansive crater that was once Dragos. "Yes sir. A very big impression."

"Sounds good. I can't wait to personally see what this ship of yours can do."

"You won't be disappointed."

"I hope not," Mariner returned. "General Lagar and I will be arriving to join you in another hour."

Fenlow was not enthusiastic about having to entertain guests at such a crucial time. But then he concluded that Mariner's presence would prove to be highly useful to the next phase of his plans. He put on a cordial face. "Then we'll see you soon." Mariner's image blinked out.

Fenlow turned back to Danton. "If you have any concerns you'll have to save them until later, Major. I have too much to do right now. Succubus, end transmission."

Danton's image blinked out.

"Walter Carnaby has been contacted," Succubus' voice announced. "He is standing by."

"Send him through."

The close-up image of Carnaby, wearing his dark gray suit with a black shirt and tie, floated before Succubus. Carnaby smiled.

"Howard, am I ever glad to hear from you," he said. "I was trying to reach you earlier. So, I hear that you're making quite a stir out there with our new toy."

"Yes, sir. The Viperhawk is fully functional," Fenlow stated proudly. "A warship completely powered by a psionic computer and weapons system. I'm anticipating a stronger show of force from the enemy so that I can really test Succubus' level of power."

"Well, you're a better man than I am for standing in the crosshairs like you are," Carnaby said. "All for the sake of conducting an experiment. Personally, I'd find it to be too unsettling."

"I'm in no immediate danger," Fenlow replied. "And this test is vital to our plan to create a fleet of ships like the Viperhawk, to maintain order throughout the Protectorate and aid in our expansion."

Carnaby nodded. "And to help keep our friends, the Brelac, in line as well. I have to admit that I was doubtful about your plans when you came to me from the research section with your proposals. Psychic computers, psychic Reploids with super powers. It all sounded a little too fantastic."

"But it was an asset that we had to pursue. When I examined my first Brelac cadaver and experimented with their psionic implants I realized the potential in what they possessed. And like them, I saw the value in taking the development of these implants to a whole new level with the second generation Reploids and their powers, with the creation of Succubus and the Viperhawk. The only thing that helped me to achieve this breakthrough before the Brelac was my development of the special regeneration gene, FG-54. Without that, the implants would gradually destroy their hosts."

"So, in this psychic arms race we've got the jump on the Brelac. But then I suppose that it will only be a matter of time before they engineer the same gene themselves. It's like that old adage about the bomb. We have it first. How long do we have to wait until they have it?"

"The bomb?" Fenlow said, confused. "I don't follow you."

"Something that was before both our times. My intelligence team also tells me that you've created some type of psychotic robots and set them loose."

"My Deltan units. A side project of mine," Fenlow confessed. "They're a slightly scaled-down version of Succubus. So far I'm happy with their performance. I'm hoping that with their power we can use them as an effective ground force."

Carnaby paused for a moment. "So much destruction. It's regrettable. But this *is* war. Vendetta's war. Our war with the United Protectorate never ended."

Quietly, Fenlow nodded.

"How are you getting along with the Brelac?" Carnaby asked.

"I've been working with a major. Clive Danton is his name. I personally don't care for him too much. I confess that he gives me an eerie feeling. The feeling that I got when I first met their leader, Mariner. But Danton manages to stay out of my way and let me operate unhindered. And Mariner has been very accommodating. He's planning to arrive here in another hour. Too bad you can't be here to meet him."

"I have spoken to him twice in the past. The next time I speak with him it will be on my terms."

"I see. And do you trust Mariner?"

"I don't trust these Brelac." Carnaby shook his head. "They are far too alien."

"But far too similar. That's what I find so unsettling. They speak our language, and their names are similar. It's almost as if they're mimicking our way of life. Just what do we really know about the Brelac? Besides the fact they're all basically clones of each other? Where are they really from? Danton says that he was born, or made, in the Mediterranean Sector. I searched through both Protectorate and Brelac databases and couldn't find reference to such a star system."

"Perhaps that information is too heavily classified," Carnaby pointed out. "After all, even they have to maintain their security. But their past history doesn't matter. What's important is that your plan to keep them in line will be effective. And that the Viperhawk prototype will perform to our expectations. Are you quite sure that this thing will be able to stand up to what the Protectorate forces can throw at it? They'll defend Maseklos Prime with everything they've got."

Fenlow smiled. "I'm not worried. Through Succubus' greatly augmented psionic power the ship is protected by a shield that will maintain its integrity and regenerate its strength if necessary, as long as the brain within the computer is fully functioning. The ship's main weapon is pure psionic force, also generated by the brain. A force that's a thousand times more powerful than any large laser or plasma cannon. And the intensity can either be increased or decreased as it is needed."

"So then, the Viperhawk has the power to destroy an entire planet?"

"That level of power is far out of Succubus' range." Fenlow frowned. "Just like Succubus' telepathic power to send and receive messages is limited. The video portion of your transmission is being presented to me as a holographic image, boosted and manipulated by Succubus. I've also noted the fact that Succubus can read the thoughts of others but it can't project its own thoughts back."

"Its *thoughts*?"

"All computers think, to a degree. Succubus' thought processes function on a more complex level. On a near human level."

Carnaby laughed briefly. "This is where things get to be a little too outrageous for me. I'm not concerned with making a machine that thinks like it's human. I just need it to hold up against the United Protectorate and the Brelac. The Brelac think that we're just going to hand this technology to them and hope that they leave us alone while they march across the galaxy on their mission of retribution and domination, if that's what they want to call it."

"They're in for a surprise," Fenlow said. "I already have that covered."

"Good. Then everything is going according to our plan. I'm starting the next phase of our operation. Within the next few hours we're going to end two wars at the same time. This current war with the Brelac, and Vendetta's war against the United Protectorate. I'll see you soon at Navarone."

Carnaby's transmission ended. His image disappeared.

Fenlow's mind went back to Danton's words, *Mediterranean Sector*. He took a step closer to Succubus.

"Patch me back into the Protectorate and Brelac databases. It's time to do a little more research."

CHAPTER TWENTY-ONE

Colin sat on the lower bunk below Diane in the large, gray-walled cell. In his opinion there was nothing more humiliating than being arrested and jailed by your own military—twice. In spite of his anger, Colin was thankful that the troopers in the landing bay had restrained themselves from using physical violence. He did not think that his body could stand up to another beating.

He had been in the room long enough to lose track of time, but at least the base medics had treated Colin's injured arm. During his examination the medics were surprised to find that his cut was healing rapidly, and had focused on the fractured ulna he'd damaged during his fight with Keith Berry back in Lenora. The medics treated Colin's arm easily by setting the bone, giving him antibiotics for infection and an intravenous calcium stimulant to increase the regeneration of the damaged bone, and finally wrapping his arm in a dark, protein fiber mesh.

They put their jail time to good use. Blair worked with them to expand the use of their powers, and Colin and Kelly practiced using their abilities until they were becoming more versatile. Kelly discovered that he could consciously alter his psionic shield's color from blue when absorbing attacks, to red when reflecting energy. Although Kelly made it clear that he was not too eager to test the durability of either shield under enemy fire.

Colin's control over his electrical-based power also widened. He could exercise a form of mental control over most electrically conductive materials, which helped explain his ground-splitting trick back on Trillion.

But can I depend on this power when I need it?

The door suddenly slid open and everyone came to attention. A captain stepped inside.

"Look alive. You're all to come with me," he ordered with a grim face.

After being confined in the room for so long, Colin felt grateful for a chance to leave. The wide corridors of Lodestar bustled with activity, hundreds of troopers moving about with haste. Passing troopers stopped to raise their hands to salute the captain.

The captain brought them to a busy landing bay. Pilots and crews scrambled to reach their ships. Colin decided that it was time to get some answers from their mysterious escort.

"Do you mind if I ask what's going on here?"

Colin noticed the captain seemed to be nervous. The man stopped and quickly scanned the area. "I'm Captain Robert Burns, Special Operations. You're all to accompany me on a highly important mission."

"What kind of a mission?"

Burns took them to an unoccupied corner. The personnel in the landing bay saluted Burns and went on with their own activities. No one stopped to question the odd group sulking about.

"A first strike," Burns replied. "Right now we're assembling our forces to make a major offensive against the Brelac. Our goal is to silence Fenlow by any means. And with your powers you have the best chance of achieving success. You can do things that an ordinary team of troopers can't. We don't have much time. We have to reach our objective while the Brelac's security is still low."

At the mention of a ship, Diane rushed beside Burns and immediately took charge. "If we're getting a new ship then we need one that has lots of leg room," she demanded. "Especially leg room up front. Our last ship was too cramped. And softer seats. The pilot's seat in that little scout ship was too damn hard. And don't forget head room."

Colin almost laughed at the inane demands that Diane was making. "Do you want a ship or do you want to drive a sedan into battle?"

They approached a spacecraft that could possibly satisfy Diane. They marveled at its design. Its long golden hulled form was twice the size of the scout ship that they arrived in and unlike their scout ship, the vessel was fully armed for combat. The two small wings on the side of the ship housed twin laser cannons and a small stock of missiles. At the rear section were two broad wings, their tips mounted with bulb-shaped gun turrets with twin laser cannons. On the top of the ship sat a dome-shaped gun turret with two laser cannons. Beneath the ship was an open ramp waiting to admit its new occupants.

"We're taking Corvette," Burns said. "It's a new variation on our assault cruiser. What do you think of her?"

"I like it," Diane smiled. "We can do a lot of serious damage with a ship like this."

"Especially after we crash it," Kelly said, the memory of the previous crash clearly still fresh in his mind.

"Let's get moving," Burns said. "We've got a battle to win."

Colin and Diane led the way up the ramp and into the ship. Burns kept a close watch over the activities in the landing bay as Kelly and Blair boarded next. After traveling in the tiny scout ship Colin was thankful that Corvette was much larger. There was a small passenger's section with four seats. Kelly sat at the left. Blair sat behind him. Colin followed Diane inside the cockpit. There would be plenty of space to sit and move in here. Diane took her place in the pilot's seat, Colin next to her.

Burns entered the cockpit. He looked at Diane with an annoyed grimace. "What are you doing?"

"I'm flying us outta here," she replied, not bothering to look at Burns.

She carefully examined the large control panel in front of her. This assault cruiser had twice the buttons and gauges that the scout possessed, many of which were not labeled. Without the proper training their functions Colin could only guess at.

"This looks complicated," he said.

"A jigsaw puzzle with missing pieces is complicated," Diane jeered back. "This is a pain in the ass."

"Flying Corvette is a job for a skilled pilot," Burns said.

"That's me," Diane returned. "Captain Diane Christy. I've got 230 confirmed kills under my belt." Diane's eyes were still going over the many buttons and switches on the panel. "Which one of these starts the engines?"

"Diane is really a great pilot," Colin said in Diane's defense. "She's just been out of action for a while and needs to get reacquainted with the controls. Perhaps you can help her?"

It was certain that Diane was not going to move from that seat. And Burns seemed to be too agitated to fight with her. He kept looking out of the window as if he were expecting someone. He exhaled a long sigh.

"Okay, Ace. Let's make this brief," Burns calmly stated. "There's a button marked power generator at the right side of the control sticks. Press it."

Diane pressed the button. A powerful vibration surged through the entire ship as its cold fusion generator came to life. There was a loud beep. Then a small monitor above the control sticks was activated. Red letters spelling out 12:00 A.M. flashed repeatedly.

"I don't think that's the right time," Diane said.

"Don't worry about that," Burns grunted. "Now go to that little panel on the left side of the control sticks. That will activate the ship's engines. There are six buttons. The two top buttons are for your main engines. The two in the middle are for your primary thrusters. The ones on the bottom are for your secondary thrusters."

Diane pressed all six buttons.

"To reduce main engine power and kick in your thrusters for takeoff and landing press the first switch on the side of the left control stick." Burns reached over and pressed a series of buttons on the panel. Four numbers appeared on a small monitor above them. "I've entered the coordinates into the hyperspace controls. Just pull back on the left control stick to lift us off. Then kick in the main engines and we're on our way."

Diane pulled the control stick back slowly. Colin strapped himself into his seat as the ship rose into the air. Then Diane slowly pushed both sticks forward. The ship tilted from side to side as it flew down the runway and headed for the opening. To Colin's great relief, the ship entered space without any unfortunate incident. Burns reached for the control panel and pressed a button. The ship's speed increased. Then he pressed a button on the hyperspace controls, and Corvette was swallowed by the bright white flash.

CHAPTER TWENTY-TWO

General Larkin hurried to reach landing bay six. He'd arrived at Lodestar a few hours ago. He'd been in the central command center trying to organize a full-scale offensive against the Brelac's powerful new warship when a trooper informed him about the loss of an assault cruiser, Corvette, and who had taken it. It was a most unusual report. Once he reached the landing bay he headed straight for the flight control booth. C.I.D. Captain Melony Carter stood waiting for him. She snapped to attention and gave a salute when he approached.

"At ease," Larkin said, "and tell me what happened."

"Two hours ago assault cruiser Corvette launched without authorization. And without its assigned crew. Then it made a warp jump and escaped before our fighter patrols were able to intercept it."

"And now they could be anywhere," Larkin added. "And its occupants?"

"Several witnesses have reported seeing a group calling themselves Silencers Squad in the landing bay. Apparently they boarded the ship and took off."

"Obviously," Larkin said quietly. He hadn't been aware that Silencers Squad was on Lodestar until now.

He was eager to learn why they would want to steal a ship and escape. No one here posed a threat. "Any idea how they could have gotten out of confinement?"

"My team and I were keeping an eye on these three back at Nocturne as you ordered. When the base came under attack and the evacuation was ordered there was pure chaos. We temporarily lost track of them. When I found out that they were locked up in a cell here I thought that they'd stay put. Unfortunately that wasn't the case. I questioned the troopers who were guarding the cell where Silencers were being held. They both stated that a Captain Robert Burns gave them a written order from you, releasing the prisoners into his custody. It had the proper clearance code."

"This Captain Burns obviously forged my signature and somehow gained access to my official codes. But now the question remains: where did they go?"

"Perhaps they went back to the Brelac. Maybe they were here to gather information about Lodestar's strength and our current location."

Silencers, spies? Larkin thought.

"That's insane," Larkin scoffed. "And no sense in trying to trace this Captain Burns. Chances are the man is just a shadow."

Whether or not it was true, Larkin could not stop what was already set into motion. In another four hours the fleet of ships that he summoned from the other sectors would assemble here. Then they would hunt down the Brelac's new super warship and destroy it before it carried out the latest threat that Doctor Fenlow had recently transmitted. The capital city of Navarone on Maseklos Prime would be destroyed unless the United Protectorate surrendered immediately.

If there was a chance that the Brelac knew they were coming, then Larkin thought that it would be wise to throw them a curve.

"I'm informing the personnel in the command center that I'm moving our timetable ahead. Instead of waiting for our reinforcements to arrive we're going to launch the defense force guarding Lodestar. We launch within the hour."

CHAPTER TWENTY-THREE

"What exactly are we going to do when we reach our target?" Colin asked.

"We're going to infiltrate our target from within and make a surprise attack," Burns explained. "I'll show you how we're going to do it. Diane, let me have the controls so that I can take us in."

With Burns' skilled hands at the controls, the ship quickly moved toward its destination. Colin saw they were approaching a large, oval-shaped spacecraft with swept-forward wings. The nose of the ship was red with a crystalline appearance. To Colin somehow the ship appeared to be dangerously familiar.

"There's our target," Burns announced. He guided Corvette in smoothly, and then stopped it next to the target ship. He then pressed two buttons on the control panel. "Extending docking tube."

Corvette was mildly shaken by the impact of the two ships connecting with a mild boom.

"Here we are," Burns said. He rose from his seat. "We're infiltrating this enemy ship."

Colin was curious about the ease in which Corvette had traveled through enemy space. "Strange how we didn't run into any fighters. Maybe the Brelac are allowing us to get this close so that they can spring a trap."

"We slipped through a hole in their defenses," Burns explained. "But we only have a limited time to act."

Burns led the group behind the four seats of the passengers section to a short corridor. The circular airlock door was on the left side of the corridor. "Prepare yourselves," he warned.

Burns pressed a button on the wall panel to open the door. The airlock slid open to reveal three robotic creatures waiting on the other side. Tall silver-bodied creatures with large oval heads with a narrow red slit for an eye. They stood on thick legs with reversed joints, their right arms long, cylindrical weapons with four triangular fins aimed directly at Colin. Colin's heart jumped; these were the same robots that had nearly killed them back on Trillion.

Burns produced a laser pistol from his pocket and jammed it into the side of Colin's head. "Nobody moves or McKenzie dies!" he shouted.

"What the hell is this?" Colin demanded.

"You said it yourself," Burns smugly replied. "It's a trap."

CHAPTER TWENTY-FOUR

Danton noticed that Fenlow looked completely calm as he stood in front of the Viperhawk's airlock door. They awaited the arrival of two highly important visitors: Mariner and General Lagar. Their ship was due to arrive any minute and dock with the Viperhawk. For that reason Danton had an entire nest of butterflies swarming inside his stomach. A visit from the Brelac's two highest ranking superiors was always just cause to restrain an urge to fly into a blind panic.

There was a sudden thundering boom of a docking tube connecting with the airlock; Mariner's personal cruiser had arrived. Danton's heart fluttered. He wished that he had more time to prepare for this visit. There was the sound of compressed air being flushed through the docking tube. While the dark, wedge-shaped vessel docked, Mariner's escort, the Elite Guardian Squadron, flanked the ship in a protective formation—the firepower of four attack carriers and six destroyers that always traveled with Mariner and would battle furiously to protect him.

The airlock door slid open. Mariner's personal guard marched out of the airlock first: ten soldiers with their rifles in hand. Then Mariner and Lagar strode out of the airlock. The soldiers lined up along the corridor and snapped to attention as their superiors passed by. Danton greeted them with a quick salute.

Fenlow smiled, rushing over to Mariner and Lagar to shake their scaly hands. "Welcome to the Viperhawk. I promise that you will both have a unique experience here."

"Coming all this way I hope so," Mariner said. "Am I to understand that you've conquered Trillion single handed?"

"Precisely," Fenlow returned with a proud smile, "save for a few weakly armed stragglers, all major opposition on the planet has been removed. Quickly and effectively, thanks to the superiority of psionically powered weaponry."

"It's a shame that you didn't wait until Lagar and I arrived. I was eager to see what this psionically powered weaponry of yours can do."

"You'll get your chance," Fenlow assured him. "You and your squadron will accompany us to our next target. Maseklos Prime."

"Eleven ships attacking the heart of the Protectorate?" Lagar said. "Only a full-scale assault by a full armada would be able to break through their defenses."

"A feat that would take you months. Trust me. We have more than sufficient power to do the job. You will see the power of this new weapon's technology in action to end the war."

Mariner hesitated, clicking his pointed teeth. "We'll see. I'm putting a lot of faith in you, Fenlow. For the sake of our survival I hope that you are right. But in the meantime, we'd like a tour of this ship. Let's start with this super computer of yours."

"Succubus," Fenlow said. "Major Danton will take you to the control center to have a look. While that's happening I have a few personal matters to attend to. I'll get back to you as soon as I can."

Without another word Fenlow turned and walked away.

"Fenlow seems to be a little over enthused about his creation," Mariner commented to Danton.

"He has a good reason, sir," Danton said in Fenlow's defense. "This ship wields awesome firepower. Conquering Trillion single handedly is an impressive accomplishment. The ship is easy to control. Its main computer, Succubus, follows verbal commands. I've accessed it several times."

"Then I assume that you can take control and manage things without Fenlow."

Danton nodded. "Yes, sir."

"Good. Then we'll have no further reason to keep Fenlow alive. We already have everything we need from him. He's already given us his advanced gene, FG-54. Back at Rantraven we've set up an experimental program to create soldiers with a greater level of psychic powers. If it works then we'll begin full-scale production and crank out an army of super soldiers."

"I still would like to see this ship in action," Lagar added. "That will give me the chance to see if it's worth constructing more."

"You won't be disappointed, sir," Danton assured him.

A soldier from Mariner's cruiser came running through the airlock, gasping excitedly. "Sir, there's an urgent message for you. It's from the research section at Rantraven. There's been an accident."

221

Mariner and Lagar bolted through the airlock. Danton followed close behind them. If this accident was serious enough that the scientists at Rantraven had to contact Mariner personally then Danton feared the worst.

The cruiser's bridge was only a short distance down the dimly lit corridor, and the dark metal door quietly slid open upon their approach. They charged onto the small, circular bridge. There were three consoles in the middle of the room, standing four feet high. A Brelac crewman stood stationed at each console, tending to the rows of glowing yellow keys on long keypads.

Behind the three stations was a short pedestal of steps and a single ottoman with a thick, dark cushion. Being the commander of this vessel, only Mariner had the privilege of a seat on the bridge. At the front of the bridge was a wide, forward window that clearly displayed a portion of the Viperhawk's broad wing and its shiny outer hull. At the left and right sides of the bridge were Brelac crewman stationed at consoles positioned in front of two large windows. The right window displayed only the Viperhawk's hull, the left the blackness of open space.

Mariner headed for the communication's station at the right, the crewman quickly stepping back as he approached. "Mariner here. What's going on?"

"This is Captain Armatige," a frantic voice responded. "We were working on the new experimental cloning section when the computers suddenly erased all our data. Then there was an explosion. Seven technicians were killed."

"What was erased?" Mariner asked, growling.

"All the project data. The formula for Fenlow's gene, FG-54, his psionic implant designs. Even his designs for the Viperhawk and the Delta Nova prototypes that he created. The computers just summoned up all the data and erased it."

"All of it?" Danton gasped.

"Can anything be salvaged?" Mariner desperately asked. His tail whipped back and forth.

"Nothing is left, sir. I'm sorry."

"Do you have any idea how valuable that data was? What about the explosion?"

"It was a very powerful blast. Obviously from an explosive device of some sort. We have no idea who could have planted it. The entire lab is a total loss."

Mariner clenched his teeth and hissed loudly. Then he let out a deep growl and slammed his fist down onto the communications console. "I want you to find the son of a bitch who set off that blast! A human couldn't possibly have breached our security, so it has to be one of our own! Find him!"

Mariner turned to Lagar and Danton. "Well, gentlemen. It would seem that we'll still have a need for our good Doctor Fenlow after all."

CHAPTER TWENTY-FIVE

"I wonder what's going to happen to us next?" Blair said. "It certainly seems that whoever is behind this went through a lot of trouble to get us into their clutches."

Colin sat against the cold metallic wall of this small, gray room, the only features the white light shining down from the middle of the twelve-foot-high ceiling, and a red lens, roughly a foot in diameter, mounted in the middle of the rear wall near the ceiling.

Probably part of a surveillance camera, Colin thought.

He felt like a complete idiot for allowing him and his friends to walk into such an obvious trap. Colin brooded over the fact that their captors could have provided a containment cell with at least one small cot or a chair. Sitting on the cold, hard floor was very uncomfortable.

"You can bet that we ain't here to sign autographs," Diane stated. "Chances are that they want information. And the way I see it, they can only get it by putting us under a brain scan and sucking our minds out a little bit at a time."

Blair recoiled at Diane's morbid description of their possible fate, scooting farther away against the wall.

"Nobody's going to do any sucking," Colin declared firmly. "We'll find a way to get out of this mess."

"Do you think those robots are still outside?" Kelly asked fearfully.

"You can bet on it. And why not? They're the perfect guards. They beat us pretty easily back on Trillion. And we don't really know how many there are. For all we know, there could be a few dozen of them manning this ship."

The fuzzy image of a man in a white lab coat suddenly appeared in front of the door. His sudden appearance startled everyone. He addressed them in a booming voice.

"You have nothing to fear from my Deltans. That is, as long as you cooperate with me."

"Deltans?" Colin asked, "So that's what they're called. And who are you?"

"It's a pity that Doctor Trevor didn't program you to recognize me as your creator. I'm Doctor Howard Fenlow."

Creator? Colin thought.

Blair moved in closer. "Doctor Fenlow? Is that really you?"

"In a way." Fenlow smiled. "You're being addressed by a holographic projection transmitted by my computer, Succubus. Succubus is the main power behind this ship. I'd like to officially welcome you aboard the Viperhawk. I trust that you are all feeling well. I apologize for the deception but it was necessary to bring you here. I originally planned to have you Reploids destroyed back on Trillion. But when I learned that you narrowly escaped with your lives I decided to alter my plans for you. Instead of killing you I had you all brought here alive."

"You had us brought here?" Blair asked. "For what purpose? To defect like you and Captain Burns did?"

Fenlow laughed briefly. "I'm sorry, but the being that aided your escape from Lodestar was not a real Protectorate officer. Captain Burns is a Reploid agent. I had him infiltrate Nocturne during the attack. That way I could have a waiting agent within the military. Then you Reploids escaped from my Deltans. That gave me the chance to put Burns to use. I needed someone to gain your trust and bring you here peacefully."

"Now that you have us here, what do you want?" Colin snapped.

"I consider the Viperhawk to be the greatest creation of my career," Fenlow said proudly. "Its power will end this insane war and start a new era for our people. I'd like for you, Blair, one of my most trusted assistants, and my creations, the Reploids, to be a part of that era. I want you all to share my triumph and join me."

Colin saw no incentive in Fenlow's offer. "That also means joining the Brelac like you did. That's not a savory idea."

"Working with the Brelac was necessary," Fenlow said. "I needed their resources, and their presence is crucial to the success of my plan. I'm going to need them to help me expand the Protectorate. Much bigger and better than before. Everyone will benefit from this. Even the Brelac. Will you join me?"

Colin stared back at Blair, Diane, and Kelly. There was a pause of silence between them. He turned back to Fenlow. "We're not interested. When we enlisted in the military we took an oath to guard the Protectorate and its citizens. We don't take that oath lightly. Maybe you shouldn't either."

"So it appears that Colin McKenzie is speaking for the entire group," Fenlow said. "You seem to be adamant on your position. That's unfortunate. But I suppose that it's my fault. I should have instructed Doctor Trevor to program you all to be more loyal to your creator. Then having you join me would not be such a problem. But in spite of this I can remain benevolent. I'll give you one hour to reconsider my offer. Agree to work with me and you can all walk out of this room. If not, then the Deltans will insure that none of you leave here alive."

Fenlow's image flashed and then blinked out, leaving the group in silence. In Colin's mind there was no real choice. He could not voluntarily join Fenlow and the Brelac. He hoped that Diane and Kelly felt the same way. As for Blair, Colin now had several vital questions in his mind, and it was possible that only Fenlow or Blair could provide him with the answers.

"Creator? Programs?" He turned and stepped closer to Blair. "What was he talking about?"

Diane and Kelly both flanked the young man closely. Blair looked down at the floor and exhaled.

"Guys, I've got a lot of explaining to do."

CHAPTER TWENTY-SIX

Mariner was highly impressed as he studied Fenlow's computer, Succubus. He had never encountered such an advanced technology of this type before. He thought that it would be fascinating to have full access to Succubus and find out exactly what it could do. But, as he explained to Lagar, there would be plenty of time to explore the computer later. For now, he would just settle for replacing the valuable data that he needed.

Mariner noticed that Succubus was studying him in return. The image of a gaping eye followed his every move. It alarmed him at first. Then Danton waved his scaly hand through the image of the eye to demonstrate to him that it was merely a harmless holographic projection. Another reason to marvel at this machine of Fenlow's.

Fenlow entered the room.

"This is quite a piece of hardware you've got here, Doctor," Mariner said. "I can just imagine what it can do."

"I doubt that," Fenlow replied in a dull voice.

Mariner shrugged off that blatant insult to his intelligence. "But still, you have to admit that this is a remarkable piece of work. A fully functioning cybernetic computer system. Part machine, part living tissue. Managing every function of this ship. And able to generate enough power to take out a Protectorate military base in a single blow. When you first described this project to me I had my doubts. Now here it is."

Fenlow stood silent.

Mariner continued. "This goes beyond anything my scientists could come up with. I have to hand it to you, Fenlow. You're a true genius. Which brings me to the point. I've received a report about an unfortunate incident back at Rantraven. There was an explosion in the lab where we were setting up our experimental advanced cloning program. The whole damn thing is a total loss."

Fenlow seemed unruffled by the incident. "That's old news. And I should know. I caused it."

Mariner whirled around. "You?" he snarled, baring his teeth.

"I sent one of my Reploids to do the job."

"How?"

"Very easily. I've established a small network of human and Brelac Reploids, infiltrating both ranks. The Reploid that I sent to Rantraven easily blended in with your scientists, planted the bomb, and left to await further orders."

Mariner was speechless. His eyeless face spun toward Danton. "Danton, how is all this possible?"

"Don't waste your time asking him.," Fenlow stated. "I did everything right under his nose. Just like I purged all traces of my data from your computers."

"You're saying that you're responsible for that as well?"

"Don't be so dense," Fenlow said. "You're standing in the room with my greatest instrument. Succubus, the most advanced computer, and the most powerful psychic mind ever created. It was easy to penetrate your computer systems at Rantraven by simply hacking into your database and slipping through your security undetected. It deleted all traces of my data just as easily as it monitored your every move. As well as your intentions to eliminate me."

"Eliminate you?" Mariner's shoulders tensed, and he rocked back on his heels. "I don't know what you're talking about."

"Don't insult my intelligence!" Fenlow bit back. "Succubus informed me that you planned to have me eliminated just as soon as the Viperhawk was completed. It pays to be able to verbally communicate with your tools. Especially tools that can read minds."

"You got me, Doctor," Mariner confessed with a toothy smile. "Why deny it? In addition to the Viperhawk I wanted your genetic data for my own plans. And of course, I still want it."

Mariner drew his plasma pistol from his weapon's belt and aimed it at Fenlow. Lagar and Danton drew theirs.

Fenlow held his tranquil demeanor. "Ah, guns, threats. I was wondering when you'd get around to this."

"You're a little smug for someone who's about to die," Mariner hissed.

"Dying isn't a part of my plan. You don't realize who's in control here. Did you monsters really think that I was going to give you the power to wage war across the whole universe? You Brelac are far too dangerous to be allowed to remain as a dominant military force. Far too aggressive. Too mysterious. But what I find most disturbing about you is that you're all too familiar."

"What the hell are you talking about?" Mariner snapped.

"Danton. When I asked you where you came from you told me the Mediterranean Sector. When I first tried to locate this place in both Brelac and Protectorate databases I couldn't find any star system with that name. Now, curse me for being so stupid, but it dawned on me that I was searching in the wrong area. Your Mediterranean Sector isn't an area in space. It's an area on land. Protectorate historical data lists an area called the Mediterranean Sea on the planet known as Old Earth."

Mariner, Lagar, and Danton remained silent. Slowly tilting their heads to the left and right as they listened.

"Old Earth," Fenlow went on. "That name has a legendary aura. The last time I heard that name was when I was a teenager in school. The first home world of the human race. The historical database also listed something that you, yourself, mentioned to me the first time we met. You called it Pandora's Kiss."

"A past affliction," Mariner hissed. "A ghost story that doesn't interest me."

"But it interests me. Especially since you're referring to a viral outbreak that infected Old Earth centuries ago. This same outbreak killed millions and forced the uninfected members of the human race to abandon the planet and search for new homes out in space."

"First ghost stories, now history lessons!" Mariner shouted. "You're starting to bore me, Fenlow!"

"How did you Brelac come to Old Earth?" Fenlow asked sternly.

"I've heard enough!" Mariner spouted out, stepping back and raising his gun higher. "If you won't give me the data that I need then at least I'll still have this ship."

"You don't even have that." Fenlow shook his head. "Looks like you've come up empty through all this. Too bad. Now I'll have Succubus disarm and restrain you."

Mariner sneered. "The computer? What's it going to do? Whip us all to death with its extension cord?"

"Succubus, disarm the Brelac."

Mariner, Lagar, and Danton's plasma pistols were suddenly wrenched out of their hands by a strong and unseen force. Lagar and Danton's guns struck the side of Succubus and remained fixed there as though they were magnetized. The gun from Mariner's own hand flew toward Fenlow. Fenlow snatched it out of the air and pointed it at his three targets.

The doctor grinned smugly while Mariner stood in bewilderment.

"Telekinesis," Fenlow proudly stated. "It's simply another manifestation of Succubus' power. You have to admit that it comes in handy for situations like this. You were right when you said that you couldn't imagine all the things that Succubus could do.

"Succubus, execute hyperspace jump to Maseklos Prime. Order Mariner's fleet to do the same. Use his voice and image. It's time to put the final phase of my revised plan into action."

CHAPTER TWENTY-SEVEN

Walter Carnaby was thrilled as he entered the conference room, a sharp contrast to the grim looks on the faces of Rodger Bannister, John Steiner, and a few others seated at the table. On his way here he'd envisioned the memories of the countless meetings that he had in this dreary room. Now, his thoughts turned to the future holding of meetings within the hallowed walls of the presidential conference room. The United Protectorate was about to undergo a sweeping change, and the current government would be the first target; President Drennen and many others would soon be removed.

Carnaby noticed that the large video screen against the left wall was in the middle of receiving a transmission, projecting the glowering face of John Crane, Secretary of Defense. A high ranking member of this clandestine group who kept his association with them a tight secret.

"Gentlemen, why the sour faces?" Carnaby asked, taking his seat.

From the video screen Crane spoke out first. "Some of us are sharing the same concerns about your man,

Fenlow, and his role in our plan. His approach is just too bold. He could expose us all if he's not careful."

"And what if he does?" Carnaby asked. "When the plan succeeds, we'll reveal ourselves as the leaders of the new empire that we've envisioned."

"And what if the plan should fail?" Crane demanded. "Undoubtedly, Fenlow now has the entire military agitated after he made the second ultimatum. Threatening to attack Maseklos Prime will not be taken lightly. Defenses are being bolstered. I'm not sure if he'll have the power to prevail. What if the Viperhawk is damaged or destroyed, and Fenlow is captured?"

Carnaby scoffed, shaking his head. "Nonsense. The results at Trillion speak for themselves. Nothing can stand against this new psionic weapons technology."

"Perhaps," Steiner said. "But I'm still worried about bringing the Brelac into this plan."

"I've already told you that the Brelac are a vital pawn in our plan," Carnaby said. "They provided the means to create this weapon under the guise of an alliance. And in turn, we will have the means to control them. With the Brelac neutralized as a threat and the Protectorate under our power, we will be able to finally realize our goal of establishing the new independent territories. A new United Protectorate of independent states, banding together in the presence of any common threat."

"And in reality governed by a new central power. With you at its head," Bannister added with a smile. He laughed. "If the rank and file only knew that they were fighting to put a pretty new label on the same old can of worms."

Carnaby frowned and shook his head. "On the contrary. We're giving them a new government dedicated to expansion. The Protectorate hasn't grown in decades. We need to add new worlds into our sphere of influence."

"Before we conquer the universe let's concentrate on gaining control of our own back yard," Steiner said slowly, holding up a hand.

Carnaby rubbed his chin in his hand as he considered Steiner's advice. He gave a nod. "Perhaps it would be realistic to take this one step at a time. If there are no objections then we can begin the final phase of Operation Broad Axe. I've already ordered our fleet of shuttles carrying our assault troops to launch for Maseklos Prime. On my command they will land and garrison themselves in Navarone."

"And what if President Drennen happens to be more stubborn than you realize?" Crane asked. "What if she refuses to surrender?"

"Then Navarone becomes a crater," Carnaby said, bringing his fist down on the table top. A scowl appeared on his face. "Our assault troops will land in the nearby city of Manheim. There we will establish a new capital and declare a new government."

"I still don't know about all this," Crane returned. He sat back in his chair and crossed his arms. He tilted his head back and let out a loud sigh. "This plan had better work. I'll be putting my ass out in the open with the rest of you. I don't have to remind you of what will happen if this whole thing should fall through."

"Think positive," Carnaby advised. "I don't conceive any possibility of failure. Now if there are no further subjects to discuss I suggest that we board our shuttle. We'll accompany our assault troops when they arrive at Maseklos Prime. This is the day that Vendetta takes control."

CHAPTER TWENTY-EIGHT

"You guys are not who you think you are."

"Really?" Kelly asked, sarcastically. "Then who exactly are we?"

"The three of you are actually complex computer programs created by Doctor Trevor, and placed into cloned bodies that were rapidly grown through an in-vitro process. Your programs are patterned after the lives of real troopers."

"Real troopers?" Kelly asked in a skeptical tone. "So, who exactly are these people?"

"I have no idea. But that's not important. You three were the survivors of a shipment of Reploids that the Brelac were planning to use to infiltrate Helios. Your ship was shot down and we recovered you. We reprogrammed you to be Protectorate troopers. Your programs are quite complex, really, each having your own personal identities, the ability to think independently and make your own decisions. All the qualities you need to be the perfect fighting machines."

"I'm already the perfect fighting machine," Diane stubbornly boasted. "I'm an ace fighter pilot with 230 kills on my belt."

"Diane, you're not an ace pilot," Blair impatiently explained. "You only think you are. Doctor Trevor obviously failed to program you with the proper knowledge of flying. And you have to practice to gain the skill of an ace pilot. There were some instructional flight programs available. He could have converted them into his program for you. I'll never understand why he didn't."

"Are you trying to tell us that we're not...real?" Colin asked, his throat tightened.

"No. I'm not saying that." Blair shook his head. "At least, not altogether."

"Not altogether? Sounds like you're giving me two separate answers in the same sentence," Colin said. He was growing more impatient with Blair's logic. He reached into his back pocket and brought out the printed pages with his parents photographs. "I've got a family. Parents. Are you going to tell me that my parents aren't real?"

Kelly glanced at the pages in Colin's hand. "You have parents?" he exclaimed in amazement.

"Yeah, I have parents," Colin growled back. "Where the hell are yours?"

Diane spoke up for Kelly. "Both dead. Like mine."

"Let's just calm down and let me explain," Blair demanded. He paused for a moment as if to gather his thoughts. "As I said before, you guys are Reploids. I'm sure that you know how Reploids come into being. The Brelac capture human subjects, clone them, and then program them to commit acts of sabotage and terrorism against the Protectorate. When the Brelac are done with the original human subjects they dispose of them. Knowing the Brelac the way we do, that usually doesn't involve locking them up and feeding them for the duration of the war. Colin, this means that there was a real Colin McKenzie. And those people really are his parents. But you're *not* that Colin McKenzie. You're just a convinced copy. That goes for the rest of you too,"

Colin looked down at the pages with his parents pictures. His fingers squeezed the pages in his hand, crumbling their images. "I've got other relatives," he said. "People that are alive. I've had contact with them."

"I wish you hadn't done that," Blair replied, his brow furrowed. "That's really going to complicate things."

"This is crazy," Kelly shouted in disbelief. He stood and put his fists to his temple. "I'm not a clone of anybody. Just because I don't have any family doesn't mean that I don't know who I am."

"And how well do you know that?" Blair asked. "Your eighteenth birthday. What did you do that day? Did you blow out all the candles on your cake? What kind of presents did you get? What about other birthdays? Christmas? Your mother's birthday?"

Kelly pressed his hands harder on the sides of his head, his eyes squeezed shut. "Let me think."

"What about school? Who was your best friend back in high school? Who was your first date?"

"I don't know."

"When was the last time you were with your parents?" Blair asked. "You say that they're both dead? Which one of them died first?"

"Look, I don't know!" Kelly shouted back to him, quickly pointing his finger. He was growing more frustrated. "I don't know yet. Give me a minute to think."

Diane stepped toward Blair. "Leave the kid alone," she said softly. She turned to Colin. "Tell me what you think about all this."

"It all makes sense," Colin muttered in a cheerless voice.

"Don't tell me you believe all this?" Kelly yelled.

"It has to be the truth," Colin replied. "It explains a lot of things. How we came from those cylinders back at Scorpis. These powers of ours, and the nightmares…" He shrugged. "Blair's explanation fills a lot of gaps in our lives."

Diane scoffed. "The only gap in your life is the one between your ears. I'm Captain Diane Christy. I'm a fighter pilot. I have 230 kills on my belt."

"No, you're only an ace pilot in your own mind," Blair corrected her. "But your skills are improving. You handled Corvette really well."

"Yeah. And look where we ended up," Kelly chided. He turned to Colin. "If this is all true, then what do we do about it?"

"What can we do?" Colin quickly snapped. "I'm still me. Sergeant Colin McKenzie. That's the only identity I know. I admit, I'm really shocked about this. But that doesn't change the fact that I'm alive. And I'd like to keep on living. You don't expect me to commit suicide over it, do you?"

"Suicide?" Diane walked to the wall and sat down on the floor. She hugged her arms around her lap and covered her face with her knees.

"So, we're fake." Kelly gave Blair an almost tearful look. "That's the truth? You're the only real person in this room?" He began to pace back and forth.

"No," Blair moaned. "You've got to listen to me. You guys *are* real. As real as I am. You're just different. You're *made* differently than me."

Kelly pointed his finger. "*Made*. Bad choice of words," he bitterly corrected, his voice cracking.

"Sorry. Born. Whatever," Blair replied, flustered. "The point is that you guys still function perfectly as humans. Your emotional reactions right now prove that."

Diane raised her head. Her cheeks were red and wet. "You want to talk to me about emotional reactions?" she cried loudly at Blair. "All this tells me is that I don't have any damn emotions. I'm just reacting according to somebody's stupid plan. This is all a big sick experiment. None of what I feel and think is really me. Some evil bastard someplace types in a computer for me to like the color blue or like chocolate ice cream and those are the rules of the game that I have to live by, including how I feel about somebody. If I were to love somebody it won't really be me. It'll just be some program that somebody wants me to follow.

"Can't you see how cheap that is? How fake that is? And then here I am running around thinking that I'm this great fighter pilot. When all along you people filled my head with lies. You think that was funny? Were you a part of this?"

Blair raised his hands defensively. "No, no. I had nothing to do with your programs."

"No! You just helped to keep it all a big secret!"

"I was under orders," Blair argued. "You guys were part of a military project. I had no choice. Plus you weren't ready to know the truth."

Colin stepped closer. "And when was a good time to tell us all this? A time like now? When we're about to die? And when were you going to tell us that we were under surveillance by the C.I.D.?"

Kelly stopped pacing. "The C.I.D. was watching us?" he shrieked, raising his hands to the air. "This isn't getting any better."

Blair sighed and stayed silent.

"Look, we'll deal with this problem later." Colin replied. "Right now we have a bigger issue to deal with. If we want to survive then we have to concentrate on getting out of here and stopping Fenlow."

He turned away and examined the gray-colored walls. He knelt down and ran his hands across the cool, smooth surface of the metal floor. *Perfect*, thought Colin.

Now to see if this power can really work for me.

"I don't know about any of this," Kelly whined.

"You'd rather stay here and die?" Colin snapped back.

He looked over his shoulder to Diane. She remained sitting on the floor with her chin resting against her knees. Her reddened eyes stared forward blankly. "Diane?" he called out to her.

Diane did not respond, she just slowly rocked back and forth.

Colin sighed. *Who the hell can I depend on?*

This was a time when it seemed that his survival was in jeopardy more than ever. And he could not have felt more alone. But whether Diane and Kelly snapped out of their state of distress or not, he was determined to take this fight directly to Fenlow. He kneeled down to the floor and extended his hand.

"Get ready."

Colin's hand touched the floor. Blue flashes of energy and sparks flowed from his fingers and along the surface of the floor. He concentrated on creating a small hole. Suddenly the entire floor began to splinter. Then it collapsed. Colin and his friends noisily and painfully crashed down into an empty room below.

Small hole, small hole, Colin scolded himself.

Everyone was briefly stunned by the fall. No one moved. Colin finally twisted his head and looked around. He looked up and saw the door above slide open. The Deltans were coming to investigate the disturbance.

"Move!" Colin shouted. He jumped to his feet.

Colin started to run down the left corridor. He was relieved to see Kelly and Blair running alongside him. But Diane was not among them. He stopped to look back and saw Diane also running down the corridor, in the opposite direction.

"Diane!" Colin cried out to her.

Diane stopped running and looked back at him with her reddened eyes and a frown on her face. She turned away and ran down the corridor.

"Where the hell's she going?" Kelly asked.

"We can't worry about her now!" Colin yelled.

Fenlow was waiting.

He ran down the corridor, accompanied by Kelly and Blair. This was possibly the last time that he would ever see her again, and his thoughts were on her as he rushed into what might be the last fight of his life.

CHAPTER TWENTY-NINE

"The Silencers Squad has escaped from confinement."

"How?" Fenlow spun around. "Succubus, report."

"The Reploid, Colin McKenzie, used his power to somehow disrupt the structural integrity of the floor to their confinement area. They are now in corridor B of level two. The Deltans are in pursuit."

"It would seem that the Silencers are starting to become an annoyance." Fenlow sighed. "Maybe I should have killed them back on Trillion."

"What's going on?" Mariner inquired.

"Nothing. An obsolete experiment," Fenlow explained cheerlessly. "Ungrateful lab rats. But they'll pose no threat to my plans. I'm sure that your guards will keep them at bay long enough for my Deltans to reach them. Then their presence will be eradicated."

"Arriving at the Maseklos star system," Succubus informed Fenlow.

"Continue on course for Maseklos Prime," Fenlow ordered. "Scan the system for any defensive forces."

Within seconds Succubus revealed its findings.

"A large fleet of 390 Protectorate warships have formed a blockade at coordinates four, one, one, two, eight."

"You expect to hold off that many ships?" Mariner asked in amazement. "Even with my Guardian Squadron to back you up you don't stand a chance."

"First off, I don't expect to hold off that many ships. I expect to destroy them," Fenlow calmly stated. "Second, I don't need your squadron to help me deal with anyone. Instead, I think that it's time I deal with you Brelac before I deal with the Protectorate. Succubus, activate jamming sequence for Type One psionic implant."

"Initiating sequence," Succubus said in compliance.

The three Brelac cried out in pain, grasping their heads and bending down to the floor. Their tails thrashed wildly about. Then their heads swiveled about as if scanning the area for something that was no longer present. Mariner lifted his head and stood to his feet. He jerked his head from side to side. Lagar and Danton slowly rose and turned about as though they were lost.

"What the hell's going on?" Mariner squawked. "I can't see!" His hands clawed the air for something to touch.

Fenlow crossed his arms and grinned. "Succubus is jamming the interaction between your psionic implants and your nervous systems. In effect, rendering you what you were born to be. Blind."

Mariner snarled furiously. He turned left then right, sniffing the air loudly. He stopped, facing Fenlow. He sniffed the air again. Then he lunged forward, swiping the air toward Fellow with no hope of actually striking him. Mariner stumbled forward, barely able to break his fall with his hands. Lagar and Danton both stumbled back, desperately swiping at the air. Mariner stayed down on the floor, holding himself up by his hands. Streams of saliva spilled out from both sides of Mariner's mouth and onto the floor.

Fenlow watched as Mariner remained still before him. *Like a four-legged beast sizing up its prey,* he thought

"When you first gave me a few of your psionic implants to study I discovered a means of jamming them by projecting a stronger psionic signal along the same resonance," Fenlow explained. "At the time of the discovery, its use as an effective weapon against you had a great potential. Naturally Carp and Vendetta withheld that knowledge from the military. After all, they had their own agenda. And the jamming could only be performed on a limited basis. Only a living brain could produce the needed psionic power. On a small scale at that. We needed a larger source of power with a greater means of projecting it. That's where I envisioned the concept for Succubus. A larger, living generator of psionic power, enhanced by larger versions of your implants. Able to deliver a signal powerful enough to blind all Brelac within a vast range. Succubus, show me what's happening outside."

Succubus immediately displayed the chaotic image of Mariner's squadron in a state of disarray. The destroyers and attack carriers had stopped their engines. Several of the huge vessels had drifted into each other, causing major damage to their hulls. The sounds of panicked voices could be heard as the Brelac crews were desperately trying to maintain proper order aboard their ships while trying to comprehend the sudden loss of their psychic sight.

"Hear that, Mariner? Your ships are completely helpless. This takes your squadron out of the fight. Not that they were needed."

Mariner roared loudly and leaped forward, his mouth gaping wide open, exposing his red pointed tongue and rows of long knife-like teeth. Fenlow jumped back.

At that second, a smoky glass-like wall of energy appeared between them. Mariner hit the wall and bounced back. He rolled across the floor, knocking down Lagar and Danton. Their tails thrashed and a chorus of savage roars erupted as the three Brelac scurried to set themselves right, but they remained down on all fours. They spun their heads about rapidly, their claws scraping the floor and sniffing the air. They stopped and faced Fenlow. They remained still and hissed, long and slow.

Succubus addressed Fenlow. "I've erected a barrier between you and the Brelac subjects. I will maintain it for your protection until further orders."

Fenlow did not hear Succubus. His attention was fixed on the surprising transformation taking place with his three Brelac guests. He watched their hands, resting on the floor. Their claws grew to three inches long, by his guess. The bony spikes along their sides grew longer, nearly a foot long. Two rows of foot-long spikes sprang up along their backs. A row of spikes grew along the top and sides of their tails.

A defense mechanism brought about by the stress of losing their sight, he thought *Along with their increased state of aggression.*

Whatever the case, he shuddered at the thought of being in this room with these three without the benefit of Succubus' shield.

Mariner suddenly jumped at Fenlow, a wide spray of saliva shot forth as his mouth gaped open. Lagar and Danton also jumped up. Mariner was the first to bounce off the shield and fall back, the other two joining him a second later. The three Brelac quickly jumped back to their feet, their heads moving about as they smelled the air to again locate Fenlow's scent. Again they faced him and paused. Mariner growled viciously while Lagar and Danton both hissed. Fenlow crossed his arms, but took a step back.

"Just behave yourselves and I may find it within my heart to return your sight." Though he wondered if they could still understand him through their rage.

"A large fleet of Protectorate warships have emerged from hyperspace at coordinates eight, six, one, two, eight," Succubus droned. "Two hundred vessels. They are rapidly approaching our position."

"Reinforcements," Fenlow muttered with a sigh. "Succubus, destroy them. Then continue on course for Maseklos Prime."

CHAPTER THIRTY

Colin was anxious to get as far away from the Deltans as possible. He led the group through the corridor until they came to a four-way intersection. He glanced both ways, eyes skimming the empty halls.

But in a ship this big, where's the crew? So far we haven't run into anybody else yet. Fenlow and those three robots can't be the only ones here.

"For all we know we could be walking into another trap," he murmured. "We'd better find a way to get off this ship. Maybe we can find a shuttle or some escape pods someplace."

"I would agree with that idea under normal circumstances," Blair panted. "But we can't leave. Not until we find Fenlow. We have to try and stop him, or he could destroy the Protectorate."

"Any idea how we can make this happen?" Kelly asked. "We're stranded on an enemy ship, and those robots that kicked our asses back on Trillion are right behind us."

"Then we work fast." Colin shrugged. "Though you're right, our best chance to get off this ship alive is to deal with Fenlow first."

But where do we find him?

A man emerged from the right corridor, a laser pistol in his right hand.

Captain Burns.

"Silencers!" Burns cried out. "Thank God you've escaped. I need your help. That Fenlow is a madman!"

"Save it!" Colin snapped. "Don't insult our intelligence. We know what you really are!"

"I see that you won't be on the recall list for brains, McKenzie," Burns replied. "It's a shame that you have to be eliminated."

"We're not going to waste any time with you, Burns," Colin said, pointing a finger. "Drop the gun. You're outclassed."

Burns laughed. "Outclassed? By who? You and Lytton? You're both clueless amateurs. And Van Doren? He's only human."

"I'm losing my patience. Drop the gun and back off." Colin's left hand clenched into a tight fist. He bent his knees slightly and shifted his weight to his heels. "Final warning."

Burns pointed his gun toward the ceiling. He raised his left hand. "You want the gun? Okay, take it. I don't need it." He dropped the pistol onto the floor and kicked it toward Colin. "Where's your girlfriend, Christy? The Ace? Is she out flying a bombing mission, or did one of my friends get to her?"

"Your friends?" Colin asked, confused.

Burns turned and ran down the corridor. A second later the intersection was filled with the sounds of animalistic grunts and snarls as ten Brelac soldiers came charging down from the left corridor, running on all fours like a pack of wild dogs. They moved about clumsily, bumping into each other and the walls. Colin noticed the Brelac appeared to be covered by long, sharp spikes from back to tail.

Those things look sharp enough to rip a victim to shreds on contact, Colin thought. *Not to mention those oversized claws.*

"It's a trap!" Colin shouted to Kelly and Blair. He raised his hands and fired an electrical bolt that knocked two of the Brelac into the air and back down the corridor.

Kelly quickly sent crimson beams of energy from his hands that burned through the bodies of three Brelac. The remaining five Brelac were thrown into complete chaos as they scampered about in disarray. One Brelac turned to face Colin, teeth bared and nostrils flaring. Colin's hand fired a bolt that lifted the creature off its feet and sent it bouncing against the left wall.

A sudden unseen force suddenly ripped through the corridor and threw Colin, Kelly, Blair, and the four remaining Brelac off their feet to hurl down the hall. Colin's body went spinning. He hit the wall and then fell to the floor. Blair and Kelly landed behind him. The four Brelac landed in a twisted pile near his feet. The back of Colin's head ached, and felt as if a heavy rock had been thrown against his chest. It hurt to breathe.

"Shit," Colin groaned. "What the hell was that?"

He looked up to see Burns slowly walking down the corridor, an evil smile on his face. Burns raised his hands, fingers outstretched. A large sphere of the air in front of him blurred.

The four Brelac were the first ones to rise. They leaped to their feet, turning their heads wildly about as if they were lost again.

"You idiots aren't the only ones with special abilities," Burns said.

As if to prove his point, Burns aimed his right hand at one Brelac. Instantly, a blurred stream of energy shot out from the sphere and struck the Brelac on the top of its head. The Brelac's head exploded with a loud, wet pop. Colin's body was showered by a spray of blood, scales, and chunks of brain matter. A wide pattern of blood splattered across both walls. Before the Brelac's body fell to the floor, Burns quickly turned his hand to a second Brelac and fired a stream of energy into its chest. The Brelac's chest expanded to twice its size, until the flesh ripped and blood burst out from bubbling skin, leaving a gaping hole.

Colin struggled to his feet. Behind him, he heard Kelly and Blair follow suit. A Brelac, startled by Colin's sudden movements, spun about and swiped its claws into the air, catching hold of Colin's ankle. It let out a hoarse wail as its mouth gaped open wide to deliver Colin a lethal bite. Colin heard an explosive force behind him. He turned to see Diane bursting through the right wall behind him. Upon seeing the Brelac she let out a piercing battle cry and sprinted forward. She reached for the Brelac that had grabbed Colin, seizing it by its neck. She lifted it up and slammed it back onto the left wall with a force that produced a moist crunch of breaking bones and a thick splatter of blood. The last Brelac wheeled toward Diane, baring its teeth and hissing loudly. Diane released the dead Brelac. Its body slid to the floor. She bolted forward and quickly thrust her fist into the last Brelac's head with a muffled crunch, killing it instantly. Diane's hand had a coating of blood and small white blobs as she yanked it out of the Brelac's head, letting the body drop.

"Ace," Burns called out. He was still smiling. "Glad you could make it. Now I can kill you all together. My plan with these Brelac didn't work out, so I'll have to get the job done myself." Burns stretched his arms straight out and moved his hands closer together. "Die!"

Kelly jumped to his feet and held his hands out to form a blue wall of energy in front of the group. The blurry sphere of energy in front of Burns' hands exploded into a stream of force that shot down the corridor and collided with Kelly's shield. The corridor was filled with the sound of an explosion combined with the whipping of a gale force wind. Kelly cried out as he was pushed back a few inches, his shoes squeaking against the floor. When the attack finally subsided the sides and top portion of his shield had eroded away, leaving jagged blue edges.

"Psychically generated concussive force!" Burns shouted. The blurred sphere reformed in front of his hands, larger this time, and a bit more solid. "I told you I didn't need any gun, McKenzie. You keep it. Every soldier should have a sidearm with their dress uniform at their burial."

Diane looked to the floor and dove down. She picked up the laser pistol and swiftly took aim and fired a bolt into his head. Burns hands flew apart from each other, and the energy sphere faded. Diane kept firing, sending two laser shots into Burns' neck and four shots into his chest. Burns fell back to the floor, his body riddled with smoking holes.

Colin looked at Diane. He had to force himself not to smile after seeing her here. "I thought that you were done with us."

Diane casually shrugged her shoulders. "Where the hell else was I gonna go?"

"Are you okay now?"

She paused and stared back at him. "I'll be okay."

Colin opened his mouth to respond, then hesitated as movement behind Diane's shoulder caught his eye. The three Deltans stormed down the corridor toward them. He yelled and prodded the group down the right corridor, not sure of exactly where it would take them.

The odds here are definitely working against us, Colin thought. *Who knows what else is going to be thrown at us. Instead of finding Fenlow I'd be happy to find a ship docked at an airlock.*

There were doors on both sides of the corridor. Colin led the way to each door to see what was behind them, only finding each to be large empty rooms.

What the hell kind of a ship is this?

The group approached a door at the end of the corridor. The airlock hissed and slid open by itself. Colin became suspicious, knowing it could be a trap. But he knew he would rather face what was in the room up ahead instead of the three deadly robots behind them. He looked back down the corridor. The heavy, repeated thumps of the Deltans' metallic footsteps were getting louder. He bit his bottom lip and looked back at the open doorway.

"What do we do?" Blair asked.

Colin glanced back toward the Deltans, then to the doorway. "This way."

Colin led the group through the doorway. They found themselves in a large circular room paneled with gray walls and facing a large black, circular area on the floor. In the middle of this area stood a white, column-shaped device standing nearly six feet tall. There was a multicolored keypad on its side and a glowing red light above it. Above the machine floated the image of a large eye that stared back at them.

Fenlow stood in front of a metal table to the right of the machine, a pistol in his hand. He grinned triumphantly. At the left side of the room were three Brelac. They appeared to be in the same feral state as the group that were in the corridor, crouching down on all fours, snarling and hissing like mindless animals as they tilted their heads from side to side. They were confined to this side of the room by a wall of dark, smoky energy.

That energy looks damn familiar, Colin told himself.

"It's about time you people showed up." Fenlow approached the group. "I hope you wiped your feet before you came in here."

CHAPTER THIRTY-ONE

"Doctor Fenlow," Colin said.

"In the flesh this time," Fenlow declared, still wearing a proud grin on his face.

The three Deltans appeared in the doorway. They were about to enter the room when Fenlow ordered them to stop. They stood at attention outside the room as the door closed and locked.

"Don't worry about them, they won't hurt anyone," Fenlow assured the group. "Not unless I give the word. Welcome, Silencers, to the nerve center of the most powerful weapon ever conceived. Also, you have the honor of meeting my associates and benefactors. Major Clive Danton, General Owen Lagar, and the Brelac's supreme commander, Governor General Bane Mariner."

Colin looked upon Fenlow's Brelac guests with disdain. "With all the threats that you've made against the Protectorate, I'm not surprised to see your Brelac masters here."

"You're clearly mistaken by the appearance here. I'm the only master in this room," Fenlow corrected. "Mariner and his two flunkies are also quite harmless, as long as they stay behind that barrier. But, as a military threat, his forces outside are currently thrown into a state of disarray thanks to the power that I hold over them."

"What the hell did you do?"

"This ship's main computer here, Succubus, is transmitting a signal that's jamming their psionic implants. In effect, rendering them completely blind. Did you know that with the power of their implants it's impossible to sneak up on a Brelac? They have a full 360 degree scope of psychic vision. And now look at them. With their implants disabled they've reverted to savage monsters. I theorize that the implants not only grant the Brelac sight, but also help them to maintain a level of sanity."

"An interesting science lesson," Colin said. "But we didn't come here to get a lecture. We came here to stop you."

He took a step toward Fenlow and raised his hands, but a powerful and unseen force threw Colin and the others backwards against the wall. The impact sent a wave of pain through Colin's body. His back was pinned tightly to the wall and he glanced to his right; Kelly and Blair seemed equally helpless. Diane appeared to be unconscious.

"You assumed that I was just standing here helpless without the Deltans?" Fenlow bellowed in a tone of triumph. "Succubus possesses not only telepathic abilities but telekinetic power that could crush you all quite easily. But I've decided to allow you to live so that you can witness the historic victory that you ungrateful lab rats were stupid enough to pass up."

Succubus beeped. "There is a second fleet of ships emerging from hyperspace at coordinates three, four, seven, three, two. Seventy destroyer class vessels."

"Vendetta's fleet sent by Carnaby," Fenlow declared. "Just as I expected."

"Vendetta?" Blair inquired. "Carnaby?"

"Both one in the same." Fenlow grinned. "Are you so naive as to think that Vendetta had completely melted into oblivion? If it weren't for Carnaby, Carp Technologies, and a few others bankrolling them and pulling their strings, the entire organization wouldn't be able to organize a bake sale, let alone start a civil war."

"There is an incoming message from Walter Carnaby," Succubus announced.

"As I expected," Fenlow said. "Send him through."

The smiling holographic image of Walter Carnaby appeared above Succubus' eye.

"Hello Walter," Fenlow greeted cheerfully. "You're right on time."

"We're reshaping history. I'd be a fool to be late for such an event like this. I assume that you have our Brelac allies under control?"

Fenlow nodded. "Of course. The psionic jamming signal transmitted by Succubus is working perfectly. Mariner's forces have been immobilized. All that remains is to head for our prime target. But first, I'm preparing to warm up with a little target practice. Succubus, give me an outside visual."

Carnaby's face was replaced by the image of the blockade of ships waiting out in space. The Protectorate's huge triangular battle cruisers and destroyers were joined by the carriers—enormous rectangular ships with large cylindrical engines mounted at the left and right ends of the ships, broad triangular wings attached to the sides of both engines. From a wide, square opening at the front of the carriers, countless swarms of fighter craft launched and streaked toward the Viperhawk with their laser cannons blazing.

"Fire at will," Fenlow commanded, his hands folded behind his back.

The Viperhawk unleashed a red blast of energy from the main weapon at its nose that incinerated ten of the large ships. Their confederates quickly maneuvered to surround the Viperhawk while firing their powerful weapons. With each weapon strike a thick section of the Viperhawk's unseen protective shield appeared, making it impervious to the combined firepower that would have quickly destroyed any other vessel.

The Viperhawk slowly turned around and fired again. This time, its wide fiery beam consecutively destroyed another seven ships, each exploding in a bright white flash and an expanding cloud of fire that quickly dissipated in the vacuum of space. Large glowing chunks of debris bloomed out from the explosions. Mangled sections of the destroyed hulls that floating about aimlessly.

The wide stream of devastating energy the Viperhawk fired steadily diminished the Protectorate's numbers. Among the sounds of thundering explosions the terrified screams of the dying echoed throughout the room. Panicked voices shouted desperate orders to evade the Viperhawk. The numerous fighters continued flying circles around the Viperhawk, firing their lasers against its shield but causing no damage. The Viperhawk's multiple laser turrets fired and struck each fighter accurately, turning the small ships into exploding fireballs.

The Viperhawk pivoted around to follow a large group of destroyers attempting to maneuver behind it.

Huge chunks of twisted debris from destroyed ships floated in its line of fire. They were no hindrance as the Viperhawk fired. The debris and Protectorate ships all exploded in the lethal stream of fire.

Pressed against the wall, helpless, Colin felt sickened by the collective sounds of the ships crews dying out in space. *We have to stop this*, he thought. *But how can we? We're going to be next.*

Fenlow smiled obviously pleased with the results of this lopsided battle. "I almost feel sorry for the poor fools. Desperately trying to penetrate the Viperhawk's shields while waiting to be swatted out of space. It's a shame that you can't see it, Mariner."

Mariner responded by baring his teeth and giving a loud hiss.

"You're still under the effects of Succubus' jamming," Fenlow said. "I need you to be a little more coherent, so I guess I'll have to fix things. Succubus, terminate jamming sequence."

The three Brelac froze. They rapidly shook their heads left to right. Then they moved their heads about slowly, as if scanning the room. Mariner hissed again, then emitted a long and low growl.

"Fenlow."

"I've decided to restore your sight," Fenlow explained. "It's been restored to your forces outside as well. I'll allow you to keep it as long as you cooperate and stay on my good side."

Mariner was silent. He slowly stood up, taking an unsteady step backward, the muscles in his leg tensing. Lagar and Danton also stood. Mariner cleared his throat. "You won't get any trouble from me or my forces."

"Good," Fenlow said sharply. "Glad to hear that we're friends again. Succubus, drop your barrier."

The smoky wall faded.

Colin's confusion grew. "If you have such a powerful weapon to use against the Brelac, then why not use it to help end the war?"

"Ending the war in favor of the Protectorate did not fit into Vendetta's plans. When we first made contact with the Brelac, we carefully negotiated an arrangement with them. We would grant their ships access to our hidden bases to resupply and make repairs, as well as access to certain bits of tactical information from time to time. In exchange, certain targets connected to Carp Technologies and Vendetta would remain untouched by Brelac aggression."

"So in other words, you sold the rest of us out in order to cover your own asses."

"I prefer to call it buying time," Fenlow corrected, tilting his head to one side and chewing on the inside of his cheek. "It wasn't our goal to live under Brelac rule either. We had to work with them and keep them pacified until we could find an effective means of withstanding their power. And they handed it right to us."

"The psionic implants," Blair said.

"The implants," Fenlow repeated, nodding. "A technology possessing an awesome potential. Unfortunately, the Brelac lacked a specially engineered gene that I gave you three. It was fortunate that I was able to develop this gene first."

Colin digested Fenlow's explanation. *A sinister tale of clandestine treachery.*

"So, what are you going to do after you take over the Protectorate? Create an army of Reploids equipped with your special implants?"

"No, you Reploids are obsolete," Fenlow replied, laughing. "I intend to use my Deltans to enhance the military forces of my new empire. They're quicker to manufacture and far more powerful than all of you combined. But then you've already found that out. I'll also need them to police my human and Brelac joint forces and guard against any resistance."

"Joint forces?" Blair gasped. "Are you out of your mind?"

"Why not have the Brelac join us? We seem to have a lot in common with the Brelac. We share the same origins."

"Origins? What are you talking about?"

"Do you know where the human race came from?" Fenlow spun about. "How the United Protectorate came into being? It's all traced back to an ancient point in deep space. Old Earth."

Blair's face turned pale. "Old Earth? I've heard about that from high school history. The human migration. But that was centuries ago."

"Yes, humans were forced to leave the planet and find a new home among the stars because of a deadly viral outbreak. The Pandora Simplex. But what wasn't recorded was the fact that some remained behind and survived the virus. They grew and evolved until they became what you see before us. An alien enemy completely bent on destroying the human race."

Blair's wide-eyed gaze dropped to the floor. Then he looked up at Fenlow again. "If this is true, then we have to tell somebody. People have to know."

261

Fenlow laughed. "We'll film a documentary," he said, throwing his hands into the air, "I'll even let you narrate. Assuming that I change my mind and let you live."

"And what about us?" Mariner inquired. "Do you intend to kill us along with them?"

"No. You're still useful to me, I'll allow you to leave and go back to Rantraven. By the looks of things outside, your squadron won't be facing too much opposition from the Protectorate forces."

Colin glanced back to the scene being projected by Succubus. The Viperhawk continued to destroy any ship within its gun sights, the blackness of space alight with the explosions from destroyers and battlecruisers that would never fight again. Frantic voices from the remaining ships relayed the order to retreat. The small group of survivors began to quickly disperse as the Viperhawk continued firing at them. Five more battlecruisers were destroyed as they fled for safety.

"Succubus, cease fire and proceed to Maseklos Prime," Fenlow commanded. He turned to Mariner. "Are you deciding to stay?"

"I'll stay," Mariner answered. "I'm curious to see how this whole thing turns out."

Fenlow smiled. "A wise choice. I would rather have spectators at my side that can appreciate the historic events that I'm about to create. Not unlike my ungrateful creations and my associate, Doctor Van Doren."

"There is another transmission coming in from Walter Carnaby," Succubus announced.

Fenlow turned to Succubus. "Send it through."

Carnaby's face replaced the image of space outside. Jubilant laughter rolled from his lips. His face cracked with a broad smile.

"That was magnificent," Carnaby chuckled. "That ship is more awesome than you first described to me. You went through that entire fleet like a jackhammer on an anthill. Our scanners show the Protectorate ships scattered beyond the system. But they appear to be attempting to regroup and launch another assault."

"They no longer concern me," Fenlow said. "My focus is on Maseklos Prime. In just a few moments we'll see whether Drennen and the others are stupid enough to defy me."

"We'll remain a safe distance behind you until it's time to make our move and occupy the capital. Carnaby out."

Carnaby's image faded to be replaced by the scene outside. The Viperhawk was rapidly nearing the blue planet that was the center of the United Protectorate. Maseklos Prime, a planet now sitting vulnerable before this powerful invader. Standing between Maseklos Prime and the Viperhawk was the planet's last line of defense. The huge, white octagon form of a starbase orbiting the planet.

"Starbase Redoubt," Fenlow commanded. "Succubus, destroy it."

Blair engaged in a frantic struggle to break free of the wall. "Doctor Fenlow, please. There are over three hundred people on that base."

"There are even more down on the ground," Fenlow stoically replied.

A stream of energy blazed out from the Viperhawk and burned through the Redoubt. The entire structure exploded into three white flashes. Countless glowing fragments shot out in all directions and a huge burst of fire erupted and quickly faded in the cold vacuum of space.

Colin joined Blair's struggle but it lasted briefly. Succubus' telekinetic power holding him was far too powerful for his muscles to overcome.

Succubus beeped in. "The remaining units in the defensive fleet have regrouped and are heading on an intercept course."

Fenlow gave an annoyed sigh. "Give me a visual."

Succubus displayed the image of several battlecruisers and destroyers flying on a direct course toward the Viperhawk. After the merciless thrashing that the fleet had earlier endured, Colin was amazed that the survivors would either be courageous or insane enough to try and wage another futile assault against this ship. He heard an array of voices barking out orders. There was one voice that Colin thought that he recognized. Apparently Fenlow picked up the voice as well. He raised his hand.

"Succubus, stop. Patch me into the ship that made that last transmission."

Succubus instantly obeyed, showing the image of a ship's bridge. Dozens of crew members were seated in front of their consoles. A few high ranking officers stood behind several consoles in a supervisory role. There was one officer that Colin's eyes quickly focused on.

Fenlow clasped his hands. "General Larkin. I thought I recognized your voice. Nice to see you. If I had known that you were attending this little party, I would have taken the time to eliminate every damn ship out there. Starting with yours."

Larkin looked up, his face surprised at Fenlow's transmission. "Fenlow," he shouted, "I had a feeling that you would be on that ship. As soon as we get within firing range we're going to blow you out of space."

Fenlow laughed. "Just where were you during the last attack? In the john working on a crossword puzzle? You were lucky to escape with your life the first time. Maybe I should give you a little demonstration of what's in store for you if you get in my way. Succubus, bring us about."

The ship turned slowly until it faced the small semi-circular fleet of ships that followed it. The ships manned by Vendetta personnel.

Fenlow pointed his finger at the image of three of the vessels. "Fire."

CHAPTER THIRTY-TWO

The Viperhawk's main weapon unleashed firepower that obliterated the ships in an instant.

Colin jerked against the restraining force. *Fenlow firing upon his allies' ships?* "All this power that you're wielding must be driving you insane!"

Fenlow ignored Colin's insult as Succubus announced that Carnaby was sending another message.

"Fenlow, what the hell's going on?" Carnaby bellowed, his face red and scrunched. "Tell me that was an accident or a malfunction!"

Fenlow seemed to remain calm and confident in his power. "I can't tell you what you want to hear, Walter. But if you need an explanation, then I can tell you that there's been a slight change in plans."

"What the hell are you talking about?"

"What I mean is that I've decided weeks ago that I should be the one to exclusively benefit from this power. After all, I've done all the real work. You just sit in the safety of your cushy office and make plans. And I'm supposed to just hand everything over to you? What's my compensation out of all this? A gold watch? An office party in my honor?"

"Damnit, Fenlow! You are a member of Vendetta and an employee of Carp Technologies. You work for me! Now I order you to stand down and surrender that damn ship! I'm getting somebody else to handle this operation."

"I don't think so, Walter," Fenlow returned, waving his finger. "Perhaps you've forgotten the compliment that you've paid me earlier about the Viperhawk's power. Maybe I should give you another little demonstration to jog your memory."

Carnaby said nothing. He simply held an infuriated grimace on his face.

"Just keep your nose clean and stay out of my way, Walter," Fenlow warned. "Leave Maseklos Prime to me. Succubus, bring us back to the planet."

"I'm curious," Colin said. "Is there anyone in this universe that you're really loyal to? So far you've taken your Brelac buddies, Blair, the Protectorate, Vendetta and your boss, and managed to stab them all in the back on the same day."

Fenlow stood a few short feet away and looked into Colin's eyes. "Your limited Reploid programming can't comprehend the concept of how to use power. When you're holding a smoking gun and half your enemies are laying dead at your feet, you don't need to show loyalty to anyone."

"I understand more than you realize. I understand that you have to be loyal to something or someone. Otherwise your life will be pretty damn empty."

"As empty as *your* life?" Fenlow chided in an irritated tone. "You and these other Reploids are nothing more than complex computer programs run amok. But I suppose that it's all my fault. Diane and Kelly were originally part of a larger group of Reploid infiltrators.

The plan was to have them penetrate Helios military base on the planet Meridan and blend in with the human personnel as you did. But the Brelac ship that carried them was shot down and they were the only two that survived. Then you were captured by Protectorate troopers. So we needed a little damage control to deal with that problem."

"If we were such a problem then why didn't you just kill us?" Colin asked.

"Believe me, I wanted to quietly terminate the three of you, but Doctor Trevor had a better idea. He wanted to program you to be independent. To think for yourselves. Not like your previous programming, where your lives revolved around your programmed missions. Since you were programmed to think for yourselves Trevor claimed that your primary concern would be to maintain your survival. And to that end you would refuse to cooperate with the Protectorate and not work for them. That would ultimately result in you being eliminated by the Protectorate."

After hearing that explanation, Colin was compelled to admire and feel grateful for Doctor Trevor's failed plan.

"That way the Protectorate would do your work for you by terminating us. A good plan. So tell me what happened to change all that?"

"What happened? Trevor's stupid idea failed. Obviously, what happened is that you three formed a sort of camaraderie. You developed sympathy for the Protectorate. In short, you three rejects have become the annoyance that I've feared. But I'll deal with you after I've concluded my business with Maseklos Prime. Besides, I enjoy having an audience."

Colin had finally gotten what he had previously sought after. The remaining details about his, Diane, and Kelly's true origins. For the first time, he experienced the concept of irony. The Silencers were originally created to help destroy the very government that they were now risking their lives to save.

"You'll never pull this off, Fenlow," Colin said in defiance. "It's a big empire. Somebody will find the means to stop you."

"And who might that be? The Protectorate is already beaten," Fenlow declared. "Perhaps the Protectorate will forge an alliance with the Brelac. I'd be halfway tempted to wait around until that actually happened. That way, I can prove to both factions once and for all that I'm wielding the ultimate power. Succubus, transmit my final ultimatum down to the city of Navarone. Broadcast it on all frequencies."

Colin put his mind to work in desperate overdrive to think of some way to stop Fenlow. He needed a workable plan within the next few seconds. The sound of a loud moan caught his ears. He twisted his head around to the source of the noise. Diane was regaining consciousness.

Fenlow smoothed out his hair and straightened his collar as Succubus made connection.

"Attention! This is Doctor Howard Fenlow," he called out triumphantly. "I am speaking to you from a ship positioned in space directly over the capital city of Navarone. I have effortlessly penetrated the paltry defenses that were set up to hinder me. I am here to issue my final ultimatum. President Drennen and the Central Commission will address me within ten minutes or I will destroy the entire city, leaving no survivors. Remember, ten minutes. Don't waste time debating."

Colin could only guess as to what President Drennen and the Central Commission would say. Assuming that they would even respond. "You won't get Drennen and the others to cow down to you so easily," he said. "They'll find a way to fight you."

Diane was now fully awake. She scanned her surroundings. "My damn head hurts," she said in a groggy voice. "What the hell happened?"

Succubus announced that an incoming message was being transmitted from the city. Colin hoped that President Drennen would not be intimidated by Fenlow enough to quickly surrender to him.

Succubus brought forth the image of President Drennen, seated at a large oval table with all eighteen members of the Central Commission. The white dress that Drennen wore gave her an angelic aura that was unbefitting of the dour frown on her face. Standing behind Drennen were several other men and women who looked as equally grim.

Fenlow issued a hearty greeting. "President Drennen. What a pleasure to see you. And I see that you have the entire gang all assembled just for me. Even Defense Secretary Crane is among you."

"What do you want, Fenlow?" Drennen asked in a cold tone.

"Nothing else."

"Nothing else? I assume that you did not travel all this way, cause so much death and destruction just so that we could chat."

"I want nothing else because you've already provided me with everything I need. The entire central government is assembled with you. I just wanted to know for sure if all my targets are in one location. This will make my job a lot easier."

Standing behind Drennen a thin black man with receding hair stepped forward. "What the hell do you mean, Fenlow?"

"Secretary Crane. Deciding now to break your anonymity?"

Drennen and the others seated at the table all looked up at Crane.

"Don't be so puzzled, everyone," Fenlow said with a gleeful smile. "Secretary Crane is a member of Vendetta. He's been in the closet for quite some time now. He's been riding on the coattails of the original plan to overthrow the government."

Crane nervously looked about the faces in the room, all eyes now focused on him. "I don't know what the hell he's talking about. Look at him and what he's done. He's obviously a lunatic. Crazy."

"You're about to die and all you can do is stand there calling names? That sounds pretty damn insane to me," Fenlow pointed out. "If I were you, I'd be making every effort to get my ass out of that city before it's too late."

Crane panicked and drew a pistol from a pocket inside of his suit. He stepped back and waved it around the room. "Nobody move! All of you get back!" he shouted. "Fenlow, get Carnaby! I demand to speak with Carnaby!"

Fenlow ordered Succubus to end the transmission, disappointing Colin. He'd been eager to see the outcome of Crane's rampage. But at the same time he hoped that someone among Drennen's security forces could safely disarm the man before he caused any harm.

"I don't have time to watch the outcome of that little drama," Fenlow told his captives. "Besides, this shows me what an idiot Crane really is. Now I won't regret killing him with the rest."

"What's the point in destroying the government without even making any demands?" Blair desperately pleaded.

Fenlow sauntered over to his former assistant.

"Colin put it quite accurately when he said that Drennen and her cronies would find some way to fight me. They might surrender to avoid bloodshed on a massive scale, but they would never be loyal to me. I don't need to keep looking over my shoulder for potential uprisings. It would be more logical to exterminate Drennen and the others when I have them all in one spot."

"If you kill Drennen and the others," Colin said, "then wouldn't that make the job of managing the entire United Protectorate by yourself a bit difficult?"

Fenlow spun about to face Colin, a sneer spread across his features. "I don't intend to eliminate President Drennen and her flunkies just yet. Allow me to demonstrate. Succubus, activate Drennen Program one point zero."

Colin was amazed to see the holographic image of President Drennen's face appear before Succubus. Appearing exactly the way she did in the first image— with her short brown hair, green eyes, and wearing her white dress. Colin looked at the faces of his friends. They were equally in awe of this new development that Fenlow revealed. It came as no surprise to hear the image flawlessly speak with Drennen's voice.

"Even though President Drennen and the other members of the central government are about to be terminated, their presence will still be needed to maintain order," Drennen articulately recited. "To that end, this simulation of President Drennen, as well as the other members of the government was created. Shortly after Navarone is destroyed, President Drennen will deliver an address to all planets within the Protectorate. She will assure the people that she, as well as the other members of the central government, escaped the catastrophe by retreating to a shielded underground bunker. Then a few days later President Drennen will deliver another address to the Protectorate."

Fenlow stepped forward. "That address will announce that a cease fire agreement has been reached between the Protectorate and the Brelac," he concluded. "The populace will be jubilant. Hopefully, the mood will be so upbeat that no one will bother to question the improvements my President Drennen will make. Such as a full scale program to create an army of Deltans and a small fleet of ships similar to the Viperhawk. Of course, there might be a few questions raised when we announce that the Brelac will be annexed into the Protectorate, but none of that will happen if we keep wasting time and give our targets a chance to escape. Succubus, target the city of Navarone and charge main weapon to maximum power."

CHAPTER THIRTY-THREE

Colin was not going to remain trapped on this wall like some helpless insect. He tried to concentrate and send a surge of current through the floor toward the computer.

"You still have a few obstacles to go over before you crown yourself king of the universe," Colin said. Sparks flew out from his fingertips but he still remained pinned against the wall. He yelled out in frustration. "This thing can't fight against all of us together," he urged his friends. "If we fight hard enough we can push it to its limit."

Diane, Kelly, and Blair all followed suit and strained to tear themselves away from the wall. Kelly's hands and face took on a red glow. Diane clenched her teeth and grunted in a high tone as she tried to move her limbs. Even Blair, possessing no extraordinary powers, mimicked Diane's agonizing struggle to force his freedom.

It was a noble effort, Colin thought.

Remaining silent up to this point, Mariner spoke out against the physical drama that was taking place. "You've got them trapped here. Kill them now before they break free."

"I prefer to kill them while they try to break free," Fenlow said, smiling. "These fools still can't accept the fact that they're fighting a lost cause. In spite of their combined powers they're no match for Succubus. This is no simple hunk of hardware. Its power comes from its mind, a mind that I created. Succubus is as powerful as it thinks it needs to be to destroy any enemy. And its confidence is always unbreakable."

Colin instantly realized that Fenlow had just given him a fighting chance against Succubus. "As powerful as it thinks it needs to be!" he shouted loudly "That principle also applies to us! Our powers come from the same source. Our minds and these implants!"

For a moment, Colin felt the pressure easing up on his arms and he thought that maybe the combined power of the group's increased efforts were starting to wear Succubus down. Then he felt the sides of his head being painfully compressed, and his arms weakened. The pain prevented him from generating an electrical charge or even thinking clearly. He managed to look over at Diane, perhaps for the last time in both their lives. She was physically the strongest member of the team, but he also wondered if even she could prevail against this machine that would soon kill them all. The tone of her grunting and growling changed from defiant rage to pain and desperation. Her face reddened, but she did not stop fighting.

Colin felt the pressure on his head start to weaken. Diane let out an enraged snarl and managed to rip her right arm away from the wall. Then her right leg took a step forward. Colin realized that Succubus was diverting power from its other prisoners to deal with the one that it considered to be its prime threat. *Diane.* She pulled her left arm away. Colin felt the pressure across his body relaxing. This was all the relief that he needed.

A flash of light exploded from Colin's body as he directed streams of electricity toward Succubus. Unfortunately for Fenlow he stood in the line of fire. He received a jolt that knocked him to the floor. The powerful current continued along the floor and surged through the computer and disrupted its systems. A high-pitched screech from Succubus filled the room and its telekinetic hold on the group broke. Colin pushed away from the wall and sent two more electrical blasts from his outstretched hands. Just as quickly, Succubus created its wall of smoky energy to block the attack. Kelly sent a beam of crimson energy from his hands but could not penetrate Succubus' shield.

A strong force suddenly pressed around Colin's throat. He felt as though a pair of invisible hands were strangling him, and out of the corner of his eye saw Kelly, Diane, and Blair fall to their knees beside him, grasping their necks and folding over to the floor, gasping for air.

Succubus is attacking again. With his hands desperately clawing at his neck Colin sunk to his knees. His lungs burned, starving for air. His vision darkened. His left hand dropped to the floor.

The floor.

Colin's hand was already touching the metallic floor. He generated a surge of electricity and sent it streaking through the floor, under Succubus' shield, and straight to the computer itself. Large explosions of sparks shot out from the computer, emerging from every seam and screw hole. Colin raised himself up and bathed Succubus in another surge of electricity.

Kelly jumped to his feet, face pale and eyes red, and sent a beam of fiery energy that burned a large hole through the center of Succubus. They watched as the red light above the keypad grew dark.

Colin tiptoed to Succubus with care. Black smoke rose from its scorched column shape. Colin hesitantly touched its surface. Heat from the computer seared his fingers. He jerked away and stuck his fingers in his mouth. He needed no further evidence to tell him that this monstrosity was damaged beyond repair.

Diane dashed to the floor to retrieve her fallen laser pistol. She darted over to the three Brelac standing at the other side of the room. "You die first!" she shouted at them.

Mariner quickly raised his clawed hands as if to surrender. He stepped back, growling at Diane.

There was a sudden pounding on the closed door. A metal fist broke through the door with no effort.

The Deltans, Colin thought. He was not about to remain here while his executioners casually strolled into the room.

"Kelly, do what you can to try and hold those things back," he ordered. He needed some time to think up an effective way to fight these machines.

The Deltan's hand grabbed the edge of the hole that it made. It started to peel a large strip of metal away from the door. It did not look like it would take the Deltan long to make an opening large enough for it and its comrades to enter the room. Diane backed away from her three Brelac prisoners and aimed her weapon toward the door, but also keeping them within her view.

Kelly rushed over to the door. He held out his hands and focused his power toward the door.

A large panel of shimmering blue energy materialized in front of him, effectively blocking off the door. Kelly held his hands steady. The panel slowly grew thicker until it was nearly six inches thick.

It looked almost solid, Colin thought. *But would it be strong enough to stop those things?*

The Deltan raised its gun arm. With a crimson flash it fired a plasma beam at the barrier. The blue shield easily absorbed the powerful assault. The Deltan fired a second burst into the barrier and it continued to hold up. Though after absorbing a third burst, a shower of small, blue energy fragments broke off from the barrier, evaporating before they had a chance to touch the floor.

"Colin," Kelly's voice raised an octave, "we've got a problem."

"I'm working on it," Colin assured him. His anxiety mounted as he pondered a quick and effective solution. He dreaded the idea of having to face the Deltans again.

"Diane, we need an exit," Colin told her. "Blair, keep an eye on our guests."

Diane handed Blair her pistol, then followed Colin to the wall at the opposite side of the room. Blair kept his weapon and gaze fixed on Mariner, Lagar, and Danton. Colin instructed Diane to rip a large hole into the wall. At first she hesitated. Then her right fist sank deep into the metallic surface and her hand quickly tore away two huge sections of the wall. She grimaced and examined her hand; her knuckles had small, reddened wounds where her skin was broken. A thin stream of blood trickled out from each wound. They turned and looked through the wall and found an empty room.

"Everything under control, Kelly?" Colin asked.

"Under control?" Kelly shrieked. "Oh sure. He looks like he's getting a little tired."

The Deltan was not letting up on its efforts to reach its victims. It had taken a more intimate approach to attacking Kelly's energy barrier by hurling a steady stream of punches into the barrier. Kelly was trying to persevere, using his power to try and maintain the barrier, but his efforts were failing. Large fragments broke away from the barrier with each punch landed by the Deltan. Finally its fist punched through, leaving a gaping hole.

"Let's get the hell out of here," Colin said, pointing toward the new exit that Diane had created.

There was a loud moan from Fenlow. Apparently he had survived the electric shock that Colin had inadvertently given him.

"What do we do with him?" Diane asked.

"Leave him," Colin replied bluntly. "Leave the Brelac too. They'll only slow us down."

Kelly abandoned his weakening shield and joined the others as they darted into the next room. Without his power to maintain the barrier's stability it quickly faded away and the Deltans quickly entered the room, single file, to hunt down their prey.

Colin led the group out of the room and into the corridor. He ordered Kelly and Blair to position themselves a few feet down the corridor. He and Diane continued on a few more feet.

"Follow my lead and shoot at the ceiling," he ordered.

No one moved. They remained silent. The multiple thumps of the robot's heavy footsteps echoed through the corridor. At first they were faint. Then they quickly grew louder. A powerful explosion shattered the door into fragments. The Deltans stepped out into the corridor, accompanied by Fenlow. His face was red. He gnashed his teeth, grimacing in pain as he moved. His brow was furled and his eyes narrowed, his right hand grasping his chest.

"Are you idiots making a stand here?" Fenlow snarled. "I was hoping that you wouldn't make the chase too easy for me! You may have destroyed my plans to build a new empire, but I can still have the pleasure of watching you all die!"

"We're not here to make a stand," Colin yelled back. "We're here to see you off!"

Powerful bolts of lightning blazed from Colin's hands and flew down the corridor. In an instant, one of the Deltans erected a defensive shield, just as Colin expected it to. Colin redirected his firepower to the ceiling above them. Kelly followed suit and released a huge burst of flame from his hands. Blair immediately opened fire with his laser pistol. The concentrated firepower ripped a gaping hole into the ceiling, resulting in an explosive decompression of the corridor. Fenlow and his Deltans were caught off guard by the sudden powerful air current that jerked them off their feet. Despite their awesome power, the Deltans were sucked up through the large hole in the ceiling and out of the ship.

And Fenlow with them.

Colin felt the powerful air currents tugging at his clothes. Breathing was difficult. He yelled over the rushing wind. "Kelly! We need that hole sealed!"

Kelly heard him and quickly complied. He raised his hands and summoned his power once more. A circle of glowing blue energy appeared to effectively seal the hole. The vacuum in the corridor stopped.

Colin and Diane both gasped to catch their breath and waited to see what would happen next. Looking down the corridor Kelly remained still with his hands outstretched to hold his shield in place. Blair had a broad smile on his face.

"We actually did it. We saved the United Protectorate. We won."

"We can't celebrate just yet," Colin advised. "We still have to get off this ship,"

A sudden tremor shook the corridor nearly throwing everyone to the floor.

Something exploded outside, the rocking force powerful enough to rip Kelly's shield into dissipating fragments. The strong current of the decompressing air pulled at Colin and the others. Two of the Deltans reappeared and crawled head first through the hole in the ceiling and dropped down into the corridor, the long cylindrical thrusters on their wings spouting short streams of blue flames that cut off as the Deltans righted themselves and landed on their feet.

"Just our luck," Colin moaned. "Those wings aren't just for show."

The Deltans swiftly kneeled down and dug firm handholds into the metallic floor, firmly anchoring them so they would not be sucked out of the ship a second time.

"Kelly!" Colin shouted. "Plug that hole back!"

Kelly raised his right hand. His blue energy disk reappeared to again block off the large hole. The rushing current of air instantly stopped. Then he thrust his left hand forward and erected a wall of his blue energy shield to protect himself and Blair. Upon seeing this, the two Deltans turned their attention to the most vulnerable targets. Colin and Diane. The robots marched down the corridor.

Colin was at a loss to think of what to do next. His plan to deal with the Deltans had failed. At least he had the consolation of knowing that the third Deltan was not present.

I just hope that it's not on its way here.

"Ok, plan A didn't work," Diane frantically concluded. "What do we do now?"

Colin thought quickly. Trapped on this ship with powerful killing machines that would track them down relentlessly, there was only one course of action to take.

"It's them or us," he said. "We'll have to take them down."

If only that job were so easy, Colin thought.

He quickly kneeled down and brushed his hand against the metallic floor. With blazing speed a wide strip of the metal floor shifted and buckled toward the Deltans. When the strip reached them it violently buckled and splintered, knocking both Deltans off their feet.

Diane dashed forward to attack as the Deltans rose to their feet.

"Diane, get back!" Colin cried.

Kelly created a small round opening in his shield that was large enough to allow Blair to fire his laser pistol through at the robots. After firing four shots, the only result was to gain the attention of one of the Deltans. It charged toward Kelly's shield and began to punch its fist onto it. The second one rushed for Diane and gave her a backhand strike to her chest and sent her crashing into the wall.

Colin moved to fire an electrical bolt at the robot, but it stepped too close to Diane and he didn't want to risk it. The Deltan struck out again and connected with Diane's head. She let out a high-pitched cry as the back of her head smacked back against the wall. The Deltan lifted one arm and a long, sharp blade thrust out from its wrist. Colin yelled out as the Deltan stabbed the blade through Diane's left shoulder. The blade emerged out of her back to lodge itself in the wall. She threw her head back and screamed. Colin was still helpless to act. The Deltan was too close, and he knew a bolt of electricity could end up killing Diane in the process. He glanced over to Kelly, who looked just as helpless, as the second Deltan pounded its fist away at his weakening shield.

Diane suddenly shoved the robot back. The blade ripped its way out of her flesh, spraying blood. She turned and leaned against the wall, grasping her wound. Blood oozed between her fingers, a red spot quickly expanded on her gray camouflage shirt. The Deltan rushed forward and grabbed her in a tight embrace. Diane screamed out in pain, and then she pushed herself and the Deltan back against the wall. The robot's body struck the metal wall with a loud crash, the impact putting a large dent in its polished surface. Diane rammed the robot back against the wall a second time, then a third and a fourth. A large dented panel in the wall buckled and collapsed, and the Deltan finally released its grip around Diane to steady itself.

Diane grabbed the Deltan's arm and ripped it from the armored shoulder, and sparks jumped sporadically out from exposed black wires. A green fluid squirted out from three severed plastic tubes at the end of the limb and the Deltan's shoulder. The severed arm's fingers continued to twitch. Diane swung the limb like a club, smashing it into the Deltan's head. The Deltan staggered back as Diane struck it a second time. A third strike shattered its horizontal eye lens. The Deltan fell back against the wall and crashed to the floor.

"Diane, back away!" Colin shouted.

The Deltan rose to its feet and staggered back against the wall, the tip of its gun arm starting to take on a reddish glow.

"Diane, get down!"

They both ducked down to the floor as the Deltan sent a wild, fiery beam of energy burning across the wall. The Deltan spun around to Kelly's direction and fired again. The beam burned across its partner's back. The Deltan dropped to the floor, its back ablaze. The first Deltan stepped back and fired again. Kelly's shield changed from blue to bright red, and instantly reflected the attack back to the Deltan's gun arm, exploding the arm. Flaming debris scattered about the corridor. The Deltan staggered back as flames danced from its shattered stump.

Colin and Diane stood back up. Colin blinked.

"I don't think they can shield themselves and attack at the same time!" he shouted.

"Like this?" Kelly cried back.

A thundering blast of energy exploded out from the center of Kelly's shield and hurled the Deltan to the floor.

Colin's eyes widened. *How the hell did he learn that trick?*

He turned to the Deltans as they struggled to return to their feet. Colin now had a clear shot at them both. His outstretched hands exploded with a blue flash, and sent a powerful stream of electrical energy burning through the air, stopping just short from hitting its targets as the Deltans' panel of energy shielded them from his attack. Colin fired another blast, but it was also deflected. He fired again and gained the same result.

"Come on, Sarge," Diane gasped. She had one hand pressed against her bleeding shoulder. Her legs buckled and she dropped to one knee. Her head drooped.

Colin fired another blast. He raised his hand and sent an electrical stream up to the ceiling. He directed the powerful charge along the ceiling until it reached the Deltans, then the energy crackled down on the robots like a bolts of lightning from the sky. The shield that they had created dissolved under the attack. Colin took advantage of this opportunity and sent another blast of energy that struck them both. A thick hail of sparks leaped out from the Deltans' bodies as their once-silvery forms became completely scorched black. The smell of ozone filled the corridor. One Deltan remained on its feet but clumsily staggered backward.

Colin warned Diane to back away. Blue fire radiated from his hands and crawled up his arms and shoulders. Jagged forks of energy leapt out from his fingertips. He screamed, and the entire corridor exploded in a chaotic storm of electricity that burned through the air and bounced off of the metal walls. Jagged metal shrapnel, large twisted panels, bent pipes, and beams ripped themselves from the walls, floor, and ceiling. The floor erupted from under the Deltans' feet and hurled them into the air.

"Let's finish this," Diane urged, leaning forward, still clutching her bleeding shoulder.

Colin lifted his hands. They began to glow with an intense blue aura, much brighter than before. Several small bolts of energy flashed out from his body, bouncing off of the walls. Colin fired a ball of energy from his hands that shot through the air as large streams of electricity traveled along the floor, walls and ceiling, all of them converging onto the Deltas. Within this area Colin concentrated his power over electrical energy and his control over electrically conductive matter.

In his mind Colin visualized the intense electric current burning through every wire, processor, and circuit within these two machines, while feeling their metal bodies bend and shred. Both Deltas suddenly shattered with a bright blue flash and four large bursts of sparks. Tiny metal fragments scattered throughout the area, clicking as they settled against the scraped metal flooring.

Colin slowly lowered his hands, gasping for breath. He licked his lips and focused on keeping his knees strong.

"We done here?" Kelly spoke out in a jittery voice.

Colin chuckled and nodded. "We're done." He slowly turned to Diane. "Are you okay?"

Diane grimaced in pain. She was breathing heavily. "I'm still alive. I'll be fine after I get a chance to rest."

Kelly lowered his shield in the corridor but kept the one in the ceiling intact to seal the hole. Blair rushed over to Diane, his hands reaching for her wound.

The corridor suddenly shook, accompanied by a thundering roar that echoed off of the remaining walls.

"What the hell was that?" Diane cried.

"It's probably the reason why we should get off this ship." Colin frowned. "General Larkin and the defending fleet that attacked this ship earlier are probably making a second attack. Only this time the ship is dead and has no shields to protect it."

"Fenlow mentioned that those Brelac had a ship docked with us." Blair stood, wiping Diane's blood off his hands and onto his pants. "If we can reach it then we might have a chance."

Several more tremors rocked the ship. Then a door lock suddenly swished open to allow five armed Protectorate troopers into the hall. The troopers stormed up to them and stopped a few feet away from the group and aimed their weapons.

"Don't move!" one of the troopers snapped. "Where's Fenlow?"

"He just stepped out," Colin answered. "He won't be answering his voice mail."

"Fenlow's gone," Blair said. "But we do have three Brelac prisoners waiting in the room beyond this one."

Two troopers broke away and dashed into the room. Within seconds they returned.

"There's nobody in there," a trooper reported.

"They probably slipped out through the other door," Colin said quietly. "They might be getting away right now."

"We've no time to look for them," the first trooper said. "We were given only a few minutes to try and find the traitor Fenlow alive. Looks like you four will have to take his place. Now we'd better go before this ship is blasted into particles. Let's move out of here. Don't any of you try anything funny."

The troopers hastily led the group down the corridor. There was a large hole in the hall wall waiting for them, connected to a docking tube that extended from another ship.

The group was guarded closely as they were herded through the tube and into the next ship. Colin guessed that they were probably in the corridor of a battlecruiser. The airlock door slid shut behind them with a metallic bang. The docking tube retracted with a loud hiss.

The troopers kept their weapons trained on the group, but permitted them to go to a small window to observe what was taking place outside. The ship raced away from the Viperhawk and they received a clear view of the enemy ship being bombarded with multiple energy bolts from the Protectorate ships surrounding it. A series of explosions shattered the vessel into several small fragments.

Fenlow's ultimate weapon was destroyed.

CHAPTER THIRTY-FOUR

"I can't believe that we are still putting up with this shit!"

Colin sat at his new desk in the large supply room and listened to Diane's enraged tirade. He was certain that her screaming voice was causing the dozens of metal shelves standing behind him and their contents to vibrate. The proper medical care may have been administered to her wounded shoulder, but her temper was still raw. Kelly and Blair stood quietly by and looked on while Diane ranted wildly about the injustice that had been inflicted upon them.

"There's gotta be something we can do besides keeping our mouths shut and looking stupid!" Diane yelled.

"Try to calm down," Colin told her while trying to maintain his own composure. "We have our orders."

"We have our orders," Diane mocked with clear resentment in her voice, her hands on her hips. "We risk our asses to save the president, this city, and the whole Protectorate. And do they treat us like heroes? Hell no. From the moment we left the Viperhawk we were treated like prisoners of war. Then they give us jobs that were worse than the last ones they stuck us with."

It was too early for Colin to compare his new position against his old one. After the conflict with Fenlow was concluded, the group was assigned to new jobs on Navarone. Colin was now an assistant supervisor working in a military supply warehouse. After her shoulder had been treated, Diane was assigned to a construction and maintenance battalion. Kelly was put to work at a reception desk in the main lobby of the Judge Advocate General's Corps, a high-profile position where he could be closely and easily watched. As for Blair, he was assigned to the First Veteran's Hospital as a resident surgeon.

"Look on the bright side," Colin shrugged. "At least they didn't really split us up and send each of us out to different sectors or planets."

"I still say that we deserve better," Diane groused. "I guess that means they'll keep us filed away until they need us again."

"I suppose you can say that," Blair replied. "But then, you guys are programmed to think for yourselves. The question is if they call you together again, will you decide to go?"

"Would you?" Diane countered. "We're in the same military just like you. We follow orders. It's the only life we know. But I'd still like to have my life as a pilot."

Kelly rolled his eyes and shook his head in frustration, letting out a bitter guffaw. "You're still holding on to that fantasy? Captain Diane Christy, psycho pilot. It's a fabrication."

"It's all I've got," Diane returned, a note of sadness in her voice. "If I really am a Reploid with a programmed identity, then I just can't sit in a corner until I figure out who or what else I can be."

Colin nodded in sympathy. "Reploids or not, we're all going to have to go forward with this. We can only improve on who we are and keep building our lives."

"Building our lives?" Kelly scoffed. "First, Diane hangs on to her pilot fantasy. Now, I suppose you're still gonna walk around with those papers in your pocket. The ones with the pictures of the *real* Colin McKenzie's parents."

Colin reached into his back pocket and brought out the crumpled and slightly faded papers. He unfolded them and took a long look at the images on them. "You know, you're right. Maybe it's high time that I got a wallet to carry these in."

Diane stepped closer to get a better look at the pictures. "You know, Sarge. I envy you with these pictures."

"You envy me?"

Diane nodded. "Yeah. At least you can frame yours and sit them on your desk like the other big shots that I've seen."

With that, Diane reached into her back pocket and brought out three pages of her own. She showed them to Colin. On one was the photograph of a middle-aged woman with long brown hair wearing a blue sweater. The second photograph had the smiling face of a man with short dark hair, round glasses, a thin moustache, and a gray shirt.

"I always believed that my family was dead," she explained. "And I got a little jealous of your pictures so I went on the macronet and did a little digging. This is my mother, Janet, and my father, Dave. They're both dead. But I found out that there are surviving members of the Christy family. I even contacted some of them."

Kelly shook his head. "I don't think this family stuff is a good idea. I mean, you're stepping into somebody else's life. If you meet these people, what are you going to tell them?"

Diane tilted her head. "I admit that all this is still complicated. I want to go ahead with my life. But then I look in the mirror and wonder if I am going ahead with my life, or Diane Christy's? Then I wonder if I'll have the same doubts about myself a year from now. A year's worth of life and new experiences. Will *any* of us feel the same way after a year?" She shrugged. "And look on the bright side. We could have been made to be somebody worse than we are now."

"You all originally were," Blair sighed. "Fortunately, the three of you evolved into something better."

"What about Doctor Trevor? As well as Carnaby, Crane, and the others?" Colin asked.

"Doctor Trevor has vanished, along with Walter Carnaby. From what I've been told, Carnaby's secretary stated that he's temporarily away on official company business and can't be reached. As for Secretary Crane, he refuses to answer any questions regarding Carnaby, Carp Technologies, or Vendetta. From what I understand, Crane's attorney is trying to use an insanity defense, caused by the stress resulting from Crane's life being threatened by Fenlow. He supposedly threatened the president and the Commission with a gun without really knowing what he was doing."

The frown remained on Diane's face. "Why do I get the feeling that if they were to choose between Crane and us, we would end up in prison?"

"Don't worry," Blair assured her. "Nobody is going to walk away from this incident untouched. An investigation is being launched and our testimony will help bring Carnaby and the others involved to justice. But in a small way it would seem that they have won a victory. I've heard a lot of talk about the Protectorate establishing a new program for deep space expansion and exploration."

"Expansion and exploration?" Colin asked. "When we should concentrate on the Brelac and Vendetta?"

"They're the main reason. We were lucky to win against Fenlow's Viperhawk, Succubus, and his Deltans. But our enemies could easily send more of them against us. As well as more Reploids with powers like yourselves. We don't have the ability to fight both the Brelac, Vendetta, and these powerful new weapons."

On that point Colin agreed. As did Diane and Kelly.

"Then we need help," Kelly surmised. "This expansion and exploration is more about finding allies in the war.

"In an unofficial capacity," Blair stated. "It would hurt morale if word ever got out that we were desperately looking for help. We need to find new strategic points in space, more resources, maybe contact alien cultures and gain new technologies. But the main hope is to learn what happened to the other groups of explorers who migrated from Old Earth. In the past, there have been several small-scale missions to explore deep space and find out what happened to them. But the war placed that project low on a long list of priorities.

"History tells that the Protectorate grew from one of six separate groups that headed out to different locations. After all these years it's possible that we could be the only ones who flourished. But if any of the other groups survived and built up civilizations that equal or surpass our own, then they would make valued allies."

A noble endeavor, Colin thought. *One that could certainly prove to be beneficial. But such an exploration would not come without its pitfalls. Space is a vast and dark mystery. After all these years they could finally reunite the separate civilizations of humanity. Or they could encounter a threat that could be far more horrific than the Brelac.*

Colin found himself being drawn to the shrouded mystery of deep uncharted space. Especially looking behind him at the warehouse's rows and rows of shelves holding their goods.

"I hope they have fun with this deep space exploration," Diane scoffed. "A hell of a lot more than I'll have."

Blair backed away, heading for the door. "Well, I've spent enough time here. I've got to get to the hospital and make my rounds."

"And I have to go start my new career," Diane said. "If I work hard enough then maybe they'll at least give me a driver's license."

Kelly placed a gentle hand on Diane's shoulder. "Or maybe one day you'll fly again. I wouldn't want to see psycho pilot grounded forever."

For a moment Diane stared back at Kelly. Then she formed a smile. "Thanks kid. I mean, Kelly."

"Nice to see that you two can get along," Colin complimented them both, smiling. "I hope that this won't be the last time that I see this."

Now Kelly smiled. "Of course not. After all, we are a team." He turned and headed for the door. "Unlike the rest of you people, I've got the day off. I'm going to spend the day having fun and building up some memories of my own."

Diane followed behind Kelly. "We'll keep in touch," she said over her shoulder. She headed toward the door, stopped and hesitated, then turned back to Colin. "You know, you did a pretty good job of managing this bunch of screw ups, Sarge."

"Thanks," Colin said slowly.

Then as he watched her leave the room, he decided that he could appreciate even a brash compliment from Diane. Her style may have been unceremonious, but he enjoyed the intended result. *Feels kind of nice*, he thought.

With his friends gone, Colin stood and looked at the shelves and all the materials behind him. For a minute he thought about some of the issues in his life that were still unresolved.

Questions about his past activities with Ed Driscoll, and a question of their possible involvement with Vendetta. Colin also wondered who had sent his impersonating cousin Keith Berry to contact him, then try to kill him.

For now, Colin thought that it would be wiser if he kept some of the dark allegations of his past to himself.

Colin picked up a small stack of papers off his desk. He glanced down at the list of items that would have to be packed up and shipped out to various destinations: uniforms, boots, field ration packs, computers.

Colin sighed. The first day in his new life was destined to be a very long one.

www.ingramcontent.com/pod-product-compliance
Lightning Source LLC
Chambersburg PA
CBHW020915200626
46814CB00001BA/356